"HERE HE COMES!" SOMEONE CRIED. "HERE COMES MURALES!"

Longarm jumped. His boots caught Murales' right shoulder a glancing blow. The man went spilling to the ground as Longarm landed heavily on the boardwalk. A rotten board snapped under his weight, his left foot driving down to the ground beneath. Murales swung the rifle stock with wicked precision and knocked Longarm's Colt flying.

A gleaming smile on his dark face, Murales levered a fresh cartridge into the Winchester. He raised it to his hip, and leveled the muzzle on Longarm . . .

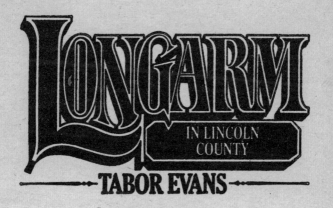

LONGARM

IN LINCOLN COUNTY

TABOR EVANS

A JOVE BOOK

LONGARM IN LINCOLN COUNTY

A Jove Book / published by arrangement with
the author

PRINTING HISTORY
Jove edition / September 1979
Fourth printing / July 1982

ISBN: 0-515-06950-7

Jove books are published by Jove Publications, Inc., 200 Madison
Avenue, New York, N.Y. 10016. The words ''A JOVE BOOK'' and the
''J'' with sunburst are trademarks belonging to Jove Publications, Inc.

Chapter 1

For a full hour before the shot, Longarm had smelled
trouble. When the shot came, he had been riding across
a shallow saddleback. At once—as the rifle's crack
rolled like thunder after him—he leaned well over the
buckskin's neck; jabbed spurs to the animal's flanks,
and galloped down the slope toward the thin trickle of
a stream gleaming below him.

Now, with his horse crowded against a dark clump
of juniper, and his eyes on the ridge behind him, he
waited with his Winchester in his hand. The stream's
cool murmur—it was only a few yards beyond the
juniper—was the only sound to break the silence of the
clear, brilliant day. Longarm would have liked the
acrid taste of a cheroot between his lips, something to
clamp his jaws down on. But things were falling in
upon him too fast for that; the cheroot could easily
disturb his aim. He didn't need that. Apaches seldom
gave a White Eyes more than a second chance, and according to those Apaches beyond the ridge, the towering deputy marshal reckoned, he was already on
borrowed time.

Longarm's gunmetal-gray shirt was heavy now with his perspiration. In this silent, withering heat, it was beginning to smell the way he felt—stale and old. He was a lean, muscular man with shoulders that tugged against the shoulder pads of his brown frock coat. His face was wind-cured and rawboned, his skin tanned to a saddle-leather brown. There was no softness in the man, not even in the gunmetal blue of his narrowed, careful eyes. His close-cropped hair was the color of fresh tobacco leaf, as was the neatly waxed longhorn mustache that flared proudly upon his upper lip. His hat was a snuff-brown Stetson, the crown telescoped in the Colorado rider fashion, positioned carefully on his head, dead center and tilted slightly forward, cavalry style—a legacy from his youth, when he'd run away to ride in the War.

An Apache, dressed in buckskin shirt, breechclout, and knee-high moccasins, darted into view, his thick hair flying, rifle in hand, and flung himself across the ridge. Longarm levered and fired almost in a single motion. A plume of dirt erupted at the Apache's feet. Longarm fired again, more carefully. The Apache left his feet and flung himself behind a clump of giant saguaro cacti. Another Apache followed the first over the ridge. Longarm levered and swung his Winchester around—just as his left foot was yanked suddenly, with such violence that he was flung sideways out of his saddle.

He clung grimly to his rifle as he looked up at the reeling blue sky, then felt his back slam with breath-robbing force into the ground. He did not let himself lie still on his back. Even as he hit, he rolled over once, twice, then lurched up onto his knees. By this time, a circle of Apaches had formed around him. As they closed in, Longarm fired at the nearest of them. The shot went high. On his feet by that time, he swung the rifle like a club. The Apaches pulled back. One of them smiled—his teeth brilliant in his broad, chocolate-brown face. A knife flashed in his hand and, as the rest fell back to give him room, the Apache ducked under Longarm's second furious swing and lunged.

Longarm parried the knife with the rifle's barrel, then drove the barrel with vicious force into the Indian's midsection. A weaker man would have lost his breakfast. The Apache just bent over and went down on one knee, grasped the barrel with one hand, and flung it aside. Longarm dove at the Indian, catching him about the waist and driving him back so suddenly that he lost his footing and went down under him. Longarm sledged a few blows to the Apache's face, but they appeared to make little impression. The two men grappled for position, rolling over and over in the alkali dust, while the silent, impassive Indians kept the enclosing circle moving with them.

The Apache had long since lost his knife, but he had found a rock and was using it to some effect on Longarm whenever he could work his right hand free. At last, after a particularly numbing blow to the side of his head, Longarm flung himself back and felt the Apache lift himself from him. Feigning unconsciousness, he looked up through slitted eyes and saw the Apache towering over him. Another Apache handed the brave his knife. Again the Apache smiled and raised it over his head.

Longarm had already palmed the derringer from his vest pocket. The Apache's eyes widened in surprise when he found himself staring down the twin barrels of the marshal's .44 derringer. The pistol fired with a dull splat, and the .44 slug plowed into the Apache's knife hand, which seemed to explode in a spray of blood, bone, and sinew. The knife went flying.

Sitting up, Longarm reached across his belly for his Colt, worn high in its cross-draw rig under his frock coat, but froze in the act as he heard the Winchesters around him levering almost in unison. Looking around the impassive circle, he counted at least five muzzles trained on him. Slowly he let his hand ease away from the grips of his Colt.

The shot Apache was on one knee, holding onto his shattered hand, his dark eyes blazing with fury. He turned to his tribesmen and yelled something at them. It sounded distinctly like a command to Longarm, and he had little doubt as to what the Apache had commanded them to do. Looking back at the ring of Indians, he saw the resolve harden on their round dark faces.

A horse's pounding hooves shattered the pulsing silence. The bleeding Apache flung himself about angrily as the ring of Indians broke apart. An Apache woman rode through the break and flung herself from her pony with all the casual skill of a Plains Indian. She took one look at Longarm, then spun on the Apaches, who immediately shrank back from her angrily blazing eyes. She spoke up then, scolding them in their own tongue. What she said, Longarm had no idea, but it certainly had an effect. The rifles were suddenly lowered and the Apaches, with the single exception of the brave whom Longarm had wounded, took still another step back. The woman turned to face Longarm.

She was a dark, handsome woman with the round, rather flat face of the typical Mescalero Apache, but her hooded eyes gave her away. She was a breed. The eyes were a bright blue—almost as blue as the sky overhead. She was dressed in a buckskin skirt and jumper. On her head she wore a black bowler with a small red feather stuck in the brim.

"What are you doing on our land?" she snapped. There was no trace of an accent. Her voice was deep and musical, though, at the moment, she made no attempt to conceal her anger.

8

"Just riding through," Longarm replied, "on my way to Paso Robles."

"You are on Mescalero land!"

"I know that."

"Who are you? What is your business in Paso Robles?"

"Custis Long. I'm a deputy U.S. marshal out of Denver, Colorado," Longarm replied. He bent to pick up his hat. As he slammed it against his thigh to rid it of the alkali dust, he looked at the woman. "And before I tell you my business, who might you be?"

"I am Nalin."

"Thank you, Nalin. I got the distinct impression you saved my life."

"You say you are a deputy U.S. marshal. Prove it."

Longarm reached into his breast pocket for his wallet, opened it, and showed Nalin the federal badge pinned inside it. She studied it intently for a moment, then nodded curtly. "You've come to investigate the murder of Fred Bernstein, is that right?"

"Among other things. Governor Lew Wallace is a mite upset at what's been going on in these parts, so I've come to have a look-see. Seems like I ran into a hornet's nest real quick. You people do know how to welcome a lawman, and that's a fact."

Before Nalin could reply, Longarm looked up to see a party of four mounted agency police clearing the ridge. They were not punishing their horses. The four Apaches were dressed in motley, some with army blouses, some without. All were wearing campaign hats and were heavily armed, with bulging cartridge belts around their middles, rifles across their pommels, and sixguns in oiled, flapped army holsters. Two of them wore cavalry britches.

The Apache who had attacked Longarm took one look and slipped off through the junipers, with the rest of the Apaches following. The agency police pulled up to watch the fleeing Apaches, then started up again, two of them peeling off to follow the Indians, the rest riding on toward Longarm and Nalin.

As the two Apaches pulled up before Nalin, she spoke to them rapidly. The riders listened impassively, their cold eyes flicking in Longarm's direction only once, then nodded and rode off after the ambushers. Again, Longarm noticed, they were not punishing their horses at all. They were a most leisurely police force.

"I spoke for you," Nalin told Longarm. "You had better be who you say you are."

"And who the hell, ma'am, are you? The Mother Superior?"

She took a deep breath, then smiled. The smile was dazzling, and it completely disarmed the marshal, despite his growing impatience. "I guess I deserved that, Mr. Long. I run the agency school. I also serve as a nurse, and, more often than not, I am the only one who seems capable of interceding for my people when they run afoul of your law."

"Now just hold it a minute, Nalin. I think we better just eat this here apple one bite at a time. What was it set those people of yours onto me just now?"

"Last night an Apache woman was raped and killed by two white men, not far from here."

Longarm frowned and let that sink in. "That Apache who came after me. Was he—?"

Nalin nodded. "Yes. She was his woman. His name is Toklani. I do not believe he will forget you."

"I didn't rape his woman."

"That doesn't matter, I am afraid. It is enough that you are a White Eyes."

"Well, it matters to me."

Nalin mounted her pony in one quick jump, Indian-style, and snatched up the reins. "Follow me and I will take you to my school. We can talk there, if you want."

"I want," Longarm said, reaching down and picking up his Winchester. He had already slipped his derringer back into his vest pocket. He patted it absently, then dropped the rifle into its saddle scabbard, and mounted.

Nalin led him along the streambed for better than a mile, then cut sharply through a pass. A half-mile farther along, they came to another stream and, just beyond that, a tableland, wooded somewhat more luxuriantly than the dry, bone-white land through which they had just ridden. Close in under some oversized junipers, a frame school building had been erected, with an outhouse just in back, tipping precariously on the stony ground. On the other side of the junipers, covering the tableland like a series of festering sores, were the Apaches' wickiups—brush shelters fashioned of leafy branches and rotting army blankets flung over cone-shaped frameworks. A few army-type wall tents broke the monotony. The Apache settlement was not an imposing sight, nor were the Apache squaws, who were barely animated bags of bones squatting in front of the wickiups or hobbling about, tending fires. Only the children seemed truly alive and vital as they darted about in small gangs, playing their games and shrieking wildly all the while. Most of them were as dark as Nalin, and many were completely naked.

Once they caught sight of Nalin and Longarm riding across the tableland toward the junipers, they came running, their dark eyes gleaming as they encircled Longarm's horse. A few commands from Nalin dispersed them, however, and the two continued on to the schoolhouse without further incident. The white-haired squaws seemed too exhausted even to look up at them as they rode past.

They dismounted in front of the schoolhouse, and Nalin led the way into the frame building. The single classroom was neat, but stiflingly hot at the moment. The odor of chalk dust hung heavily in the air. Nalin led the way through the classroom into an apartment in back, consisting of a small kitchen and two bedrooms. A back porch containing a table and two benches also led off the kitchen, and Longarm made himself comfortable at the table while Nalin rustled up some coffee for him. He took the time to brush himself off a bit more and reload the derringer. This surprise among his armament had bailed him out of many a tough spot; it was a .44-caliber weapon with a brass ring soldered to its brass butt. A long, gold-washed chain with a clip on the end of it led from his left watch pocket where Longarm carried his Ingersoll pocket watch. He was just placing the derringer back into the vest pocket, allowing the gold chain to drape innocently across his vest front, when Nalin brought out cups and a steaming coffeepot.

As she placed the cup and pot down in front of Longarm, she smiled and put a finger to her lips, then disappeared back into the kitchen to return a moment later with a bottle of Irish whiskey. "For your coffee," she said. "I imagine you would appreciate it, after what you have been through."

Grinning gratefully, Longarm poured his coffee and added a healthy dollop of the Irish to it.

Quickly she took the bottle off the table and went back into the kitchen. He glanced in through the open kitchen door and saw her hide the bottle well under the sink. She took pains to make sure it was hidden completely.

Out of politeness, and in consideration of his disadvantageous position, Longarm chose to overlook the illegality of the presence of liquor on an Indian reservation. He was sure the woman must be as aware of the law as he. Normally, he would have considered it ungentlemanly to drink in the presence of those who chose, or were forced, to abstain, but in view of his recent, somewhat unsettling experience, he decided to make an exception in the present case.

She turned and saw him watching her, and said, "If any of the Apache men knew I had that there, it would be gone on the instant."

"What about yourself?" Longarm asked.

"I know. I've got Indian blood. I should be just as liable to abuse the liquor, shouldn't I?"

"That's what I hear."

"It's a lie—a damned white man's lie."

Longarm grinned at her and sipped his coffee. "I just asked."

"I know. I shouldn't get angry. It's just your ignorance."

"I reckon. Tell me, Nalin—how did you get to learn so much, you being an Apache and all?" Again Longarm smiled at her, hoping she would understand that his question had no malicious intent.

The answering gleam in her eyes assured Longarm that she understood. "I was educated in Texas," she told Longarm, "in a schoolhouse run by a very remarkable woman, Mrs. Russell Olafson."

"Texas?"

"My mother was a white woman, a Texan captured by the Mescalero Apaches. My father was a famous Apache warrior who was killed by a band of Texas Rangers who tracked him and his war party, killed him, then raided our settlement. My mother was killed in the attack, but before she died, she convinced one of the rangers to take me with him. That man was Russell Olafson. He was a good man, and he kept his promise. And his wife became more than a mother to me; a teacher and a friend."

"So what are you doing back here? This is some distance from Texas and Mrs. Olafson."

"She and her husband are dead now—and I have

learned there is only one kind of white man: the full-blooded variety. With the Olafsons gone, I found I really had no one that I could call a friend. The men who courted me—they wanted me because I was part Indian, a breed from whom they could expect all sorts of things." She looked away from Longarm's face and picked up her cup of coffee, holding it with fingers that trembled ever so slightly. "And so," she finished, "I came back to my people. To teach them the white man's ways, to care for them." She shook her head. "Because they are not as civilized as the white man, they accepted me almost without question. Here, at last, I have found a home."

"How old were you when Olafson took you back with him to Texas?"

"Ten years old."

Longarm nodded. "Are you paid by the federal government?"

"I am paid by no one. I was fortunate that the Olafsons left me a considerable sum. With that I have been able to build this schoolhouse and provide myself with those luxuries I had come to depend on in Texas."

"Like Irish whiskey."

She smiled. "Yes, like Irish whiskey. Now, Mr. Long, why are *you* here?"

"My friends call me Longarm," he told her.

"All right, friend Longarm. Why are you here? Is it not more than the death of that clerk, Bernstein, as you suggested earlier?"

Longarm studied the girl, wondering how much he could tell her. He still had a few questions he would like for her to answer. "Nalin, how'd you happen to come upon me when you did?"

"You mean, did I have anything to do with that ambush?"

"I have to be careful, Nalin."

"I had just dismissed the children. It was close to

noon. I saw one of Toklani's brothers hurry into the camp. Soon after, the rest of the men drifted out of camp, all of them armed. I knew something was up and that it had to do with Toklani's wife. I sent word down the valley to the agency, and then left as soon as I could without attracting attention."

"It took you a while to catch up."

She smiled thinly, and for that instant Longarm saw the Indian in her, clearly and unmistakably. It blazed in her eyes. "I am sorry I did not arrive sooner, Longarm. If I had, you would not have Toklani as your enemy. But I lost their trail when they split up before the ridge. Besides, I kept well back. I did not want them to know I was following; they would not have allowed it."

Longarm nodded. "All right, Nalin. The governor, Lew Wallace, asked my office for assistance because a territorial agent he sent to Paso Robles has disappeared. Governor Wallace sent the agent in because there've been quite a few shootings in the past two months, in addition to the murder of Bernstein. Wallace wants to know what's going on. And," Longarm concluded, pausing to get her reaction, "of course there's always a chance that Billy the Kid could be behind these shootings."

"Billy the Kid?"

"You've heard of him?"

"Vaguely. But I know no such person."

"He is an adenoidal lout who's recently made a name for himself as a regulator in the Lincoln County War. He goes by a whole bunch of handles—William Bonney, Henry McArty, Bill Harrigan, Kid Antrim, to mention a few." He grinned at her. "Any of those names sound familiar?"

Nalin shook her head.

"I didn't think so. You're pretty well away from it up here. How long a ride is it to Paso Robles?"

"A good three hours. If you punish your horse, you could make it in less time. And then, of course, I don't know how good a rider you are."

"I could take some lessons from you, I reckon. But I'm in no hurry. Tell me, is there anything out of the ordinary going on in Paso Robles?"

"Out of the ordinary?"

"New faces, new activity, settlers moving in, things like that."

"There are some new people—Anglos—moving into Paso Robles, I believe. But it is still mostly a Mexican settlement. It is those white men moving through our reservation at night that bother my people," she said. "They use our land to get to the pass. And the cattle they drive before them are not their own, I am sure." She smiled slightly at this, pleased to contemplate the depravity of the White Eyes. "I would not be surprised if some of these rustlers and rapists come from Paso Robles, but this would be unusual. The Mexican ranchers and those living in the town have always been a peaceful lot." She smiled slightly. "They are too frightened of the Apache to be anything else."

Longarm nodded. Cattle rustling could be behind all the shooting, he realized. It was quite possible. The pass leading through the Sacramentos came out onto the Jornado del Muerto trail, which, in turn, led to El Paso—a good place to unload rustled beef for a good price. But this did not entirely square with what Marshal Vail had told Longarm back in Denver, which was that since General Lew Wallace had been brought in to calm things down, both sides in the Lincoln County War were keeping their asses down. That should have pretty well stopped the thieving. Unless, of course, Billy the Kid was behind it.

Longarm finished his coffee and looked across the table at Nalin. It had been a long trip from Denver. He had taken a train from Denver, getting off at Roswell in neighboring Chaves County. From there he had taken a stage up the Rio Hondo into Lincoln County. At Fort Stanton he had picked up the buckskin, preferring to ride the rest of the way on horseback. The stage had been, as usual, a numbing exercise in boredom. The only pleasure in it had been the brief acquaintance he had struck up with a Mrs. Kate Ballard, a very enterprising young widow who had confided to Longarm that she was going to open a saloon in Paso Robles. From the look of her, Longarm had judged that she was a soiled dove of some experience who had been smart enough to salt away her nefarious earnings in a sock and then hang onto it. He did not believe for one minute that she had inherited her modest fortune from her dead husband.

Longarm had found much in the woman's endowments to admire, and he was looking forward to meeting her again. Still, a three-hour ride did not strike Longarm as a very pleasant prospect, despite the likelihood of the widow Ballard's company at the end of it. As a matter of fact, he now found Nalin's company considerably more intriguing. She made excellent coffee.

But, of course, he had to be invited—and he was still, after all, in the middle of a comparatively hostile settlement. Toklani would soon be back in camp, anxious to cut out the liver of the White Eyes who had shot up his right hand and who might still be, in his eyes, the rapist who had despoiled his woman.

"Thanks for the coffee, Nalin," Longarm said, standing up. He did not try to keep the reluctance he felt out of his voice. "I reckon I better be on my way."

"You have a long ride," Nalin observed, getting to her feet also. "Would you prefer a fresh start in the morning?"

"Now that sure does appeal to me, at that."

She smiled. "You realize the dangers if you stay here?"

"And the advantages."

Nalin frowned. "You understand, Longarm. I am just another woman. There is really nothing special about me—nothing in my Indian nature to make me any more . . . exciting than any other companion you might find on your lonely journeys."

"That's as it may be, Nalin, but why don't you let me be the judge of that."

She inclined her head slightly in his direction, as if to concede the point, and Longarm thought her already dark complexion grew a shade darker. "I do like you, Longarm," she admitted. "But again, I feel I should warn you of the danger if you remain here overnight."

"Thank you. Now I think I better see to my horse."

She smiled. "I'll go with you. When the women see me with you, they will understand that you are to be trusted. They will speak to their men."

As they stepped through the schoolhouse door, Longarm heard a commotion beyond the junipers. Apache children came running toward the schoolhouse, their eyes wide. Nalin called to one of them, obviously asking what was causing the disturbance. When the answer came, she looked at Longarm with a sympathetic smile.

"We have visitors, Longarm. The Indian agent and two of the agency police. It seems they have come to escort you from the reservation."

Longarm sighed and waited by the buckskin as three riders appeared, south of the schoolhouse. The agent was in the lead, with two of his dark-skinned keepers of the peace at his back. The agent was dressed in a dark suit, and wore a bowler hat similar to Nalin's atop his bald skull. A thin string tie was knotted at his throat. His shirt appeared filthy, even from this distance. He waved a gnarled hand in greeting as he passed through the camp on his way to the schoolhouse. When he got close enough, Longarm could see the man's bulbous, inflamed nose, the indelible mark of the inebriate. The man's cheeks were sunken, his eyes watery. He appeared to be holding himself atop his mount with some difficulty.

He reined in his horse sloppily and looked blearily down at Longarm. "You the feller shot Toklani?" he asked.

"It was self-defense. I could have aimed to kill him."

"Maybe you should've. What's your business here?"

"Just passing through."

"You got a name?"

"Custis Long, deputy U.S. marshal. What's yours?"

"Caleb Longbough. I'm the agent for this here reservation. You got proof you're who you say you are?"

Longarm had started to reach for his wallet when Nalin spoke up.

"I saw his badge, Caleb. He's a lawman, all right. All the way from Denver, on his way to Paso Robles."

Caleb shifted uncomfortably in his saddle. "All right, then. I got word Toklani is still out there, fixing to even the score with you, Long. So I'm ordering you off this here reservation, and I'm giving you an escort. These two agency policemen are the best I got. They'll see to it you get out of here and safe on your way to Paso Robles."

Longarm took a deep breath. "All right, Longbough. Thank you. I'd purely appreciate the escort. But I'd like a chance to water my horse."

"You can do that on your way. There's a stream west of here. You'll pass it."

With a shrug, Longarm turned to Nalin. The smile on her face was understanding. "Reckon I'd best be riding on, after all," Longarm told her softly.

There was a mocking light in her beautiful eyes. "You can't win them all, Longarm," she replied just as softly. "But perhaps you will pass this way again."

Longarm touched the brim of his hat to her and swung into his saddle. Catching up the reins and looking back down at her, he said, "I'll make it my business to do that, Toklani or not."

"Toklani has asked me to be his woman," she said, stepping back from Longarm's horse, a direct challenge now in her eyes. "Nevertheless, I will look for your tall figure on a horse."

Longarm pulled the buckskin around and galloped ahead of his guardians out of the Mescalero encampment. Toklani wanted Nalin for his squaw! He shook his head at the thought, then put his mind to the ride ahead. Three hours to Paso Robles, Nalin had told him. Hell, with angry Apaches at his back, he should make it faster than that.

Chapter 2

Paso Robles lay bright and clean under the wash of a full moon. It sat in the fertile bowl of a long valley cut by a broad stream—a pale ribbon of moonlight that snaked through the entire length of the valley.

Astride his buckskin atop a ridge less than a mile away, Longarm had no difficulty picking out the church; it was the tallest adobe structure in the town. A neat, empty square fronted it. Extending in both directions from the church was a single line of one-story *jacales*. Narrow sidestreets behind the church contained other adobe living quarters, making a sharply defined pattern of light and shadow under the bright night sky.

Across from the church were the false-front frame buildings of the Anglos, with more substantial two-story frame dwellings extending up the side of a broad hill behind the business district. This way, Longarm noted ironically, the Anglos in Paso Robles had no difficulty at all in looking down on the greasers.

Kneeing the horse's flanks, he left the ridge and angled down the slope until he reached the stream. It didn't take him long to find a rutted road. He followed it into Paso Robles. Turning down a narrow street that led into the Anglo section of town, he dismounted eventually at a livery stable and led his horse into the barn.

The hostler was busy forking fresh hay into a stall. He glanced up and, after leaning the pitchfork against the wall of the stall, started toward Longarm. He was a young fellow, close to twenty, with alert, wary eyes set in a friendly face. His front teeth protruded slightly. The Levi's he wore were filthy, and his red cotton shirt matched them in accumulated grime. His hat was a sorry thing with a torn brim that hung down over one ear.

"Well now," the hostler said, taking the reins of Longarm's buckskin. "This here sure is a nice-looking piece of horseflesh."

Longarm could tell at once that the fellow knew it was army stock even before he saw the brand, and that, as a result, the hostler was on the alert with him. "Take good care of him," Longarm said. "He's had a long ride. All the way from Fort Stanton. He deserves a rest." There was no sense in trying to hide what was already obvious, Longarm realized. That sort of thing only increased suspicion. "What's the best hotel in Paso Robles?"

"The *only* hotel is down the street past the Dry Gulch Saloon." The hostler indicated the direction with a nod of his head. Then his eyes narrowed. "You army?"

"Nope."

"A lawman?"

The tall man nodded affably. "That's right. You got anything against lawmen?"

The hostler shrugged. "Depends on the lawman."

"Name's Long. Custis Long. You take good care of that horse, hear?"

"Sure."

Longarm tossed the hostler a silver dollar he took from his trousers pocket, then untied the saddle bags and the bedroll, lifted his rifle from the sling, and started from the stable.

"Thanks, Mr. Long," the hostler called after him, flipping the coin.

Longarm paused in the doorway and looked back at the hostler. "What did you say your name was?"

"I didn't. But my friends call me Hank."

Longarm nodded and left the livery stable, his saddle bags and bedroll slung over his shoulder, his rifle in hand. He was passing the Dry Gulch Saloon when a drunken drummer reeled out through the batwings and into the street, where he collapsed facedown in the white dust and began to snore loudly. The fellow had barely noticed Longarm as he staggered past him, but Longarm recognized him as one of the passengers on the stage he had taken as far as Fort Stanton. *Widow Ballard must be in town,* he thought, and proceeded up the street to the hotel, a dismal two-story frame building. The word HOTEL had been painted in large block letters on the false front, but the blistering New Mexico sun had almost completely bleached it to the color of the wood it was painted on. Entering, Longarm found himself in a small, dusty lobby. A bespectacled night clerk wearing a green eyeshade was napping in a chair behind the desk. Longarm set his gear down on the desk as loudly as possible, but the clerk did not stir. Longarm slapped the bell. The clerk rose out of his seat as if he had been bitten by a scorpion, almost losing his eyeshade in the process.

"Yessir, what can I do for you?" the clerk asked, fumbling with his eyeshade. He had a round, owlish face, and his thick glasses gave his eyes a looming, grotesque prominence.

"I didn't come in here for a drink," Longarm drawled, "and I didn't come in here for supplies. This isn't a barbershop, this is a hotel. What in blazes do you *think* you can do for me?"

The man snatched up the pen from the desktop, and dipped it into the inkwell. Handing it to Longarm, he said, "Just sign the register, sir. Just sign it right there. Would second floor front be all right?"

"That would be fine," Longarm said, signing the register.

The clerk handed Longarm his room key. He glanced at the number on the tab, gathered up his gear, and started for the stairs. He was tired, very tired. All he wanted now was a good night's sleep. As he started up the stairs, the clerk made no offer to help with the law-man's gear, but sat back down in his chair, tipped its back against the wall, and closed his eyes.

Longarm found his room, entered, dumped his gear on the bed, and, with a sulfur match, lit the single lamp he found on the dresser. He closed the door behind him and looked about the room in the dim, flickering light from the lamp. The furnishings were in the traditional Spanish style, with a heavy wooden bed and two large dressers elaborately carved and decorated. A white porcelain-enameled washbasin, with a graniteware water pitcher standing in it, was on top of one of the dressers. The chamber pot sat on a marble-topped commode next to the dressers. It had been cleaned out, but still exuded a faintly unpleasant odor. Longarm paid that no heed, and swung the pot in under his bed where it would be more handy.

He lifted his rifle off the bed and leaned it against the wall by the headboard. He was taking off his hat when he heard a soft rapping on his door. He swung about, his eyes narrowed thoughtfully. It couldn't be the clerk, and he doubted that it was the hostler. Who the hell else knew he was in town? That drunken whiskey salesman hadn't even seen Longarm when he staggered past him.

24

"Who is it?" he called through the door, his hand resting lightly on the grips of his holstered Colt.

"Mister Long?"

Kate Ballard, the widow. Longarm relaxed and pulled open the door. The tall woman was standing nervously in the dim hallway, an uncertain smile on her face.

"I hope you won't think I'm shamefully forward, Mr. Long," she said, "but I couldn't help noticing you as you walked up the street toward the hotel. I am afraid I would recognize that impressive stride of yours anywhere."

The marshal smiled, inviting her into his room with a sweep of his arm.

She took a hesitant step toward the door. "Are you sure you don't mind? That must have been a very tiring ride."

"After such a ride, your pleasant company will be most welcome, Mrs. Ballard. Do come in."

Without further hesitation, the widow entered, blushing a bit. Longarm closed the door after her. He spotted a somewhat battered wicker armchair in the corner by his closet and quickly brought it over for the widow, holding it for her as she sat down.

"Now then," he said, sitting on the edge of his bed. "What can I do for you, Mrs. Ballard?"

"You may call me Kate."

"And you can call me Longarm, if you're of a mind to. I hope the rest of your trip was all right."

"Tiresome, Longarm. Terribly tiresome. I simply hate stagecoaches. It is *not* a very refined torture. We got in early this morning."

"And you found your partner, did you?"

"Yes," she said, "I found him." Her voice revealed a sudden grimness. "Drunk and stone broke. I wish you could see what condition the saloon is in. It will take considerable capital to fix it up for business."

"I'm purely sorry to hear that."

"Fortunately, my rival has generously offered to help."

"Your rival?"

"A Mr. Charles Kilrain. He owns the Dry Gulch, among other establishments in town. He is also running for mayor."

"That was nice of him."

"Oh, the monetary aid he has extended to me is not without strings, Longarm, not at all. He is charging me ten percent interest."

"I see."

"Mr. Longarm, what is your profession?"

Longarm frowned. During the long stagecoach ride with the widow, he had avoided revealing his occupation to her. He'd found it generally a good practice not to own up to what he was about until it became inconvenient not to do so.

When he didn't answer immediately, she went on, "I need a partner, Longarm. I cannot rely on that drunken fool."

"I see."

"He still owns fifty percent of the saloon, of course. But aside from that, he is useless. I would split my half with you."

"Twenty-five percent."

"That's right."

"I have no capital," he said with a shrug.

"Your capital, Longarm, is your strength, your size, your competence as a man. I have the feeling I will need those qualities in this place."

"Kate, you do me an honor. But I don't think I'm cut out to be a saloonkeeper."

"You didn't answer me, Longarm. What *is* your profession?"

Longarm realized he couldn't politely avoid the question any longer. "I am a lawman, a deputy U.S. marshal."

She leaned back in her chair, the light in her eyes showing triumph. "I thought so! Just the kind of man I need! Your duties would simply be to keep the riffraff in line, something you could do with a sharp word alone, I am sure. Certainly, you don't want to remain a federal marshal for the rest of your life. A good saloon never lacks for patrons, Longarm—not in this man's world. Anything which caters to a man's appetite has a long and profitable life. I know from experience."

He smiled a mite wearily. This was far from the first such offer he had ever received. "No, Kate. Thank you for the offer. But I guess I'll just have to stick to doing what I do best—and wearing a badge seems to be it."

She looked at him for a long while, her shrewd eyes searching his face for any sign that she might still be able to prevail upon him. At length, satisfied that he was sincere in his refusal of her offer, she shrugged and smiled.

He found her, in that instant, a most handsome woman indeed. More striking, in fact, than she had appeared in that dusty, rocking stage. She was a tall woman with sharp, angular features; her thick hair was swept back in a tight bun. Longarm imagined it untied and cascading freely almost to her waist. Her eyes were dark and luminous, the brows that arched over them very dark and cleanly outlined. Despite the fact that she would never see thirty again, her flawless complexion was without wrinkles or sags. Her nose was straight, her mouth firm, her lips sensuous. Longarm's instinct told him that if she had made her bundle in a sporting house, she must have been the top of the line, able to command a very high fee.

"I understand, Longarm," she replied, undaunted. "But if you won't join me in this venture, would you do me the kindness to come downstairs with me and talk to this damned partner of mine? He is no gentleman and has already struck me once because of our disagreements. He is, I am afraid, an unmitigated cur."

"You want me to put the fear of the law into him?"

She smiled, relieved. "Yes, precisely. I would appreciate that very much." She paused, her eyes watching him closely, measuring him. "And you will find that I can be very generous to those men gallant enough to stand by me at such times."

Longarm waved a hand, dismissing the suggestion. "It's my job. Keeping the peace, as they say."

She stood up. Again Longarm was impressed with the way she carried herself. "I'll get my wrap," she told him. "I won't be long. My room is just down the hall."

Longarm got to his feet also. "I'll wait," he said, reaching for his hat—and pushing the thought of sleep reluctantly from his mind.

As Longarm passed the Dry Gulch with Kate Ballard at his side, he noticed that the whiskey drummer was no longer sleeping off his load in the middle of the street. He had crawled or been dragged closer to the buildings and was lying now, still facedown, beside a fresh, steaming pile of horse manure under one of the hitch rails. A tall, sleek Morgan saddle horse was standing just beside him, nervously twitching its tail.

Past the Dry Gulch, they turned a corner, crossed a narrow street, and entered a saloon as large as the Dry Gulch, but considerably less lively. There was not enough light in the place, it seemed to Longarm. There was a long mahogany bar on his right that extended better than thirty feet. Beyond the bar was a gaming room. A faro table, a roulette wheel, and four poker tables were visible, their green felt tops gleaming softly in the dim light from the lanterns that hung from the low, beamed ceiling. Tables and chairs filled the rest of the place. Sawdust covered the rough flooring. The place was crowded, but there was not a dark face in sight. This saloon was for Anglos only, Longarm realized. Any natives of New Mexico would find themselves thoroughly unwelcome.

At Kate Ballard's entrance, the saloon's noise level dropped noticeably. As Longarm followed her and escorted her to one of the tables, the place became unnaturally quiet. Those patrons holding up the bar made no effort to conceal their appreciation of Kate's endowments, while the rest of the men in the place fixed Longarm with an unwavering, suspicious scrutiny.

Leaving Kate at the table, Longarm moved up to the bar. Kate had told him she wanted only a glass of wine. The barkeep had a broad, flat face that was beet red. His thinning red hair was plastered straight back over a shiny, freckled scalp. When he smiled, he revealed crooked, yellow teeth.

"We don't have no wine, mister. Just whiskey. You want wine, why don't you ride back to Denver and try one of them fancy hotels."

Without comment, Longarm paid for two whiskeys and brought them to the table where Kate was waiting. As he sat down, he looked around the saloon. The conversation was coming back to life. He could hear the snapping of poker chips, the clicking of the roulette wheel. Cheerful sounds, usually. But this saloon had a mean feeling about it.

"Is he in here?" Longarm asked. "This partner of yours?"

"He's coming through the door now."

Longarm followed Kate's gaze and saw a burly fellow with a bulbous nose, beetling brows, and eyes that squinted unhappily through the smoke at them both. He walked with a rolling, belligerent swagger, and his underlip was thrust out in a kind of defiant surliness. He was a most unpleasant-looking man who caused

Longarm to wonder how in hell the widow Ballard had ever let herself go into partnership with him. A business partnership was as bad as a marriage, and Kate Ballard had impressed Longarm as too savvy to let herself get roped into anything as confining as that without exercising considerable care.

"Who's this?" her partner demanded, hovering over the table like a scavenger bird. "This is between you and me, Kate. We don't need this fellow."

"I think *I* do. Sit down, Fred, and meet Custis Long." She smiled sweetly. "He's a deputy U.S. marshal."

The partner's face went only slightly pale. As he slumped into a chair between them, he did not offer to shake the lawman's hand. Kate looked at Longarm disgustedly.

"Forgive Fred's manners, Longarm. He may look like a slob on the outside, but inside he's pure shit."

Fred's face paled. Longarm could see the man's pudgy fists clench. This time, however, the man was forced to keep his temper in check. He glared at Kate Ballard and spat: "Have it your way, bitch. I'm backing out, unless you can come up with another five hundred. And I'm not selling you fifty percent, only twenty-five. Take it or leave it."

"The deal was fifteen hundred!" Kate replied furiously. "For fifty percent of this business. That's what it said in the ad! You can't back down now! Not after I've come all this way!"

"Sure I can. I'm backing down right now," he sneered. "This is still my saloon. We deal on my terms, or we don't deal at all. Two thousand dollars for twenty-five percent." Fred leaned back in his chair, smirking at Kate. "And no more lip from you. That's part of the deal."

Kate looked at Longarm in sudden dismay. Evidently her earlier confrontation with this insolent crook had prompted him to decide he didn't want Kate as a partner. Longarm finished his whiskey and wiped his mouth with the back of his hand.

"Do you have a copy of that ad, Kate?" he asked.

She took a wallet from her wrap, withdrew from it a tattered piece of newspaper, and handed it to Longarm. Longarm took it and read it twice. Then he glanced up at Fred.

"This ad says half interest in a thriving saloon. Write for details. Half interest, Fred. That's binding." Longarm glanced at Kate. "Did you write him?"

"My lawyer did," she replied triumphantly. Before Longarm could ask for the correspondence, she handed it to him.

He took it and read the letters quickly. The lawyer's jargon gave him some pause, but the gist of the agreement was perfectly clear: half interest in the saloon located in the town of Paso Robles for the sum of fifteen hundred dollars, American. It was all there, as clear as silk. And in an answering letter, which contained Fred Bushnell's barely legible signature, the terms were confirmed.

Handing the letters back to Kate, he smiled easily and looked at Fred. "Your signature on that letter makes it a bona fide contract," he told the man, lying outrageously. Longarm knew little about contracts and such things, but he was certain this huckleberry knew even less.

Stymied, Fred looked from Longarm to Kate, then back again. At last, in a show of prodigious self-control, he passed his meaty hand over his face, then fixed Kate with a despairing look. "All right then. So it's a contract. We're partners. But you just try and get any help out of me. And I'm not sinking another cent into this saloon. You may not like it, but it suits me fine just the way it is."

"Why did you put that ad in the paper, Fred?" Long-arm asked.

"I needed the money."

"Gambling debts," Kate Ballard told Longarm. "And that fifteen hundred is not going to be enough."

"That so?" Longarm asked Fred.

"Yes, damn it, if it's any of your business."

"How much?"

"Three thousand," the man groaned in a despairing voice. "It's either that or the saloon."

"You mean your interest in it," Longarm corrected him.

"No. The saloon, one hundred percent of it." He looked balefully across the table at Kate. "That's why I been trying to discourage this here widow. There's someone who will give me four thousand."

"I see. But he wants full ownership, right?"

"And if I can deliver it to him, he'll give me enough to clear up my debts."

"And clear out."

"Yes, damn you."

"And who might this gentleman be?"

"Charlie Kilrain, I'll bet," said Kate Ballard.

"It's Kilrain, all right," Fred admitted. He looked then with sudden hope at Kate Ballard. "Now you see my pickle, you got to help me out! What do you want with a saloon in this godforsaken place for, anyway?"

"Never mind why I want it," Kate replied icily. "I want it, and that's enough for me. Mr. Long has explained the legalities to you; you may now do as you wish. But I'm staying in Paso Robles."

Fred lurched wrathfully to his feet, the legs of his chair scraping harshly along the rough wooden floor. He loomed over the table, glaring furiously at Kate Ballard. "Damn you!" he spat. He glanced at Longarm. "And your lawman friend!"

With that parting shot, he spun on his heels and

stalked the length of the saloon, disappearing through a door in the game room. His furious exit caused a sudden, tense silence to fall over the place. All eyes were now on Kate Ballard and Longarm.

Kate got to her feet and, thrusting her shoulders back, stared at the patrons in return, her eyes flashing. "Drink up, gents," she told them in a sharp, clear voice that was remarkably close to a command. "As my guests, your next round is on the house!"

The patrons broke as one for the bar and were soon three deep, shouting out their orders to the astonished barkeep. Kate sat back down and smiled at Longarm. "I'll bet Fred never did that—not once. That's the first change I'm going to make. The next one is to fire that barkeep."

"Why?"

"For the way he addressed you when you asked for our drinks."

"I don't think you're out of the woods yet," Longarm cautioned her.

"I know that. But I think I've got Fred Bushnell on the run. He won't be trying to discourage me anymore. I figure he'll take the fifteen hundred and light out— without paying his debt. Good riddance, I say." She stood up. "Are you coming?"

"Where?"

"Back to the hotel. It has been a very long day for me. And for you too, I should think."

Wearily, Longarm rose to his feet. "I'd be honored to escort you back to the hotel. And it *has* been one hell of a long day."

Kate Ballard took her tall companion's arm. "It has at that," she said.

Stopping in front of Kate's door, Longarm took the woman's arm and turned her gently to face him. She smiled slightly. In the dim light from the single lamp on a shelf far down the hall, her face was only a pale oval. But her fine, luminous eyes looked up at Longarm with warmth and understanding. She moved closer to him so that the length of her body was pressed lightly against his.

"Yes, Longarm," she said softly, "I did promise you I would be generous in payment for your help."

Longarm laughed quietly. "I wasn't thinking of that just now. Something just occurred to me."

"I must admit I am not very flattered," she said teasingly, pulling slightly back from him. "But what is it? What has occurred to you?"

"If Fred can get his hands on those letters and that newspaper clipping, he might figure he has a chance of reneging on the deal. To his mind, those papers are all that's standing in his way."

"Oh. I think I see what you mean," Kate said, frowning. "That leads to a very nasty thought."

"Yes. You might very well have a gentleman caller this evening—either Fred or one of his cronies."

She looked carefully up at Longarm. "You must have an idea how I can handle this."

Longarm nodded. "I do."

She smiled. "I knew I could count on you."

"Go into your room and get whatever you need. I'll go back to my room and get my gear. We'll switch rooms for the night."

"But then you'll be the target. In the dark, Fred might think you're me."

The marshal smiled thinly, twisting the end of his mustache between his thumb and forefinger. "He might at that. It should be a nice surprise when he discovers who he's wrestling with."

"It's dangerous, Longarm. Cornered rats are not very predictable."

"Let's just eat this here apple one bite at a time, Kate. We aren't at all sure Fred will show up. Besides, this is my job, and it's a mite more sensible to stop a crime from being committed than to wait for it to happen. Go in and get your things, Kate."

Kate did as Longarm told her, and soon she had settled herself in his room, and he was in her room, unpeeling his britches, when a soft knock on the door caused him to turn.

"It's me," Kate whispered through the door. "Can I come in?"

Longarm strode to the door and spoke through it. "I'm in my longjohns, woman."

"Wait until you see what I'm in!"

He started to protest, then thought better of it. There was only one thing worse than taking a woman against her will: *not* taking her when she was willing. He opened the door and let Kate in.

What she was wearing was very pretty, very simple, and very seductive—a long blue nightgown with delicate lace along the bottom, at the sleeves, and about the neck. It buttoned all the way up the front, and Kate had contrived to leave the top four buttons unbuttoned. What this carelessness revealed was enough to make a strong man perspire, no matter how exhausted he might be. Longarm closed the door.

"This is *not* the way to turn the tables on Fred Bushnell, Kate. Hell, this way he's going to end up getting two birds with one slug."

"I'm willing to chance it," she said, leaning boldly against him. "Besides, like you said, we aren't absolutely sure anything will happen."

Longarm sighed. He reached out and pulled her against him. His lips found hers. With a sinuous, practiced movement, she let her nightgown drop to her ankles.

His arms still around her naked shoulders, his lips still on hers, he turned and moved toward the bed. The mating dance was a short one-step that took them onto the bed, Longarm's knees astride her ample hips. Her lips remained locked to his, her impudent tongue probing with maddening effect. Pulling his lips free of hers, he moved his mouth across her shoulders, down between her full, upthrust breasts, then up again, fastening his lips at last upon the rigid, puckering nipples. He teased them expertly with his tongue, nipped delicately at them with his teeth. She moaned uncontrollably and lifted her thigh under him.

"Oh, Longarm! Jesus! You're still dressed! That's not fair!"

"Undress me then," he said, pulling back and smiling down at her. "You know how to do that, don't you?"

"It will be my pleasure."

She kissed him again, and with her lips still hard upon his, she unbuttoned his shirt, slipped it back off his shoulders, then peeled down the top of his balbriggans. Her fingers moved with a swift, heated urgency that aroused him even more and he felt his erection, raw now with desire, probing at her moist entrance in a deliberate delay calculated to drive her even wilder. It succeeded.

"You bastard!" she cried out. "What are you waiting for? I want you! Now!"

He went in full and deep, thrusting powerfully, grunting with the exertion. She moaned from deep within her and fastened her lips to his again, her tongue probing almost down his throat as she brought her legs up and locked her ankles around his back. With each thrust she hugged him tighter, her hips grinding, pulling him deeper into her.

Pulling back, careful not to leave her completely, he thrust deeper than he had been able to thrust before. He felt her rock under the impact. She opened her mouth to gasp, her head thrown back, her eyes shut tightly, as he continued his long plunges. Keeping it up steadily, driving fiercely into her each time, he felt himself moving toward orgasm. He moved faster, thrusting deeper. Tiny cries erupted from her throat. She began twisting her head from side to side. Still deeper he thrust, rocking her violently, going so fast now that he felt as if a switch deep in his groin had been turned on and he was now completely out of control.

Kate gasped. Her eyes flew open. He felt her go rigid under him. Her inner muscles tightened around him. He bore in then with a grim, abandoned thrust that nailed her to the bed—and in that instant, both of them came at the same time in a shuddering orgasm that left Longarm pulsing deep within her again and again in an uncontrollable series of spasms. At last it was finished. A blissful and total relaxation fell over Longarm. He fell forward onto her, his shaft still within her, still enclosed in her soft, warm snugness.

For a moment both of them were still. Kate stirred. He looked into her face. She smiled. "Heavens, Longarm. I used to do this for a living—but never like *that!*"

"I guess I'll just have to consider that a compliment."

"Oh, it is, Longarm!" She kissed him impulsively. "But we're not finished yet! I want more! Please, let me get on top! I want to ride you! I want to feel you deep inside me while I sit astride that lovely—"

Longarm placed a finger over her mouth. "Suit actions to words, Kate," he told her softly, rolling over onto his back. "We don't have all night."

"Oh, what a shame *that* is!"

Then she was on top of him, her head thrown back, the lines of her neck muscles taut. And then she raised herself, delicately almost, while the lips of her vagina held his erection, caressing it. Then down again, driving hard. She did this slowly at first, with maddening deliberation, while Longarm felt himself growing still larger.

She moaned and increased her tempo. He reached up to hold her breasts, cupping them in his big, rough hands.

She nodded her head frantically to indicate that this was what she wanted. Soon Longarm could feel the erect nipples thrusting against the palms of his hands. Her movements became more violent now. Short explosive sounds escaped from her half-open mouth. She rose and came down on his shaft with a violence that threatened to sunder her—or injure him. He dropped his hands from her breasts and held her hips, his big hands clasping her firmly, keeping her from riding too high and helping him to bring his own thrusts into unison with hers.

"Faster!" she said with sudden, hoarse fierceness. "Faster! Deeper, damn you!"

She flung herself forward suddenly, her lips finding his. He opened his mouth and she darted her tongue wildly between his teeth. He lifted his buttocks while he continued to thrust, so that he was almost flinging her over his head. Her teeth clashed wildly against his, as she uttered short, guttural sounds that seemed to have been wrung from a part of her that even she was not aware existed.

He let go of her hips and encircled her shoulders, holding his mouth hard against hers, their tongues interlocked in a wild embrace of their own. Her hips were grinding now as well as bounding upward, with a control that was as amazing as it was effective. Longarm found that he had achieved a synchronization with her movements. They were welded together. It was all instinct now. His hips rose to meet her downthrusts in a wild, but perfectly controlled coupling. She cried out—a tiny mewling cry.

Then came the inevitable, headlong rush to climax. Plunging upward, he felt himself exploding within her. She flung back her head, keening, as her inner muscles continued to suck his erection clean. Then she too shuddered to a climax. It lasted, he could tell, for a few seconds, until she collapsed, laughing delightedly, onto his chest. Swiftly she covered his face with soft kisses, then leaned past his face to nibble affectionately on his earlobes. She was in a transport of delight that pleased Longarm as much as it seemed to please her. She slid off him.

"I've got another idea," she told him eagerly. "I'll roll over onto my back. You can enter me from—"

"Hold it, Kate," Longarm told her sadly. "It's all over for now. I was mighty tired to begin with. That big fellow is just a little mite now. Fact is, he must be raw and red by this time. You'll just have to let me sit out this dance."

She giggled. "You underestimate me, Longarm. I have a hundred tricks. I can get you up again, don't you worry."

Her fingers traced lightly down his cheeks, then down his heavily corded, deeply tanned neck to the tightly coiled hair of his chest. She kissed his shoulder. He felt the moist heat of her tongue sliding along the slope of his shoulders to the strong cords of his neck. All this time, her fingers had continued on down to his crotch. She began to stroke him. Her fingers were inspired, and gradually her lips began moving down his chest. He felt a flame of desire quickening him—but it was a feeble flame, not enough to handle the needs of this lovely wanton.

He rolled away. "Sorry, Kate. I gave you all I had— more even than I thought I had. There ain't any sense in going to the well again tonight. You'll only come up with an empty bucket."

She sat up and looked down at him. "You must think me shameless."

"You must think I'm two men."

"All I know is you're very well named, Longarm." She leaned close then, and kissed him almost demurely on the lips, her hand brushing his cheek in a surprisingly tender caress. "I'm serious, Longarm; that was very nice. It did a lot for me, you have no idea."

"Think you can sleep now?"

"Oh yes. A blissful sleep, Longarm. Truly blissful," She got off the bed and bent to pick up her nightgown. She buttoned it all the way this time, opened the door, waved, and left.

As soon as he had locked the door behind her, Longarm got off the bed, picked up his scattered longjohns and shirt, and proceeded to prepare himself for any uninvited guests. He tipped the wicker armchair onto its side just in front of the door, to create an obstruction an intruder would not know how to deal with, especially in the dark while he was doing his utmost to be absolutely silent.

His vest, with his derringer in the right-hand pocket, was folded neatly on top of his dresser. He withdrew his double-action Colt Model T .44-40 from the open-toed, waxed, and heat-hardened leather holster he had placed on top of the vest. He chided himself when he recalled how vulnerable he had been in Kate Ballard's arms with his weaponry so far out of his reach. *But hell,* he told himself as he inspected his weapon, *a man has to get carried away once in a while, or his life isn't worth protecting the rest of the time.*

He swung the gun out over the rumpled bed, emptied the cylinder on the sheets, dry-fired a couple of times to test the action, holding the hammer with his thumb, then reloaded—holding each cartridge up to the light before thumbing it back into the chamber. This time, deliberately, he dug a sixth cartridge out of his coat pocket and fitted it into the Colt's cylinder. Ordinarily he loaded only five rounds, allowing the firing pin to ride safely on an empty chamber, but he had a feeling about this night and this town. Not even the recent pleasantness with Kate Ballard could shake that feeling. He wanted that extra round tonight.

Longarm pulled on his longjohns, tucked the Colt under his pillow, blew out the lamp, and climbed into his bed. The mattress filling was a little noisy under him and perhaps even a mite lumpy; but as soon as Longarm fitted his right hand around the polished walnut grips of his Colt, he closed his eyes and was asleep.

The scream—faint, but shattering in its evocation of terror—cut through his sleep like a knife. Longarm was out of bed even before he was fully awake, the Colt in his hand. He reached the door and found his feet entangled with the chair he had set on its side in front of it. Managing, nevertheless, to pull open the door, he attempted to kick the chair out of his path. The sleep that was still fogging his brain caused him to kick a little too hard and he went down heavily, sprawling forward into the hallway.

At that moment, someone down the hall fired at him. The round whistled over his head, disintegrating the window directly behind him. Longarm's sixgun was in his extended right hand. Without thinking, he fired at the shadowy figure crouched at the head of the stairs. The gunman fired again, and the orange flame lancing from the muzzle of his weapon filled the narrow hallway with a garish light. This time the round came much closer. Longarm heard it slamming into the doorjamb beside his shoulder. He fired again, his left hand steadying his right hand, all sleep now burned from his brain.

The gunman staggered back, turned, then vanished from sight. Longarm heard his heavy body falling down the stairs. At that instant, in the doorway of the room that had been his, Longarm saw someone poke his head out, then duck back. Kate screamed sharply. The scream was quickly muffled. Longarm could imagine

Kate struggling, kicking, her screams throttled by brutal, desperate hands.

Even as he visualized this, he was on his feet racing down the hall. Plunging into the room, he saw two figures struggling in the darkness, and another figure standing before the window. Something shiny gleamed in this second figure's hand. Longarm saw the hand come up, and fired swiftly from his hip; the detonation was deafening in the small room. The intruder by the window gasped and buckled forward, his own gun discharging harmlessly into the floor. As he sagged to his knees, Longarm turned to the fellow who had Kate.

This one flung Kate onto the bed, the gun in his own hand thundering. Longarm felt something hot and heavy—like a well-landed punch—strike him in the side and spin him completely around. He slammed into the wall, his feet almost sagging out from under him. His Colt clattered to the floor. He was amazed at the ease with which he had been flung about by a single slug.

He hated it. This was not the way he wanted this mission to end. It was too damned inconsequential—helping an ex-madam to salvage a saloon deal! He spun about, steadied his watery knees, then launched himself at the fellow who had shot him. Startled by Longarm's recovery, the fellow attempted to fire a second time at Longarm, but the shot went wild, and, by that time, Longarm had the man's neck between his powerful hands, his fingers closing about the man's windpipe.

In a panic, the erstwhile assailant tried to free himself from Longarm's tenacious grasp by flailing away at him with the barrel of his sixgun. Longarm paid no heed. The bloodlust was upon him now, and all he wanted was the feel of this jasper's neck crunching beneath his fingers. The fellow dropped his weapon and, with both hands, began plucking frantically at Longarm's viselike grip. With a sudden surge of fury,

Longarm bore the man ahead of him, driving him backward onto the bed; Longarm stayed on top, his fingers tightening remorselessly about the fellow's scrawny neck.

The man's struggling grew feeble. His tongue protruded; his eyes began to bulge. Longarm felt his own face crease into a grin. A weakness, deadly and insistent, was falling over his limbs, but he managed to channel every last ounce of strength down his arms, through his wrists, and into his fingers. And they kept on tightening, tightening. He thought he felt something snap beneath them, reminding him of when he had been a boy on his father's farm in West Virginia, wringing the neck of a chicken for a Sunday dinner.

Kate screamed. He glanced up reluctantly through a fog of weariness, aware of a heavy flow of blood thickening over his thigh and creeping down the length of his leg. The shadowy figure that Longarm had cut down in front of the window had roused himself, and was now looming menacingly over him. There was something heavy in his hand. Kate screamed and tried to wrest it from him. The fellow spun her backward with a single, brutal swipe, then brought the gun barrel down on Longarm's skull. Longarm tried to duck away, but he no longer had the strength. The blow landed solidly. Longarm felt as if the hotel had collapsed on his head. Lights exploded deep within his skull.

Kate's scream faded as he tumbled wearily back into the sleep from which he had been roused so abruptly only a few moments before. . . .

Chapter 3

Longarm stirred and opened his eyes. The sudden explosion of light caused him to wince, and he shut his eyes quickly. His head was pounding. It felt like he had the granddaddy of all hangovers. He opened his eyes, carefully, a second time. Squinting in the brightness, he turned his head away from the thick adobe wall on his right and the large window in it, through which flooded the brilliant New Mexico sun.

He was lying on a large bed. Beside it, sitting on a ladderbacked chair, was a Franciscan priest. His head was bowed and the man was obviously praying, his rosary beads clutched in his brown, gnarled hands. Glancing up, the priest saw Longarm squinting at him and smiled suddenly, crossing himself as he did so. Then he got up quickly and padded from the room, his long, coarse frock faintly brushing the rough-hewn plank flooring.

Longarm lifted himself up onto his elbows, his head pounding in protest against the exertion. Treating the discomfort the way he had heard that the ancient Greeks treated headaches—with contempt—he swung his feet down onto the floor. His bare ankles were clean.

And not only had he been bathed, but his face had been shaved as well. He was in clean longjohns, with the top cut off, apparently with a pair of shears. A tight bandage was wrapped around his waist. The wound under it throbbed softly, but Longarm could tell from the feel of it that it was not serious. It was his head that worried him, especially when he stood up.

He waited on unsteady feet for the room to stop rocking, then glanced over to the ornate dresser where his gear and clothing had been piled. He walked over to it, found his shirt and put it on, then pulled his britches on. He had to curse a little more than usual to get his fly shut, because of the bandage about his waist. Gritting his teeth against the pain in his throbbing dome, he bent double and hauled on his woolen socks, then grunted mightily as he pulled on his low-heeled cavalry stovepipes.

His vest he found folded neatly atop his brown frock coat, the double-barreled .44 derringer and the Ingersoll watch still tucked safely in the pockets, the gold-washed chain connecting them. He slipped into the vest, then examined the derringer to make sure it was still loaded. It was. His Colt was in its rig, the supple cordovan gunbelt folded under the holster. In strapping the gunbelt high around his waist, he winced a little and found he could not pull the belt as snug as he would have liked. Still, the cross-draw rig rested easy above his hip. The wound in his side had not incapacitated him. He had put on his Stetson and was slipping into his frock coat when he heard the rustling of skirts at the bedroom door. He turned to see a tall, handsome woman regarding him.

"I heard you dressing," she said, "so I waited. Now that you are fully armed, I hope you will feel secure enough to join me in the dining room. I have instructed the cook to serve us there. You must be hungry."

"I could eat a bear, ma'am, with maybe a steak for dessert."

She smiled thinly, turned, and led Longarm from the room, down a long, dim corridor, across an inner patio, then into a large dining room—a place as cool as a pine forest. Longarm was astonished at the casual elegance of the furniture. The table at which they sat was long and highly polished, made of solid oak. Its legs were massive and delicately carved. Everything in the room, especially the incredibly intricate tapestries on the walls, bespoke wealth and culture.

"Reckon that blow on the head did it," he said to his hostess. "I have died and been sent on to heaven." He smiled. "Paso Robles sure didn't look this elegant from the outside."

"I am Maria Antonia Lugo," the woman said. "And you are Custis Long. I examined your wallet, you see. You are not in heaven, Mr. Long, but in my hacienda, just outside Paso Robles."

"How'd I get here?"

"Hank brought you here."

"Hank?"

"I own the livery stable in Paso Robles. Hank is my hostler."

Longarm nodded carefully. "I know Hank. Met him when I rode in. But how did he get his hands on me, Maria? Last I knew, I was in the middle of a bloody fandango at the hotel where I was staying."

"Perhaps you should let Hank explain that."

The cook brought in food at that moment. She was a young, sturdy New Mexican with high cheekbones. Her shiny black hair was combed sharply back and fashioned into a tight ball on the top of her head. She was wide at the waist; her breasts were full; but in her bright green skirt, topped off with her loose, low-cut blouse, she moved with an easy, silent grace that intrigued the marshal. He wondered if this was the woman who had bathed him while he lay unconscious, if it had been her fingers that carefully wound that bandage about his waist.

The meal was served on gleaming white china. A plate was set before him, piled high with tortillas, and beside it, a dish of frijoles and chili, beans and red pepper, with chunks of mutton. The amount of mutton was most generous. He set to work gratefully with a spoon, using it to pack the chili into a folded tortilla. Longarm loved Mexican food, and this was the real thing.

Maria contented herself with a cup of coffee poured from a solid silver service. Without comment, she watched Longarm eat. He asked for coffee, hoping it would quiet his headache a mite. She poured for him without calling back the cook. Longarm took the cup and saucer from her and placed them gently beside his plate.

As he sipped the coffee, he looked Maria over. Her dress was a mixture of Mexican and American. Her long leather skirt was tightly laced at her waist, but her white blouse was open generously at her neck. Over the blouse she wore a black *chaqueta,* beautifully embroidered with silk braid and bright barrel buttons. Her eyes were a dark brown, regarding him coolly over high, copper-tanned cheekbones. The woman's brow was broad, her eyebrows solid. Her nose was strong and beautifully fashioned, the lines of her mouth full and passionate—but cold now in a curiously unwelcoming set as she gazed on Longarm. She did not, he decided, approve of him. And he wondered why.

Longarm returned to his meal. It was a curious breakfast, he commented to himself, but one that was filling him up fast. Then again, it was probably well past breakfast time. He frowned and glanced out the window to get some idea of the sun's position. Then he consulted his watch. It was three in the afternoon.

"How long have I been here, Maria?" he asked.

"Since last night."

There was a stirring in the kitchen. Longarm glanced up to see Hank and the priest who had been at his bedside. The priest smiled happily at the sight of Longarm. Hank nodded, seemingly as pleased as the priest to see Longarm up and about.

"Come in," Maria said. "Sit down. There is plenty of coffee."

The two men hurried to the table. Both of them, it was obvious, were somewhat awed at being asked to sit at this magnificent table. Hank had cleaned his boots and put on a fresh shirt, and the Stetson he carried in his hand looked as if it had been recently cleaned.

"I am Father Manuel Chaves," the priest told Longarm as he sat down. "I have brought your friend Hank, the man who brought you to me last night." The priest's face grew solemn. "It was a brave thing he did, Mr. Long."

Longarm looked at Hank. "Tell me about it, Hank. Last thing I knew, I was in the hotel, fighting off three plug-uglies who had attacked Kate Ballard in her room. One of them clipped me from behind."

Maria placed cups of steaming black coffee before Hank and the priest, then returned to her chair. But she did not sit down. She took a position behind the chair and stood there, listening intently. It was clear that she knew very little of the circumstances that had brought Longarm into her house.

"I was in the livery," Hank said, "when Ti Cantrell dragged you in, slung you over your horse, and rode out, leading the buckskin. He went out the back way, and followed the alley out of town."

The lawman's gunmetal-blue eyes glinted coldly. "That must've been the jasper who hit me. But there were two others; what about them?"

Hank grinned at Longarm. "Both dead. One of them

had a broken neck, the other a slug in his heart. I heard he landed on the lobby floor."

"Where was the rest of the town while all this ruckus was going on? Somebody must have heard Kate's screams and the shots."

"They were all busting up the street toward the hotel. You're right; Kate's screaming sure brought a crowd."

"But you stayed in the livery."

"That's right. Then I followed Ti out of town."

"Why?"

Hank shrugged. "You ain't a cheapskate, Longarm."

"I see. You figured you owed me because I flipped you a dollar to take care of my horse."

Hank smiled in appreciation of Longarm's gentle sarcasm. "And I like that buckskin. I figured if you *was* dead, you wouldn't have much use for it."

"Will you *please* let him tell what happened, Mr. Long?" Maria said impatiently.

Longarm smiled and leaned back in his chair. "I'm a mite curious myself, Hank. Tell us what happened."

"I caught up to Ti at Cactus Springs. He was watering his horse. When I rode in, I told him to keep on riding, that I'd bring you back to Paso Robles."

"And he listened to you?"

"Nope. He just sat there with an empty canteen in his hand, his back against a scrub pine, looking at me." Hank grinned. "He was dead, Longarm. Your bullet killed him."

The priest exclaimed softly, then crossed himself.

"I left Ti for the buzzards," Hank went on, "and rode back with you to Paso Robles. Father Chaves suggested I take you to Maria. It was morning by this time, and nobody saw us ride through town. You never stirred once, but I knew you was alive."

Longarm turned to Maria. "Thank you for your hospitality, ma'am. And the bath," he added with a smile.

She inclined her head slightly. "I trust the bandage is not too tight."

"No. Just right."

She looked at Hank and said, "You may return to the livery." It was a command, but a light one. She seemed a trifle disappointed in Hank. It was his explanation of why he had gone after Longarm, no doubt. The buckskin had been a good enough reason for him to follow Ti Cantrell out of that livery, but it was not a motive that would have satisfied Maria Antonia Lugo.

Hank got up to go, finishing his coffee as he did so.

The marshal held up a restraining hand. "Just a minute, Hank. What about Kate Ballard? Is she all right?"

"Seems so. Saw her in the Lucky Lady on my way here."

"And Fred Bushnell?"

Hank smiled. "He left about noon, I hear tell. But I don't know in which direction. He was last seen in Kilrain's place."

"Was Ti Cantrell one of Bushnell's boys?"

"More'n likely."

"But you're not sure."

"That's right."

Hank was holding something back; what it was, Longarm had no idea, but he knew it would be useless to question him any further. As Hank stood there, something about the youthful, slouching figure, the careless glance, jogged the lawman's well-trained memory. He wondered suddenly how old Hank was, but decided he would not ask him that to his face.

"Thanks a lot, Hank. Guess I'd be wrasslin' with the buzzards myself by this time if you hadn't taken a fancy to my buckskin."

"Hell, Longarm. You'd of wrung them birds' necks and ate 'em for supper."

"Nice of you to say that, Hank."

With a wave, Hank turned and left the room. As he

passed into the kitchen, the Mexican cook came into view, brushing swiftly against him. Longarm saw him turn his face to hers. A soft word passed between them; a quick smile lit the cook's eyes, and then Hank was past her, stepping out through the kitchen door into the bright sunshine.

Longarm looked back at the priest. "Father, I reckon your prayers helped. I thank you."

"Bless you, my son. It is a terrible job you have. I do not envy you. Tell me, does it not occur to you that in dealing with such scum, you must soil your own hands—and your soul—beyond redemption?"

"It has occurred to me, Father. It has also occurred to me that somebody has to deal with the lawless—somebody in *this* world—or the meek will not live long enough to inherit the earth."

Father Chaves frowned. "I hope you do not speak lightly, my son."

"I don't, Father, and that's a fact."

Father Chaves finished his coffee and stood up. "I'll see you to the door, Father," Maria said. Longarm almost envied the warmth in her voice.

Longarm got to his feet, aware that his head was no longer pounding so relentlessly, and watched as Maria and the priest left the dining room together, walking as good friends do—close, but not too close. They spoke together in low voices, and Longarm made no effort to overhear what they said. In a moment he heard the heavy outside door close, and soon Maria was reentering the dining room, a cold look of resolve on her face.

"Your wound," she told him, coming to a halt before him, "is a superficial one. It bled profusely, I am sure, before you were brought to me—and you must be weak from loss of blood. But you are in excellent condition, considering what you went through. You may ride out at any time."

52

"I owe you a great deal."

"And Hank."

"Yes. Hank and his good eye for horseflesh."

"He is an excellent wrangler."

"Have you known him long?"

"Long enough, Marshal." Her answer was short, curt.

Longarm broke the ensuing long moment of uncomfortable silence: "Well then, I guess I'll be moving on. I'm not far from the hotel, am I?"

"Through the kitchen door. You'll see the church clearly. You'll know where you are then."

He touched the brim of his hat and then stepped past her into the kitchen. As he headed for the door, the young Mexican cook who had spoken so briefly with Hank glanced swiftly and covertly up at him. She was peeling potatoes. When Longarm met her gaze, she looked quickly back down at the potato she was peeling.

He strode out into the bright sunshine and selected a cheroot from the four that were left in his inside pocket. He unwrapped it carefully and savored the sharp bite of the tobacco. With a flick of his thumbnail, he ignited a match and held it to the tip of the cigar, then inhaled deeply, savoring the smoke's potent punch as it reached his lungs. It felt good, damn good. He took another drag on the cheroot, well pleased with it and with the warm touch of the clean sunlight on his face.

He could have been done in by those jaspers, and that was the truth. He had been very lucky, and in his line of work, he would rather be lucky than smart.

He stopped a moment to get his bearing. He saw ahead of him the low cluster of formidable adobe *jacales* of the poor whose numbers made up most of the population of Paso Robles. As Maria had told him, looming above them was the church's bell tower, and beyond that, he caught a glimpse of the false-front frame buildings that comprised the business section. He turned around. Maria's hacienda was a series of adobe structures built around a central court. The entire complex was enclosed in a massive, whitewashed adobe wall that extended as far as the river—a bright reminder of the days when the Apache had raided almost at will.

Beyond the river's bright gleam, Longarm saw the broad flanks of rolling pastureland extending into the shimmering distance. Clusters of cattle were grazing on the lush grass. On this side of the river, near a couple of adobe buildings that apparently served as the blacksmith shop and the bunkhouse, a large corral had been constructed just inside the wall. High-spirited horses— blooded stock, mostly—were trotting restlessly about inside it. Maria had quite an estate, it appeared, and, almost certainly, she ran it alone. She was one of New Mexico's *ricos,* more than likely a descendent of the area's earliest settlers.

But she spoke the king's English like a native; and where in hell was her husband? A woman like that needed a man to share her bed, a real man. Perhaps that was her problem: she could not find a man with the spirit to match hers, and so had given up on men. Was that why she had been so cold to him, so formal? *You may ride out at any time,* she had told him with a directness that had left no doubt in his mind that he was no longer welcome.

He started up again, anxious to cover the distance to Paso Robles as quickly as possible. If Maria Antonia Lugo would not help him, perhaps Hank would. He intended to overtake Fred Bushnell before nightfall, or early the next day.

Longarm was pleased to see that Hank had stashed his saddlebags and bedroll over the buckskin's stall, with his Winchester right beside them. When he mentioned

54

it, Hank laughed. "You better thank Miss Kate for that," he said. "She brought your clothes over to Maria this morning, and the rest of your gear she brought out to me early this afternoon." Hank shook his head in amusement. "She said it was just too hard to explain to anybody what your things were doing in her room. She said no one would believe her."

Longarm smiled and nodded. "Guess Kate's been doing a lot of running around today."

"And I reckon she wants to thank you personally for saving her life, Longarm."

"I'll let her do that later, as soon as I get ahold of that partner of hers. You said Bushnell rode out this noon."

"That's what I heard."

"And he left from Kilrain's saloon?"

Hank nodded.

"This Kilrain's a big man in town, I hear."

"He owns just about everything, and he's runnin' for mayor. And he'll make it. He's a real politician."

"Get the buckskin ready for me to ride, Hank. I'll be right back. I been meaning to meet this guy Kilrain ever since I rode in."

As Longarm strode down the boardwalk toward the Dry Gulch, he recalled what Marshal Billy Vail had told him about Paso Robles:

. . . but there's something else, something queer going on in Paso Robles that may have nothing to do with Bernstein's killing. Some new fellow—Charles Kilrain's his name—and his bunch have moved in and bought out the general store, the bank, and the best saloon in town. No one knows where he came from, but he's making his presence felt by running for mayor and contributing heavily to the local church. Governor Wallace has no doubt that this newcomer will put all his cronies in charge once he becomes mayor. What's this

fellow after, Longarm? There's no gold in the area, no silver. It's just a sleepy little Mexican town north of the Apache reservation. But people have been disappearing, including one Dudley McBride, the agent Wallace sent in personally to check out this Kilrain gent. Maybe Kilrain is tied in with the Kid. It don't seem likely. From all reports, Billy's a loner, and right now he's supposed to be in Texas. But find out what you can about this Kilrain—and keep your head on your shoulders, you hear?

Well, so far, Longarm reflected somewhat ruefully, he had kept his head on his shoulders, but only just barely. And that made him anxious to size up this jasper Kilrain, before he turned his back on Paso Robles and took after Fred Bushnell.

He shouldered through the batwings of the Dry Gulch and found himself in a saloon that was a far less grim affair than Kate's. It had more room to begin with, with broad stairs at the far end leading to a second floor. The bar itself was longer and more highly polished. The brass cuspidors, liberally placed about the floor, gleamed brightly. The gaming tables were well-lighted; the mirror behind the bar had a magnificent reach and did much to lend an appearance of luxury and spaciousness to the saloon. The lighting was cheerful, and the women Kilrain employed were all buxom Mexican beauties, dressed in traditional garb: low-cut blouses and bright, flaring skirts that gave an ample view not only of their ankles, but a good deal of their legs as well.

Their laughter punctuated the low murmur of the place, and men's laughter, equally gentle, evoked a pleasant, almost homelike atmosphere. The place was not too crowded at the moment, and Longarm saw at once that its patrons were not limited to Anglos. A tall, lean man in a light brown worsted suit, a brown Stetson on his head, was moving easily among the tables, joking with some, chatting for a moment with others, then moving on. He left smiles and amiable chatter in his wake. This, Longarm realized, must be Kilrain.

He saw all this as he strode casually to the bar and waited for his whiskey to be poured. Kilrain had seen him enter, had nodded slightly in his direction, then continued in his casual sally about the room. Longarm lifted his glass and sipped at it, impressed once again with Kilrain's style. The whiskey was first-rate, and even the sawdust on the floor smelled fresh.

Longarm took his drink over to an unoccupied table against the far wall and sat down. Kilrain took his time in coming over to introduce himself, and when he did, he was all smiles. He seemed genuinely pleased to find Longarm sitting in his saloon.

"The name's Kilrain," he announced happily, reaching a long, thin hand down to shake the lawman's large, calloused one. "May I join you?"

"It's your saloon."

"That it is. That it is!" As he made himself comfortable, he waved the barkeep out from behind the bar. As the man bent solicitously over them, Kilrain instructed him to bring a bottle of his best whiskey to the table. Then he turned to Longarm, four cigars appearing, as if by sleight of hand, in his fist. He handed them across to the marshal. "I see you are a man who appreciates a good smoke, Longarm. Try these."

As Longarm took them, he said, "I have been trying to quit."

The man laughed delightedly. "Myself as well—with indifferent success, I might add. If it is a vice, Longarm, surely it is one we choose for ourselves. There are worse, you know."

Longarm smiled in agreement and pocketed the cigars. They were of good quality; he could tell from their heft and expensive wrappings. Whatever he was, this Kilrain was no cheapskate. "I understand," Longarm said, "that Fred Bushnell was in here before he rode out this noon."

"He was." The man smiled. "You blame him, do you, for that ugly business last night?"

Longarm nodded. "I suspicion he had something to do with it. He was somewhat unhappy with me—and Kate Ballard—for saying he had no choice but to stick to the deal he'd made with Kate."

"For the Lucky Lady."

"That's right."

"Poor Fred. He had his problems, you see. When he advertised for a partner, he only needed a little over a thousand. By the time Kate Ballard arrived, his indebtedness had increased considerably."

"That's what I figured."

"What, then, was he after when he invaded her hotel room last night?"

"Don't you know?"

Kilrain smiled too easily. "Of course. Fred wanted his letter back, the one agreeing to Kate's terms—even though I assured him her letter could not possibly stand up in court."

"Did you?"

"Certainly. He did not have to sell half-interest to Kate." He smiled. "I would have been glad to purchase the saloon from him for what he owed me. And I would have given him some going-away money in addition."

"How much?"

"Enough to get that four-flusher the hell out of Lincoln County."

The man made no effort to hide his motives, Longarm noticed. He wanted the Lucky Lady and had driven Fred Bushnell into debt in order to get it. Longarm wondered if there was anything in this town that Charles Kilrain did *not* want.

He sat back and studied Kilrain. The man was what Longarm would term a long-boned fellow: narrow forehead, long face, long jaw, long arms, wrists, and fingers. He had no waist to speak of, giving Longarm the feeling that if he were to haul off and punch Kilrain in the midsection, he would simply break in two. His hair was so light and sandy that his mustache and eyebrows were almost invisible, giving his pale blue eyes a wistful innocence that the straight line of his mouth contradicted. Indeed, he *was* a contradiction. Though an apparent wisp of a man, he had a grim, driving vitality that seemed capable of sweeping all opposition before it.

"Which way did Fred go, Kilrain? I'd like to know."

"West—in obvious obedience to Mr. Greeley's advice." He took out a cigar and lit it. The cloud of thick, fragrant smoke coiled about his head. He smiled with even teeth through it at Longarm. "I believe he said something about heading for the pass. From there, I have a hunch he'll go south for a while to investigate the fleshpots of El Paso."

"You gave him some going-away money."

"I gave him nothing. I took all Kate Ballard gave him, and he left his IOU for the rest. Fred Bushnell was a braggart and a four-flusher. I hate the type, Longarm."

Longarm stood up. "So now Kate Ballard has a half-interest in the Lucky Lady—and a silent partner."

As Kilrain got up also, he smiled slowly and carefully. "That's correct, Longarm. And as long as Miss Kate knows which way the wind is blowing, I do not anticipate any conflict. We should do very well." He frowned, as if a thought had just occurred to him. "By the way, Longarm, you know we buried two men this morning. It was your handiwork. Would you care to contribute something to the expense? I took it upon myself to give the two blackguards a decent burial, but I would appreciate any sum you could contribute."

"Buried them awful fast, didn't you?"

"They were beginning to stink."

"Did you recognize them?"

"Strangers, Longarm. Brought in by Bushnell, I'd say."

Longarm nodded, touched the brim of his hat to Kilrain, and started for the door. "I've already given my contribution. Bullets cost money."

Longarm's two large, blanket-covered canteens were empty. For the last hour they had echoed hollowly whenever his knees had touched them. He was on his belly now on a warm crest of rock, with the canteens on the ground beside him, his buckskin ground-reined back on the trail. He could see the water hole just beneath him, less than a hundred yards away.

The pass was at his back, the Jornada del Muerto trail—the Journey of Death—stretching before him, a distant jumble of sawtoothed peaks outlined starkly against the fading sky beyond them. Longarm shoved his hat back and let it hang between his shoulders by the chin strap as he poked his head out still farther from the ragged bunching of grama grass that covered the crest. He had already levered a fresh round into the Winchester's chamber. The loose blow-sand between the boulders was still hot from the day's sun. Longarm inched his way through the grama grass to get a better look at the water hole.

The water hole was in a dark hollow at the base of a limestone rock formation. The water would be good, he realized; it had seeped through the limestone to gather in the shallow rock pans at the foot of the formation. So the water was there, all right. All he had to do was go on down there and fill his dry canteens.

But he did not move.

Fred Bushnell's trail had been too easy to follow. And Bushnell was not alone. Surely he knew that Longarm would be coming after him. What better spot for an ambush than this dark cup of water waiting beneath the limestone cliffs? He had smelled trouble now for some time. The thing was, he had to draw fire to know where they were. That there were two of them did not bother Longarm as much as the knowledge that he and his horse needed the water—and soon.

In that sense, Bushnell and his partner had the advantage. Longarm could wait until dark, he realized. But the light from the New Mexico moon would be as much a disadvantage to him as to his adversaries. He decided he had to move now, and quickly. The shots would have to come from high among the rocks, and no bushwhacker was ever as good a shot as he thought he was. As for Bushnell, Longarm could not imagine the man squeezing a trigger without first closing his eyes.

Longarm heaved himself to his feet and angled down the slope toward the well, his Winchester in one hand, the two canteens dangling from their straps in the other. He was almost to the well, close in under the wall of rock, when the first shots came. One slug whipped past his right shoulder, and the other struck one of his canteens, slamming an ugly hole in it. Longarm kept going, swept the canteens through the water, and as he felt the tug of water in one of them, flung himself in close against the cliffside.

The smell of burned powder was drifting on the wind. The two shots had come from almost directly above. Whoever the shooter was, he was using a rifle, and as Longarm sucked greedily on the neck of the intact canteen, he could still hear the echoes hammering against the rock walls above him. Putting down the canteen, he picked up his Winchester. A third rifle shot cracked the stillness. Longarm heard the round ricochet off the limestone wall just above him, and saw what was left of it explode in the blow sand on the other side of the well. It was only one man firing, from almost directly over Longarm's head. Good. Longarm had been right about Bushnell. The man was probably cowering down behind a rock while his partner did all the work. Probably.

Longarm lifted his hat off and pushed it out away from the rock wall a few inches. At once, a rifle shot cracked. Again the bullet ricocheted off the sandstone wall, but it sounded closer this time. Longarm put on his hat and, keeping close in to the rock, felt his way along the base until he was out of sight of the well. He kept going, following the clean flanks of the rock until he turned a corner and saw a worn trail leading to the crest of the formation. It was an old game trail, and narrow. Loose gravel made the footing treacherous, but Longarm climbed swiftly and steadily, grateful for his skin-tight stovepipe boots. Riding boots would have made this climb almost impossible.

Twice he had to flatten himself against the smooth wall and inch along a narrow ledge less than a foot in width. Then, close to the top, the trail broke out onto a series of steplike, striated rocks. He mounted them like a dwarf climbing into some giant's enormous castle. When he reached the top, he saw a grassy sward and two horses grazing. A broad trail led off the mesa south to the Jornada del Muerto. There were still more rocks towering above him.

Picking his way higher, Longarm heard voices. Querulous voices. One of them he recognized as Bushnell's. He kept going. He had unbuckled his spurs long before, but his silent progress was broken by the harsh click of his rifle barrel coming down on an unsuspected rock projection. With a silent curse, Longarm drew the rifle closer to him and rested his back against a flat rock.

A swarthy figure in a black sombrero appeared in a gap less than twenty yards above, his rifle tucked under his chin. The rifle lanced fire, and the round struck the rock by Longarm's temple. A cruel shower of rock shards tore at Longarm's face. He spun away, lost his rifle, and tumbled headlong down into a rocky defile, coming to rest on his side, his right arm twisted under him.

He dared not move. His only hope was to play possum, at least for the moment. He heard the rifleman moving about in the rocks above him, then heard his booted feet climbing away from him, back to his vantage point. The sight of Longarm's raw, bleeding face must have been enough to convince the man that he had caught the marshal squarely in the head, and Longarm's awkward, sprawling figure at the bottom of the rock cleft had undoubtedly clinched it. He was satisfied he had killed Longarm.

As he lay unmoving, he heard a faint cry from far above him, followed by a single rifle shot. As the sound of it slammed about the rocks, Longarm thought he could hear the sound of someone being dragged over the ground. A belt buckle was scraping against a rock face. He heard the familiar booted tread moving swiftly back down the rocks toward him. He could sense the dark figure's presence looming over the lip of the defile, watching him. He heard the man lever a fresh cartridge into his rifle's firing chamber. A second later, another shot exploded the silence.

Longarm felt the slug pass between his upper arm and his chest, close enough to the arm to take a small patch of his sleeve and the flesh of his arm with it. The instant he felt the round, he bucked violently, his chest heaving back, his face now staring sightlessly up at the swarthy rifleman peering down at him. A smile gleamed in the rifleman's dark face. He reached into his hip pocket for a small whiskey bottle. Tipping it up all the way, he drank greedily, then flung the empty bottle down at Longarm.

It took every ounce of grit Longarm could muster not to flinch away as he watched, unblinking, while the bottle hurtled toward him. It smashed on the rocks just above his skull. The stench of raw whiskey clouded his senses. With enormous relief, he saw the dark figure turn away. Longarm blinked, closed his eyes tightly, and waited. He did not know yet if he had broken anything in his fall. His thigh was sore and his right leg was throbbing mightily where it had come to rest against a protruding rock. He didn't think he had broken it, but he sure as hell must have bent it some.

He heard the sound of a horse's hooves on the grassy mesa below him. The steady tattoo died swiftly. He had only heard one horse. Fred Bushnell was still up there. But somehow Longarm no longer felt he had to worry about Kate's ex-partner.

Gingerly, Longarm moved his legs. He was right. He had bent, but not broken, his right leg. Bringing a hand up to his face, he felt the broad smear of already coagulating blood that covered his face like a stiffening mask all the way from his temple to his chin. The flesh wound under his arm had already stopped bleeding. He swore bitterly as he thought of the expense he would incur in repairing the fabric of his frock coat.

It was difficult for him to stand upright in the narrow cleft, but he managed. In the gathering darkness, he studied the rocks above him and began to climb. The headache he thought he had left behind him in Paso Robles had returned in full force by the time he boosted himself out of the defile. Straightening his hat and tugging it down firmly, he climbed farther up the rocks, heading toward the emplacement from which his assailant had first fired on him. He kept an eye out for his rifle, but saw no trace of it, and concluded that his ambusher had made off with it.

He came to a level spot finally, and in the dim light, he saw a cluster of low rocks that rimmed the ridge just above the flat. Looking closer, he glimpsed a rifle barrel poking out, and a dim, dishevelled figure sprawled just above it. Fred Bushnell. Climbing up to the body, he saw the clean bullet hole just under the right eye. He did not need to examine the back of the man's head to know what kind of a hole had been left by the escaping round. A .44-40 slug fired from a Winchester at that close range made an awful mess on its way out the other side.

Neat. Very neat. Fred Bushnell had died in a gunfight with Deputy U.S. Marshal Custis Long. But before he had died, he had managed to get off two shots that finished the marshal. By the time anyone stumbled upon the two bodies, the buzzards would have picked their bones clean and the bright New Mexican sun would have bleached them to a shiny white. One more emissary of the governor had come a cropper. Case solved.

Moving around behind Bushnell, he dragged the dead man away from the rocks. In the fast-fading light, he caught a glimpse of the man's wrists. They were burned raw from the thongs that had bound them. From the very beginning, then, Fred Bushnell had been a decoy used to lure Longarm into these rocks.

The poor sonofabitch.

Longarm slumped wearily down on a low rock and took stock of his situation. He was in poor condition to ride back to Paso Robles that night, but the prospect of camping by this water hole with a dead man didn't fire his enthusiasm much, either. With a weary shrug, he got up. His horse needed tending to, and there was no reason why he couldn't camp on the ridge above the water hole. He would get Bushnell's corpse off this ledge the easiest way possible the next morning and lug it back to Paso Robles for burial.

He had a feeling he wouldn't have to go far then to find his Winchester.

Chapter 4

Longarm arrived in Paso Robles a little before noon of the following day. Fred Bushnell rode behind Longarm, his lifeless form tucked into his soogan and draped over the saddle of his horse. As Longarm turned on to the street that ran past the Dry Gulch, a small group of Anglos and Mexicans gathered. By the time he had dropped the reins of both horses over the hitch rail in front of the Dry Gulch, a sizable crowd was watching. Longarm found not a single pair of eyes that seemed friendly.

He mounted the boardwalk and pushed through the batwings. The saloon was silent. Every eye was turned in Longarm's direction. The roulette wheel was quiet, and the poker players had put down their cards. Kilrain was standing at the bar, his head turned in Longarm's direction, the ghost of a smile on his long face.

"Welcome back, Marshal," he boomed cordially. "I see you got what you went after."

"And a little more besides," Longarm replied, advancing to the bar.

"You look like you could use a drink. It's on me."

"Thanks." Longarm looked at the barkeep. "Whiskey."

The tension in the room let up a bit. Kilrain also appeared to relax. Longarm was only slightly amused. What had Kilrain and his patrons thought he was going to do? Rush into this saloon with guns blazing?

"You gave Bushnell's buddies a real good funeral, Kilrain," Longarm said as he pulled his full shotglass toward himself. "So you can bury Bushnell himself now. He's outside on his horse, in terrible condition. I had to drop him a ways."

"That so?"

Longarm threw the drink down his throat. The fiery liquid did much to rid his gullet of the raw taste of alkali dust. "That's so." He looked squarely at Kilrain. "You wouldn't happen to know a dark, squat fellow who favors a black sombrero? Likes his liquor, he does."

"Nope," Kilrain said, a trifle too quickly. "Never seen the like around here." He frowned in sudden concern. "The side of your face doesn't look so good. Looks like you got into a fight with a bobcat."

"Something like that." Longarm slapped the empty shotglass down onto the bar, turned, and left the saloon.

He had no doubt Kilrain would do as he had been told. Kilrain did not know how much Longarm knew, and from this point on, he would be most cautious in dealing with him. For now, then, Longarm could afford to push. The thing was, Longarm himself did not know for sure just what he knew. The pieces were there, but they hadn't quite fallen into place.

He was certain Kate Ballard would be able to help.

The Lucky Lady still looked somewhat grim for a saloon, but the smell of paint and the new polish on the bar showed Longarm that Kate was indeed making an effort to spruce things up. Even so, it would be some time before she could hope to challenge the affluent style of Kilrain's saloon.

"Where's Kate?" Longarm asked the barkeep. He was amused to see that Kate had kept her word. She had fired the sullen barkeep that had served Longarm earlier.

"Upstairs," the man replied. His black hair was greased and combed straight back, his face as gaunt and white as a bleached skull. He looked warily at Longarm as his fingers polished a long-stemmed wine glass. "You want me to get her?"

"I'd appreciate that. Thanks."

Longarm was seated at a table near the back when Kate hurried down the narrow stairs behind the bar, the barkeep on her heels. As soon as she caught sight of him, she gave the barkeep an order, then hurried over to his table and sat down.

"Jesus," she said softly, noticing at once the side of Longarm's face. "What happened to you, Longarm?"

"I brought back your ex-partner," Longarm replied. "He had a friend."

"I heard about Bushnell," she said. "The whole town has, by now. What do you mean, he had a friend?"

"Never mind. Just answer a few questions, will you?"

"Of course. But first you must let me thank you for saving me from those rapists the other night. You rode out yesterday without stopping in."

"I was in a hurry."

"You could have let me thank you."

"I wanted Bushnell. I knew you'd be here when I got back. And here I am. I stopped right in."

"You went to Kilrain's place first."

"I guess you're right. The whole town's keeping tabs on me."

She blushed. "Hell, Longarm. Don't you and me have something . . . a little extra going for us?"

He reached out and took her hand. "Sure, Kate," he said, smiling. "I didn't mean that the way it sounded."

She softened at once. "What was it you wanted to ask me?"

"About Kilrain. You're in partnership with him?"

"Yes," she replied bitterly. "I have no choice, it seems. He took Fred's money, and along with it, Fred's share in the saloon."

"Half-interest?"

"Yes."

The barkeep brought over their drinks. Red wine for Kate, whiskey for Longarm. As the barkeep left, Kate indicated the man with a quick nod of her head. "What do you think of my new barkeep, Lazarus?"

The marshal cocked an eyebrow at the appropriateness of the name. "Is that what you call him?"

She smiled. "He doesn't seem to mind. He's loyal, and with that face behind the bar, no one gives me any trouble."

"He'll catch on soon. Someone's going to tell him who Lazarus was."

"He'll probably be pleased."

"That business in the hotel, Kate. How did Fred's boys know we had switched rooms?"

She frowned, then picked up her glass to sip the wine. Her face had gone slightly pale. "I don't know, Longarm. That's what I've been trying to figure out myself."

"You know, Kate, if it wasn't for Hank, I wouldn't likely be sitting at this table with you now. I would have been left out there with Cantrell, bleeding like a stuck pig, food for the buzzards."

Kate grew angry as she caught Longharm's drift. She sat back in her chair and fixed him with a cold eye. "After Cantrell clubbed you, Longarm, he turned on me. I was yelling my lungs out, so he quieted me with the same barrel he stung you with." She turned then to show Longarm the side of her face. There was a low bump just above her cheekbone, heavily powdered to hide the discoloration. "By the time the crowd got up to the room," Kate went on, "you and Cantrell were long gone—and I was in no condition to tell anybody anything."

Longarm smiled thinly. "I was just wondering, Kate, that's all."

"Damn it, Longarm, you don't trust me."

"The pure truth is, Kate, I'm feeling about as sociable right now as a centipede with the chilblains. My left side aches like a bad tooth, my face is as raw as a slab of beefsteak, my right leg's cracked some—and all this since I rode into this pile of adobe and alkali dust two days back. I don't see how I can afford to trust anybody. I feel like the only hen at a coyote party. It sure as hell ain't doing a thing for my peace of mind."

Kate's anger had subsided some by the time Longarm finished his speech. She sipped her drink and leaned back in her chair. With a knowing wink, she indicated two of her girls coming down the stairs at the far end of the bar. They were young Mexican girls, dressed very gaily. They looked as if they had just finished combing out their long dark hair. It was early yet. They had probably just gotten up. "What you need is the comfort of a healthy young woman—and maybe a little something extra." She smiled. "I got some nice girls in, Longarm—some of Kilrain's best. That fool, Bushnell, wore out his own stock something fierce."

"Thanks, Kate. But I never got in the habit of paying for it."

"I can understand why, Longarm." She smiled wryly. "It was just a thought. You didn't seem to be picking up any of my signals."

"I guess I'm not in the mood, Kate. Sorry."

"Drink up and relax then."

"I won't be able to relax until I get my Winchester back."

"Your Winchester?"

"You wouldn't happen to remember seeing a heavy drinker in here today, would you? A dark, squat fellow. Wears a black sombrero. He'd be feeling pretty good, acting a mite cocky."

Kate went pale. "No," she managed. "Why?"

Longarm knew at once that she was lying. He leaned close to her. "Damn it, Kate! If you've seen him, where is he?"

"No. Honest, Longarm, I haven't seen him. That's the God's truth!"

As Longarm started to get to his feet in disgust, he noticed another of Kate's girls, her eyes red and swollen, hurrying down the stairs. She uttered a tiny cry when she saw Kate, and ran across the saloon floor toward her.

"Mrs. Ballard!" the girl cried.

Kate turned her head. When she saw the girl's swollen face and discolored eye, she rose swiftly, almost knocking her chair to the floor.

"Rita! What happened?"

Before the girl could answer, the man Longarm was looking for stormed unsteadily down the stairs after the girl. He was shirtless, bootless, and hatless. "Hey," he cried to Kate, "that little Mex ain't worth nothing! I want my money back, Kate!"

Longarm was on his feet by this time, and when the swarthy fellow turned his whiskey-fogged attention away from the fleeing girl and saw Longarm standing beside Kate's table, he pulled up real smart—like he'd slammed full-tilt into a wall in the dark. His eyes bugged. He had been chasing a balky little whore across a saloon and had run into a dead man, a man he thought he had killed.

He backed up hastily, his hand slapping at an empty thigh. "Jesus!" he said softly.

"That's right, you sonofabitch," said Longarm, smiling mirthlessly as he started for the man. "I ought to be dead. Don't look like I am, though, does it?"

Then he lunged for the fellow. His big right hand came down hard on the fellow's scrawny shoulder. The man twisted away, however, and Longarm was left with a piece of his sweat-stained longjohns. Turning, the fellow raced back to the stairs. Longarm strode after him and took the narrow stairs three steps at a time. At the head of the stairs, he caught a glimpse of his quarry disappearing into a small room at the end of the hall. Before he got to the doorway, however, a screaming, half-naked girl was thrust out the door, a strong brown arm wrapped around her throat.

"Get back, Long!" the fellow cried. "Get back or I'll kill her!"

Longarm pulled up and ducked away. As he did so, the fellow hurled the sobbing woman at him. Longarm put up his hand to ward her off, but she stumbled forcefully into him, driving him back into the corner with such impact that his shoulder slammed into the window, smashing the pane.

As gently as he could, he disentangled himself from the distraught girl and raced down the hallway after his man. As soon as he reached the head of the stairs, however, a rifle shot thundered in the crowded bar and a slug whined past Longarm's cheek and smacked into the beam over his head. He drew his Colt and ducked back. Poking his head over the railing a second time, he drew fire again. This time the round buried itself in the railing an inch from his fist.

The screaming of Kate's girls, combined with the tumult of customers stampeding for the exit, added to the confusion as another rifle shot exploded from below. With a curse, Longarm turned and raced back down the hallway. He raised the shattered window, and stepped out onto the narrow roof. Crouching, he moved to the edge and looked over.

Townspeople were racing toward the front of the saloon from all directions, joining the large crowd that was already surging about the saloon's entrance. No one glanced up to see Longarm as Kate's girls and the saloon's patrons raced out of the place, wide-eyed, anxious for cover.

"Here he comes!" someone cried. "Here comes Murales!"

Longarm braced himself. He was about fifteen feet above the entrance. His quarry, the man someone had just identified as Murales, backed out of the saloon with Longarm's Winchester in his hand. He was barefoot and dressed only in his britches, his torn longjohns hanging in shreds from his dark shoulder.

Longarm jumped. His boots caught Murales's right shoulder a glancing blow. The man spilled to the ground as Longarm landed heavily on the boardwalk. A rotten board snapped under his weight, his left foot driving down through it to the ground beneath. Longarm tried to pull his foot free and, in doing so, lost his balance momentarily. He reached back to grab his foot. Murales swung the rifle stock with wicked precision and knocked Longarm's Colt flying.

Stepping back, a gleaming smile on his dark face, Murales levered a fresh cartridge into Longarm's Winchester. He was raising it to his hip, leveling the muzzle on Longarm with not a spectator making a move to stop him, when Kate screamed and flung herself at Murales's back. The rifle discharged, and the round tore into the boardwalk. This was all the time Longarm needed.

Dragging his left boot out of its trap, he lunged for Murales, catching him about the shoulders and pulling him to the ground. For a moment the two men rolled over and over in the dust of the narrow street. Longarm was able to land a few punches, but most of them went wild and somehow Murales managed to scramble to his feet. Longarm followed him, caught up with him, spun him around, and moved in. Before Murales could raise his heavy arms, Longarm gave him an open-handed belt across the mouth, following it up immediately with a raking backhand across the nose. With a cry of fury, Murales lowered his head and charged. Longarm stepped neatly to one side and tripped the man. Murales plowed face-first into a pile of horseshit; at the instant he hit, Longarm was astride him, pinning him to the ground with one boot on his shoulder, deftly scooping dust into his face. Then Longarm released the man and stepped back.

Murales—his face a bloody mess by this time, his eyes blinking furiously in an effort to clear them—jumped, screaming, to his feet and flung himself at Longarm. Longarm wasted no time in taking advantage of the man's condition. He drove a fist into Murales's midsection. The man's exploding breath was almost a shout, filled with surprise and pain. Longarm swung a wild backhanded blow that caught Murales on the cheek and sent him reeling back into a tie rail. The dry, sun-bleached wood snapped with the report of a rifle shot as Murales broke through it and slammed into the Lucky Lady's wall.

His eyes tearing, his pulped nose exuding a steady stream of dark blood, he was slowly sliding down the wall when Longarm saw the man's hand reach into his back pocket. A knife was suddenly gleaming in his fist. Murales stopped his slide and crouched. Longarm waited. He knew that Murales could barely see him, that he was done in by this time—and he marveled at the man's insane stamina. Murales lunged, his knife flashing in the sun ahead of him. Longarm was in the act of sidestepping the groggy Murales when a shot rang out from the ranks of onlookers. Murales caught the round in his chest. The force of the slug stopped him cold. He staggered about, a startled look on his face, the knife dropping from his hand. Longarm reached out and caught Murales before he collapsed to the ground.

He caught a dead man.

As Longarm lowered the corpse to the dust of the street, he looked up to see Kilrain stepping out of the crowd, a smoking Smith & Wesson in his hand.

Kilrain smiled thinly at Longarm. "Murales was an expert with that pigsticker, Longarm. Didn't want to lose a deputy U.S. marshal. No telling what Governor Wallace would think of that."

"You didn't need to do that, Kilrain. Murales was finished. He was out on his feet."

"Maybe. He didn't look so finished to me."

The crowd was beginning to disperse. Corpses were heavy. The exciting part was all over. Now came the cleanup. Kate, comforting the girl Murales had struck, was moving back into her saloon.

"Kate!" Longarm called, picking up his Colt and holstering it.

Kate paused and turned just before she reached the batwings.

"Thanks, Kate. That was a brave thing to do."

Her face as white as the adobe wall of her saloon, Kate nodded without a word and continued on into the Lucky Lady. Longarm retrieved his Winchester, then turned to Kilrain.

"Who was he, Kilrain? Who did Murales work for?"

Kilrain shrugged. "I've seen him in town a couple of times. He stopped coming into my place after he got himself stewed to the gills and raised a ruckus. But I don't know what brand he rode for—if he rode for one. All I knew about him was that he knew how to use that knife."

An oldtimer wearing a tattered white Stetson sidled closer to the two of them, angling for a better view of the dead man. Then he looked at Longarm. "Murales rode for Chisum, last I remember."

"That so?" Longarm asked.

The old cowpoke rubbed the white stubble on his chin with a gnarled hand. "Reckon that's the one, all right. About a year back, it was. Seen him with some other boys, raising a lot of dust on their way into Lincoln. I think the Kid was with him, too."

"Thanks," Longarm said.

The fellow nodded absently, took another look at the dead man, then ambled off in the direction of the Dry Gulch.

"Give that man a drink on me, Kilrain."

"I'll do that, Longarm."

A wagon was pulling up. A small, round individual with a jolly look in his eyes jumped down and surveyed the corpse. He was wearing a tan worsted suit and a black bowler hat. He glanced at both men.

"Another one, hey? You paying for this one, too, Kilrain?"

With a sigh, Kilrain nodded, touched the brim of his hat to Longarm, and started for the general store across the street. The undertaker glanced shrewdly at Longarm. "Don't worry none about Kilrain," he said. "He uses the cheapest pine he can find and won't pay the diggers more than a dollar apiece."

Longarm said nothing in response to the little man, but turned and walked back into the Lucky Lady. The place was almost empty. A swamper and the barkeep were cleaning up some broken chairs and lamps, while Kate was at the bar, nursing a whiskey. Longarm walked over and bellied up to the bar beside her.

"I would have told you he was here, Longarm," she said, without looking up from her glass. "But I knew what it would do to this place if you and him tangled. And I was right."

"Sure, Kate."

She looked at him then, and he saw that she was about ready to burst into tears. "I mean it, damn it! That's the truth!"

"Now look, Kate, I didn't come in here to argue with you. I came in to thank you. I suspicion you maybe saved my life out there."

"I couldn't just let the sonofabitch shoot you."

He smiled at her. "I wouldn't have liked it one bit if you had. Especially since it was my own rifle he was using."

She tried to smile, but couldn't quite manage it. She was still shaky. Longarm studied her closely. For a moment he had the feeling it was more than nerves. It was closer to fear—as if she had stepped too far over a line someone had drawn for her.

Longarm reached out and patted her on the hand. "Right now I've got to take a bath and find a tailor to stitch this here coat back together. Then, after I eat and get a little shut-eye, I'll be riding out of here. But I'll be back soon's I can. If this new barkeep of yours can hold the place down for a while, maybe we can go for a ride. Maybe even bring along a picnic basket, something as damn fool romantic as that. How's that sound?"

Kate smiled almost gratefully at Longarm. "That sounds real civilized, Longarm. I'd like that." She rested her hand on his arm and held it there for a moment. "I feel better already," she said, smiling for real this time. "Hurry back."

Chapter 5

It was close to noon of the following day when Longarm rode into a quiet, well-watered valley and caught sight of cattle bunched together under a clump of cottonwood. As he rode closer, he saw the famous Chisum brand, the Jingle Bob. The ears of the cattle had a somewhat grotesque appearance; they were slit from the tip to the base.

Longarm rode on through the small herd. Cresting a slight rise beyond, he saw a fine stand of pinyon and juniper leading down the slope toward a shallow river that knifed through the broad valley. It was the Pecos, he knew. Beyond it, he thought he glimpsed a huddle of ranch buildings, but he could not be sure. The distance was too great.

He was almost through the juniper when he heard the clink of iron shoes on stone. He turned in his saddle. Four horsemen swept out of the timber toward him. Their sixguns were out of their holsters. The gunbarrels gleamed menacingly in the bright sunlight. The faces of the riders were as hard as the guns they brandished.

Longarm pulled up.

"Raise 'em, mister!" the lead rider called. He was a long, lean fellow with a beaklike nose and eyes of a piercing, cold blue. "And I mean pronto!"

Longarm sat back in his saddle and kept his fingers about the reins. The cantle creaked under his weight. "What for?" he inquired reasonably. "I ain't done nothing to be ashamed of that I can recall. Not recently, that is."

"Damn you, stranger! Do as I say!"

"You never learned to say please, I take it."

With a sudden, violent curse, the hawk-faced rider reined in beside Longarm, reached over, and withdrew Longarm's Winchester from it's saddle sling.

"Go easy with that," Longarm warned evenly. "I been having trouble hanging onto that rifle and I'm getting a mite testy about it."

"Shut up!" the rider snarled as he commenced patting Longarm's frock coat. He felt the bulge created by Longarm's holstered Colt. Straightening swiftly in his saddle, his cold eyes narrowing, he cocked his sixgun. "Let's have it," he told Longarm. "Give that there weapon to me."

"Take it yourself." Longarm was aware that his anger was priming him dangerously. "If you think you can."

The fellow reached quickly into Longarm's frock coat. Before his hand could close about Longarm's weapon, Longarm reached around swiftly, grabbed the man's collarless shirt, and yanked him out of his saddle. The rider fell between the horses, landing on his back —and found himself staring up at the business end of Longarm's Colt.

"Drop your weapon," Longarm told him quietly, then glanced around at the other riders.

He heard the one on the ground let his sixgun fall, but the others hesitated to drop their own guns. One fellow, the closest to Longarm, had his Colt trained on Longarm's chest. He seemed to be priming himself to shoot.

Longarm fixed him with a cold stare. "Shoot me and I'll kill this sonofabitch under my horse. And maybe I'll get a shot off in your direction too, mister. Hell, turning whelps like you into salt and pepper shakers is' my profession."

The man hesitated to lower his gun, though the two riders beside him did so quickly. The rider beside the one who was hesitating said quickly, "Do as he says, Johnny! He's got the drop on Jim!"

From the ground, Jim yelled up at Johnny, "Do as he says, damn it! I think he done broke my shoulder!"

Slowly, reluctantly, his lean, clean-shaven face mean with bottled fury, Johnny lowered his gun, then holstered it.

"That's better," said Longarm. "Much better." He glanced down at Jim. "If you can get up, do it."

"I think you busted my shoulder."

"Use your feet then, damn it! And hurry up!"

Cursing a blue streak, the fellow reached up with his right hand, grabbed the halter of his own horse, and hauled himself upright. The way he carried his left shoulder, it did indeed appear that he had broken it when he landed. Longarm felt a mild satisfaction at the thought, but the anger that was goading him was not yet satisfied. He had had a bellyful of Lincoln County, and these riders had been the final swallow.

As Longarm reached over to help the man up into his saddle, he told the rest of them to drop their gunbelts and rifles to the ground. There was a mutter of protest, but as Longarm swept the muzzle of his Colt around the semicircle of men, each one complied with his request. As the weapons plopped onto the ground, Longarm smiled.

"Now get off your horses."

Puzzled and angry, the three riders dismounted. They

looked very unhappy standing on their feet. Longarm chuckled to himself. There were only two things a cowpoke feared: a decent woman and being afoot.

"Unsaddle the horses," Longarm said.

"I thought so," said Jim, holding his left shoulder. "Horse stealin's your trade. You been scouting for more of our stock! You bastard!"

The three men unsaddled their horses sullenly, lugged the saddles over to a small juniper, and dropped them there. When they had finished their task, they trekked back to Longarm, paused in the sunlight, and squinted up at him. Longarm smiled slightly when he saw one of them eyeing his gunbelt in the dust not far from where he was standing.

"Don't go for it," Longarm advised quietly. "Just turn around and start walking. I figure you're John Chisum's men, so lead me to his place. I hear tell it's on the South Spring of the Pecos."

"This here's the Pecos River, you damn fool," said Jim. "And that's the Jingle Bob spread in the distance there. If you weren't as blind as you are dumb, you'd of seen it by now."

"That so?"

"Yes, damn you."

"You got a right fast tongue, mister. And it ain't very respectful. I guess I don't need your help—and with all that piss and vinegar in your veins, you ain't going to let a little old broken shoulder slow you down a-tall. Get off the horse."

"Now wait just a minute!"

"Get off or I'll knock you off."

Slowly, painfully, the injured man slid off his saddle. Longarm didn't want to leave the horse ranging free with a heavy saddle on its back, and he didn't want to waste any more time. He snatched up the horse's reins and led it past the walking cowpokes, glancing down at them as he rode past.

"Better look after Jim," he told them. "He's so hot under the collar, he might turn to steam when he hits that river."

"You're going to regret this, mister," said the one called Johnny.

"Maybe. But right now I'm enjoying myself fit to bust."

Longarm spurred the buckskin toward the broad but sluggish Pecos River. He felt a lot better than he had when he'd started out that morning. It had been open season on him ever since he'd ridden into Lincoln County, and it had done his morale good to turn matters around some and teach a quartet of gunslicks a lesson in manners. It didn't matter who they rode for, John Chisum or God Almighty, it was the same principle. You don't ride up to a stranger with a mean look on your face and a drawn sixgun in your hand, unless you mean trouble. They had asked for it, and Longarm had been glad to provide it.

He glanced back. The four men were trudging wearily, heads down, through the dust he was raising. The horses were already out of sight beyond the ridge.

John Chisum's famed Long House was flanked by giant cottonwoods and a few live oaks the man must have brought with him from Texas. Before Longarm reached it, he rode into an expansive compound and past many adobe outbuildings, two large stables, a blacksmith shop, bunkhouses, cookshacks, and corrals. Chisum's operation was a large one, all right. As Longarm already knew, seventy to eighty thousand head grazed on Chisum land. More than a hundred riders tended that herd, their graze extending a hundred and fifty miles up and down the Pecos, almost a fifth of New Mexico. Chisum and his riders held this land simply by controlling the river's water. Chisum had never paid anyone for this open range, but he claimed it and his hardcase riders kept it for him.

All this information was in the material Governor Wallace had sent Marshal Vail, and most of it Longarm had digested. What had not been made too clear was how Governor Wallace felt about this kingdom of John Chisum's operating within New Mexico. Marshal Billy Vail had suggested that Wallace wouldn't be at all unhappy to find that Chisum had overextended himself. But Longarm was to work with Chisum if he could, since the man was a power in Lincoln County.

The fact that Vincent Murales had been one of John Chisum's riders provided still another reason for Longarm to seek the man out.

Quite a few of Chisum's men were watching Longarm, some from the shadow of the bunkhouse, others from doorways and windows. All were grimly curious. As Longarm neared the house, a storm of horsemen topped a rise east of the Long House and galloped toward him. Longarm ignored the charging horsemen and kept riding toward Chisum's impressive main building.

It was built of adobe and looked to be almost a hundred and fifty feet long and maybe forty feet wide. What looked like a canal or ditch ran through the compound, and right in under the house. As Longarm neared the Long House, he saw the water in the ditch flowing swiftly, and noted where it emerged on the far side of the building to continue on down to a meadowland beyond the house, where it watered some cropland and rather extensive orchards. By this time, the hardriding cowboys had clattered to within fifty yards of Longarm, raising quite a cloud of dust.

A tall man appeared on the long porch fronting the house, and shouted something to the riders. They broke before Longarm's path and clattered to a halt in a large circle around him. But not a rider challenged him as he rode on past them to the house. Longarm pulled up in front of the man he realized was John Chisum, touched the brim of his hat, and then folded his arms casually over the pommel of his saddle.

"You look like you've had quite a ride," Chisum said to Longarm. "Light and rest. There is always room for another guest at John Chisum's Long House."

"Obliged," Longarm said, swinging out of his saddle.

Chisum called someone's name, and in a moment Longarm's horse was led away to one of the stables. Longarm kept his rifle, bedroll, and saddlebags as he mounted the porch and came to a halt before Chisum. A dark, plump Mexican girl darted out of a doorway alongside Longarm, took his gear from him, and disappeared back inside.

Chisum smiled and stuck out his hand. "Name's John Chisum, stranger. What's yours?"

"Custis Long, deputy U.S. marshal."

"Come right in, Marshal. Consider this your home."

Chisum turned then, indicated the open door with a motion of his hand, and followed Longarm into the large living room. Inside, it was cool, the thick adobe walls an excellent fortress against the blazing New Mexico sun. The walls were hung with Mexican blankets and tapestries. The heavy furniture looked expensive and appropriately massive, with few if any frills. Buffalo robes were thrown carelessly over a couple of the leather-upholstered chairs and over one long sofa. The shorter, eastern wall of the room was dominated by a huge fireplace, over which a flintlock and an early Henry were hung carelessly, while, just above them, close under the beamed ceiling, the shaggy, not-too-well-kept head of a bull buffalo looked down. The room exhibited the careless luxury of a male-dominated household; the touch of a woman's hand was almost completely absent.

Another Mexican servant entered the room from a

distant doorway. She was older than the one who had taken Longarm's gear and considerably heavier. Her black hair was swept back tightly and wound into a ball that sat comically on top of her head. Her dress was a clean but simple, unadorned one-piece affair that reached only to her knees.

"Coffee and some whiskey for our guest," Chisum told the woman. "Is Sallie about?"

"Gone riding," the woman answered.

"Thank you, Rose."

Chisum had settled on the couch. Longarm took one of the leather-upholstered chairs, leaning back against the buffalo robe. Looking across at his host, he found himself observing a spare man, big-boned, his sun-baked skin the color and texture of old and supple leather. He wore scuffed boots with the bottoms of his worn and faded trousers tucked inside. His face was gaunt, narrowing to a long jaw. His nose was prominent, his dark brown hair parted neatly on the right side, his mustache full and bushy. The dark, piercing eyes regarded Longarm with something bordering on amusement.

"How did you get past my men, Marshal?"

Longarm smiled at the big man. "Why not let them tell you? They should be here before sundown, if they keep a steady pace."

Chisum grew more alert. "You mean they are—"

"That's right. Walking."

"Would you like to explain that, Marshal?"

"No," Longarm replied gently, taking out a cheroot and lighting it. The older servant brought in the coffee and cups on a large tray, a bottle of Irish whiskey standing proudly alongside the coffeepot.

The two men waited until both cups had been poured. With a nod, Chisum indicated that Longarm could measure out his own whiskey. Longarm satisfied himself with a small dollop, tasted the coffee, and leaned back contentedly.

As the Mexican woman padded swiftly from the room, Longarm said, "Like I said before, why not let them give you the story? I'm sure it'll be interesting. For my part, I was a mite disturbed at the brand of hospitality the men were showing. They didn't bother to identify themselves or request my identity. High-handed, I call it. And purely aggravating. I reckon you would have handled matters somewhat differently. You seem to be a right accommodating gent, most hospitable." Longarm sipped his coffee.

"Those men were under my orders, Marshal." The man's long face had become pale. Forcing his riders to walk was a worse affront than taking their weapons, though, of course, Longarm had done that as well. "Who were they?"

"One was called Jim, the other Johnny. I didn't get the others' handles."

"Jim? Jim Highsaw?"

Longarm shrugged and took a drag on his cheroot. He was enjoying John Chisum's discomfiture. "Maybe you better describe this Highsaw."

Chisum did so at once, his voice betraying his annoyance. When he had finished, Longarm nodded and sipped his coffee. "That's the gent."

"But damn it, Marshal! He's my range boss!"

"Didn't have much manners for a range boss," Longarm observed.

"We cannot afford manners, Marshal! It has become open season on my range stock. We have lost close to thirty head in the past month, and at least a dozen horses, all blooded stock. I am being nibbled to death by swarms of rustlers—with Billy the Kid leading the pack."

"You sure? I mean, are you sure it's Bill Bonney himself?"

"No, damnit, I am not. But does it matter? His example has inspired a swarm of rustlers. As a result, I have had to order Jim Highsaw to close off my range to any strangers. You, sir, were a stranger."

"You can call me Longarm," the lawman said, puffing on his cheroot.

Chisum got to his feet. "Will you tell me where you unhorsed my men?"

Longarm told him. Chisum nodded brusquely, excused himself, and left the room. Longarm heard the man's tread as he moved down the central hallway. Then a door was flung open and Longarm heard the man's voice, issuing orders. A few minutes later, Chisum returned to his guest, informing him, "I have sent some riders with fresh horses after them."

"Right decent of you."

Chisum sighed, took up his Irish coffee, and drank some of it. Wiping his long mustache dry with the back of his hand, he leaned back and fixed Longarm with a cold stare. "I don't know how to figure you, Longarm. You are a law officer. But you are a mighty high-handed law officer, and that's the truth."

"Any time a band of riders surrounds me with guns drawn, I tend to get a mite ruffled. This ain't your land, Chisum. It belongs to every citizen. I am not only a citizen, I am an agent of the federal government. I guess I could say that your spread is a non-paying tenant on the land I represent."

"This spread is mine!" Chisum insisted, his face suddenly brick red. "My cattle roam it, my men patrol it."

"How much did you pay for it?"

"Nothing!"

"It is yours by right of occupation. You took it first, so you own it."

"Precisely!"

Longarm shrugged. "I didn't come here to argue

with your right to the Jingle Bob spread, Chisum. All I am doing is reminding you that the way you treat others is important. I imagine a lot of small ranchers in Lincoln County have met your boys on occasion and not liked the way they were treated. That may account for the way your cattle are disappearing."

Chisum had no answer for that. In the cold silence that followed, Longarm heard the quick tattoo of horses' hooves as Chisum's men rode out after Jim Highsaw and his boys.

"Why did you ride out here, Longarm? What are you after?"

"Information. Help, if you can give it."

The man shook his head. "I must say, you have a queer way of approaching a man for assistance."

"Charles Kilrain shot and killed one of your riders yesterday."

"Kilrain?"

"The owner of the Dry Gulch—and almost everything else—in Paso Robles."

"Oh, yes. I have heard of him. You must be mistaken, Longarm. None of my men were in Paso Robles yesterday; I know that for a fact. What was this man's name?"

"Vincent Murales."

Chisum smiled and leaned back. "You say he is dead?"

Longarm nodded.

"Fine. Murales rode for me some time ago—until I found out how he was spending his evenings. He was rustling my stock, Longarm. We strung up a few of his associates, but Murales disappeared. I am glad that on his reapparance, Charles Kilrain took care of him so nicely."

"Murales had tried to kill me."

"Well, now. You are obviously a tough customer,

Longarm. And I suppose I can understand your testiness now a little better. Your nerves are shot."

Longarm smiled coldly. "Perhaps. Would you be kind enough to put me up for a while, and steer me to a hot bath? I could use one."

Chisum stood up. "Of course!" He called to his housekeeper and told her what Longarm wanted.

The woman padded swiftly into the living room, with the young Mexican girl on her heels. The girl was obviously the older woman's daughter. "This way, *Señor*," the woman said.

As Longarm followed the big woman from the room, Chisum called after him, "A nice hot bath should do wonders for your disposition, Longarm. Take a short nap after, if you like. Dinner will be at seven. I'll have Sallie wake you. Perhaps then we can start on a more congenial footing."

"Maybe," Longarm replied with a smile. "I sure will appreciate this bath."

"Yes, you will, Longarm. Rosita's way with a scrub brush is a revelation."

He turned then and strode from the room. Longarm turned and found himself looking down into the dark, impudent eyes of the girl—Rosita. She took his big hand.

"This way, *Señor*."

Rosita finished soaping his head. Stinging suds flowed down his forehead into the corners of his eyes. He grimaced as Rosita's strong fingers continued to massage his scalp. Abruptly she shoved his head forward. When he tried to straighten it, she pushed it down again. He understood. A moment later, a cascade of steaming water was poured over his head. He thought she might have scalded him to death as the steam enveloped him, but she paid his discomfort no heed as she reached into the steaming water for the brush and soap, and began scrubbing down his back.

It was delightful. She made no effort to hide her pleasure in her contemplation of Longarm's generous physique as she scrubbed up over his shoulders and down the front of his chest. Earlier, the girl's mother, watching Longarm step naked into the tub, had noted Longarm's formidable endowments and said something in Spanish to Rosita. The girl had laughed delightedly and set to work.

Rosita and Longarm were alone now, and as the girl scrubbed away, her fresh, round face came close to Longarm's. She smiled at him, her teeth flashing brilliantly in her dark face. Her hand in its downward thrust was destroying what little composure Longarm had left.

"Stand up, Señor Long," Rosita said suddenly, getting to her feet and brushing a stray lock of hair off her forehead with the back of her hand.

Reluctantly, Longarm pushed himself to his full height. Rosita did not embarrass him any further by commenting in any way on Longarm's involuntary erection. Ignoring it altogether, she busied herself in scrubbing down his buttocks and the back of his legs. She was quite thorough. Longarm could feel the miles of dust peeling off, and a good pound of skin along with it. Another steaming bucket of hot water rinsed him, and then she folded a huge towel around him and helped him to step out of the tub.

She patted him all over, her hands playing a maddening tune over his suddenly alive body. Slippers were waiting for him by the door. His longjohns, stockings, and the rest of his clothing had disappeared with the housekeeper. With the towel wrapped discreetly about his long frame, Longarm was led by Rosita out of the bath and down the corridor to his room. Inside, he found his gear piled neatly on the top of a dresser. The bed was turned down already for him. Longarm did not think he was ready for sleep just yet, however.

Rosita peeled the towel off him and pushed him gently down onto the bed. He came to rest on his back, looking hungrily up at the girl. She smiled and laughed delightedly at his obvious predicament, then gently but firmly turned him over onto his stomach. Longarm felt the bed jounce slightly as she climbed onto it and knelt beside his naked body. He was about to turn to her when her hands began working on the muscles about his neck. They pounded gently at first, then gained in power and assertiveness. The edges of her hands were like blunt knives as they kneaded his muscles and moved down his back.

It was incredibly soothing. He felt the tensions within his body evaporate without a trace. His maddening erection faded. Longarm found his senses drifting as the magic of Rosita's ministrations continued to flow over the length of his body. Her fingers, as they dug into the calves of his legs, were like steel, but soothing to a marvelous degree. Longarm closed his eyes and rested his head to one side, the tiny beating of Rosita's hands lulling him deeper and deeper into a profound sleep. . . .

Longarm heard her delighted laughter as she eased herself off the bed. He thought he wanted to call her back, but he wasn't sure. The sleep into which he was falling was like a benediction.

He did not hear Rosita leave the room.

He awoke to a gentle rapping on his door. He stirred and found that Rosita had covered him with a single sheet. He glanced up and saw a complete suit of clothes folded neatly on the chair by his bed. The rapping on his door was repeated.

"Yes," he called.

"Mr. Long, Uncle John told me to wake you. Dinner will be in a half-hour." The voice was that of a young girl. He guessed it belonged to Chisum's niece, the girl Sallie.

"Thank you, Sallie," he called. "I'll be dressed in a few minutes."

"I'll be back," Sallie said. Longarm heard her steps moving down the hall.

As Longarm examined the clothing on the chair, he was surprised to see that his longjohns, shirt, and stockings had been washed and dried in the short time he had been asleep. He credited this to the incredibly warm sun of New Mexico, and dressed himself swiftly. He was just buttoning his vest when Sallie returned.

"Come in," he called through the door.

It was pushed open and Longarm saw a well-tanned, long-limbed girl in a lovely print dress standing in the doorway. He saw that she had John Chisum's eyes and outthrust chin. She smiled at him.

"So you're the one that humbled big bad Jim, are you?"

"Big bad Jim?"

"Highsaw, Uncle John's range boss. I'm positively delighted! You are my hero, Mr. Long."

She stepped eagerly into the room, closing the door behind her. "You must tell me how you did it. He's been protesting, ever since he rode in, that you tricked him unfairly. I don't believe a word of it. I don't think you *had* to trick him!"

"He *was* a mite ripe for the plucking, now that you mention it, Sallie. Tried to reach in under my frock coat for my Colt."

She laughed, pleased enormously at this tidbit. With a swift movement of her hand she brushed her long auburn curls back off her shoulder. "My," she said, "you *are* big. Maybe even taller than our guest."

"Guest?"

"A man from Roswell—Pat Garrett. Uncle John wants him to be the new sheriff. He says he is anxious to meet you."

"Well then, Sallie, lead the way."

Sallie led Longarm down the inner hallway to the living room where Chisum, the man running for sheriff, Jim Highsaw, and another ranch hand were standing about, conversing quietly, all of them with fresh drinks in their hands. Highsaw had his left arm in a sling and he fell silent the moment Longarm loomed in the doorway. The man with him squared his shoulders nervously as he watched Longarm cross the room.

"How's the shoulder, Jim?" Longarm asked, his tone meant to convey honest concern.

"Why in hell didn't you tell me who you were?" the range boss demanded.

"Why didn't you ask me?"

Before Jim Highsaw could reply to that, Chisum strode over with his guest.

"Longarm, I'd like you to meet Pat Garrett, who's going to be the new sheriff of Lincoln County before long."

Longarm took Garrett's long, bony hand in his and shook it warmly. As Sallie had told him, Garrett was at least as tall as Longarm. He had direct, piercing brown eyes looking out from under a fine, broad brow. His mustache was full and dark and well cared for, his high cheekbones prominent. But it was the eyes that caught Longarm. He trusted the man at once, for the eyes told him that this was a man who would always find it impossible to sneak around and come in the back door. He was a direct, blunt, honest man—no matter what the cost.

"John's a little ahead of himself," Garrett said to Longarm. "I ain't the new sheriff yet. And maybe I won't need to be if you've come here to clean up Lincoln County—" he smiled—"and can do it."

"Cleaning up Lincoln County is not my reason for being here," Longarm said. "I'll leave that to you and Chisum, here."

"Why are you in Lincoln County, Longarm?" Chisum asked.

"To look into the murder of Bernstein and the disappearance of one of Governor Wallace's agents in the vicinity of Paso Robles."

Chisum nodded slowly. "Do you know the man's name?"

"Dudley McBride."

"And he disappeared near Paso Robles?"

"That's right. A town that a man called Charles Kilrain is rapidly taking over. Do you know the man, Chisum?"

"I've met him. Seems to have enough money and likes Paso Robles enough to dig in, looks like. A straightforward enough gent, as far as I could see."

"That's as it may be," the federal man said, "but ever since his arrival on the scene, there seems to have been an increase in violence in that neighborhood. A few townsmen have been killed in shooting scrapes, things like that. The governor wanted me to look into that as well, and find out what I could of the man. No one seems to know where he's come from."

"Where we all come from," Garrett said with a slow smile. "Someplace else."

Jim Highsaw cleared his throat. "This fellow Kilrain is in solid with the Mexicans in the town; I know that for a fact. Gives to the church, lets the greasers drink in the same saloon with white men."

"You don't approve?" Garrett asked softly.

Longarm caught the casual menace in the man's tone and grew alert. Highsaw's long-beaked face went suddenly pale. He was remembering something he should not have forgotten. The man's piercing blue eyes became clouded with sudden dismay.

As the man began to stammer a reply to Garrett's soft query, Chisum spoke up quickly: "Jim meant no harm by that observation, Pat. He just spoke without thinking." Chisum looked coldly at his range boss. "Ain't that right, Jim?"

"Sure, John, that's right. I didn't mean nothing by it."

Without bothering to acknowledge Jim Highsaw's explanation, Garrett looked at Longarm and smiled slightly. "I am married to a woman of Mexican parentage, Longarm. I have many friends who boast that heritage, and have never turned my back on any of them for that reason. When I first arrived here in New Mexico, the native Mexicans called me Juan Largo— Long John, that is—because of my height, and I was a welcome visitor to their dances and celebrations. They never turned *me* away because I was an Anglo."

"Good for you, Pat Garrett!"

They all turned. Sallie was standing in the dining room doorway. She had evidently come to call them to dinner and had caught Pat Garrett's words.

"I am glad you approve, Sallie," said John Chisum wryly. "I gather that dinner is ready."

"That's right, Uncle. Come and get it."

"Just in time," Chisum confided to Longarm, as he led the lawman into the dining room.

As Longarm might have expected, the King of the Pecos had a dining room worthy of his title. The massive table could easily have sat twenty or more people. The mantles and sideboards were polished to a magnificent sheen and were, at the moment, groaning under the weight of the food that had been prepared. The chairs were of solid mahogany, as was the table. The floor was carpeted with a deep Persian rug, most of its intricate weave colored a deep burgundy. The wall tapestries added still more splendor to the room. The candles along the wall were remote and gave just enough light. The room was cool and glowing.

Prime steak was the main course, preceded by a jerky-and-rice soup, *sopa de carne seca y arroz*, as Sallie called it for Longarm's benefit. There were heaping side orders of enchiladas and tortillas, and before Longarm could push himself away, he found himself devouring a thick chocolate dessert, *champurrado*. The repast was concluded with cigars, and wine from Chisum's cellar. As Longarm took out a cheroot to go with his wine, he felt like the frog in the fable who blew himself up to the point where he was about to burst. Only Longarm had the uncomfortable feeling he was *not* going to burst.

As Sallie excused herself to oversee the clearing of the table, Chisum looked down the table at Longarm.

"You said you were sent here to investigate the murder of that clerk from the Bureau of Indian Affairs— Bernstein. Seems to me I've heard it was Billy the Kid who killed him. The clerk's body was found shot full of holes near one of the Kid's hideouts, close to the Mescalero agency."

"It was the Kid, all right," said the ranch hand who was sitting beside Jim Highsaw.

Longarm looked at the man. At once, Chisum realized his lapse. "Forgive me, Longarm. I have not yet introduced Duke. He's my secretary, accountant, and all-around handyman. Been with me since Texas."

"You pretty sure it was the Kid?" Longarm asked Duke.

"He may be sure, but I'm not," said Garrett.

"Well," Chisum said, "you better listen to Pat, Longarm. He's the authority on the Kid. Isn't that right, Pat?"

"Nope. I saw him around a couple of times, that's

all. Never paid him much attention. Didn't know he was planning on becoming so famous. Hell, you should know all about Billy the Kid. He was fighting for your side."

Chisum sat back and waggled a hand in a gesture of dismissal. "Now you know I never took a hand in that fool war. It was out of control before I could do a thing to stop it. I heard that Billy told the governor I hired him on as a regulator, but that's not the truth, Garrett, and you know it."

Garrett chuckled. "I know it, John. You got too much sense to get mixed up in a mess like that. But that sure don't stop people from talking—especially when it's Billy the Kid doing the blabbin'."

Longarm looked back at Chisum's accountant and handyman. "What makes you think it was the Kid who killed Bernstein?"

"A friend of mine knew Charlie Bowdre. Said Charlie got drunk one night and admitted he and the Kid had come upon the Bernstein clerk near their place. The Kid tried to disarm the clerk, but the clerk got nervous and went for his gun. The Kid shot him."

"That's the first time you mentioned that story, Duke," Chisum remarked in surprise.

"This is the first time it came up. I didn't figure it was any of my business. What the hell, he was just a fool clerk from the Indian Bureau. An Apache lover, he was. I figured good riddance."

Longarm looked at Duke more closely. He realized he didn't like the man. He had a squeezed, pale face with eyes set rather close together and a chin with no heft to it. That this man should have stuck to John Chisum over the years was more a tribute to his lack of backbone than to Chisum's good sense.

"Why don't you think Billy the Kid did it, Garrett?" Longarm asked.

"I just think the Kid is being blown out of all proportion by the newspapers. Everything that goes wrong, any cattle that are run off, or horses, then it must be Billy. I just don't think the Kid's that good. Besides, I heard from a friend of mine that Bowdre's in El Paso, hiding out on a ranch down there. And where Charlie is, that's where I figure the Kid is. He'd be a fool to hang around here, especially with that five-hundred-dollar bounty on his head. Maybe he ain't the brightest outlaw in the world, but he sure ain't the dumbest."

Chisum laughed. "I thought you said you didn't know him all that well."

"If he could get out of a burning house with an army camped around it and then talk the governor into a pardon after the murder of Sheriff Brady, he must have *some* brains. It can't all be luck."

Longarm took out his wallet. From it, he slowly withdrew a folded, worn, and faded newspaper clipping. Carefully he unfolded the clipping and then passed it down the table to Garrett.

"What's this?" Garrett asked as he reached for the clipping.

"Supposed to be a picture of Billy the Kid. It was cut out of a Santa Fe newspaper and sent to the governor. He sent it along to my boss in Denver. Is that the Kid?"

Garrett squinted at the picture. "I can't tell for sure. It's pretty well faded. But it sure might be him, all right. I think I remember that hat, and the way he's standing with his head tipped to one side. Rings a bell, it does."

"He's left-handed."

Garrett looked carefully at the picture and then nodded. "Reckon so. It looks that way. I never thought about it one way or the other."

"May I see his picture?" asked Sallie.

They all turned as Sallie hurried from the kitchen

into the dining room. "I heard what you said. If that's a picture of Billy the Kid, I want to see it."

Longarm handed it to her. Sallie took it and examined it closely. "He's got buck teeth," she said in surprise, handing the clipping back to Longarm.

"What's the matter?" her uncle asked, smiling at her. "Isn't it proper for Billy the Kid to look like that?"

She laughed. "I guess not. I think I imagined him to be more romantic-looking than he is in this picture."

"Most people would, I imagine," Pat Garrett said. "But he's just a little gunslick, like any other."

"What color is his hair, Pat?" Longarm asked.

"Light-colored, I believe. I guess he's a nice enough kid. If you're his friend, that is. But, like I said, he'd be a fool to hang around Lincoln County. It's more than likely he's holed up somewhere in Texas along with Charlie Bowdre."

Longarm looked up the table at John Chisum. "Maybe the Kid killed Bernstein, and maybe he didn't. But that still leaves the disappearance of Dudley McBride. He was last seen riding out of Paso Robles, coming in this direction. I believe he had written to the governor a few days before that he was planning on talking to you about this fellow Kilrain."

"If that was his plan, it wouldn't have done him any good, Longarm. I told you all I know about Kilrain, which is pretty damn little. Besides, the man never reached this place. I never laid eyes on him."

Longarm looked at Jim Highsaw. "Any chance he might have run into you, or one of your eager riders?"

Highsaw's face purpled. He started to rise out of his chair in a fury. Before he could answer, John Chisum's voice, cold and wavering slightly in an effort to contain his anger, spoke quickly: "That was uncalled for, Longarm. Uncalled for. You are a guest in my house. This is no time to be accusing a Jingle Bob rider of murder!"

"Uncle!" cried Sallie, who had remained in the room as the conversation heated up. "I am sure Mr. Long didn't mean it to sound that way."

Longarm smiled at Sallie. "You're right," he told her. "I was just remembering the way I was greeted this afternoon on my way to this ranch."

"I suggest," said Pat Garrett, his voice ominously soft, "that you remember also how well John Chisum has treated you since."

"Enough!" Sallie cried. "Why don't you all go outside and cool off? I want to clean off this table. Now scat!"

Under the cool New Mexico stars, the five men lost a little of their heat. Longarm did all he could to keep his remarks from igniting further conflict. He let Chisum ramble on about his early days in New Mexico, his decision to build what he called his Long House, the loyalty of his riders. He seemed pleased enough with the way things were when he started recalling his early years in the territory; but as he began remembering events of the past four or five years, he began to express surprising bitterness.

He missed the old days, as he called them, when men rode for a brand and were proud of their affiliation. They stood by the owner, and he stood by them. Chisum recalled when one of his trail hands had been killed and he and his riders had trailed the killer to his *jacale*, dragged him out, and made a "cottonwood blossom out of him." In short, Chisum had been able to fight fire with fire until the Lincoln County War. He sympathized with the Tunstall-McSween faction, but he prudently refused to aid them directly and had to stand helplessly by as they were ground under and buried beneath the rocky soil of Lincoln County. He repeated his contention that, despite what Billy the Kid maintained, he had never hired the Kid and others as gunmen to seek retribution for the deaths of McSween and his followers.

And now it was open season on Chisum's cattle. Rustlers, like swarms of summer gnats, were sweeping down on his herds, decimating them. That was why Chisum had written a letter to the governor, suggesting that Pat Garrett be deputized to guard both ends of the Pecos River Valley. Though the governor had turned Chisum's request down, he had decided to back Chisum's plan to run Garrett for county sheriff.

John Chisum seemed to be pinning all his hopes for survival on the election of this tall, lanky, quiet-mannered individual, who had somehow managed to impress Chisum mightily. In the dim light of the porch, Longarm studied Pat Garrett and wondered if perhaps Chisum had not finally found a man who deserved his confidence. Certainly, in backing Tunstall and McSween, Chisum *had* been a loser. If, on top of all that, Bonney was also on his payroll, that would be proof positive that Chisum was a master in misjudging character.

But not so with this Garrett. Listening to the big man's quiet voice, his easy laugh, Longarm was impressed.

Garrett turned suddenly to Longarm, his dark eyes alight with a thought. "Longarm, it is said that this Kilrain has done well with the Mexicans and small ranchers around Paso Robles. That about right?"

"So I hear," Longarm confirmed.

"And the gent has become a power in the town."

Longarm nodded.

"Well, then. Maybe I'd better ride to Paso Robles and make the man's acquaintance. I'm John's candidate in this upcoming election, which means I am not going to get much support from the small ranchers or from the Mexicans. Perhaps a word from Kilrain would help. I'll need every vote."

John Chisum spoke up quickly: "Garrett, that's nonsense. You're going to win!"

Highsaw and Duke chimed in quickly in support of their boss's contention, but it was obvious that Garrett took their assurances with a grain of salt. Without angering them, he assured them he felt the most prudent course was to take no chances.

Sallie appeared in the doorway behind them at about that time to announce that nightcaps were on the sideboard. With weary sighs, the men filed into the living room for a last round before retiring. The quiet, civilized manner in which life was conducted on Chisum's ranch was a welcome pleasure to a man who spent half of his time living in cheap, loud, garish hotels, and the other half living out of his saddlebags.

As Longarm finished his drink, said good night to his host and hostess, and started for his room, Garrett called out to him, suggesting they ride out together the next morning. Longarm agreed with pleasure.

Longarm had just climbed in under the clean sheets and stretched his long body luxuriously when he heard his door open and close swiftly. Light, bare feet padded across the room toward him. The bed sagged and he felt the bedclothes being lifted as a lithe, warm body slid in beside him.

It was Rosita; he could tell from the warm smell of her. She moved her warmth against him, then snuggled still closer, her hands again working the knot of muscles behind his shoulder.

"No more of that, Rosita," he told her softly, as he turned gently to face her. She smiled and kissed him on the lips and let her arms encircle his neck. He slid effortlessly onto her. She opened her legs and locked her ankles behind his back. He was inside her before he was aware of it, while her lips remained fastened to his.

It was like coming home after a long, weary journey.

Chapter 6

Longarm and Pat Garrett, as they rode silently along together, were an impressive-looking pair. It was no surprise that a warm affinity had grown between them in the short time they had known each other; both men were tall and solidly built, and dressed and carried themselves in a remarkably similar manner. Each wore a vested tweed suit—Longarm's was brown and Garrett's gray—and each sported a neatly trimmed, full mustache. Beneath Longarm's flat-topped Stetson and Garrett's equally characteristic derby, their eyes had the calm but electric quality that comes only from years of living in vast openness, combined with the carefully cultivated ability to size a man up instantly from across the width of a card table. Such eyes are not easy to distract, and provide no hindrance to the gun hand of a skillful lawman. They rode with the easy assurance of men to whom a world without the smell of horseflesh and saddle leather would be incomprehensible.

They had almost reached the Pecos River before Pat Garrett cleared his throat. That he had something he wanted to tell Longarm had been obvious from the outset. Unwilling to push the man, Longarm had waited patiently. Now, with the river in sight, Garrett pulled up abruptly, hooked one long leg over his pommel, and looked at Longarm.

Longarm pulled up also, chucked his hat back off his forehead and waited.

"I've been thinking over what you told us at the dinner table last night, Longarm."

Longarm nodded and took out a cheroot.

"About this agent the governor sent to Paso Robles."

"Dudley McBride."

"That's the one."

"What about him?"

"I think I know the gent."

Longarm bit down on his cheroot. "That so?"

"From way back, when I was hunting buffalo in Texas. He dropped by our camp one day, and left without saying goodbye a few days later. Trouble was, he took some of our hides with him. We caught up with him outside Abilene and punished him some before we took back our hides. That was the last I saw of old Dudley."

"Can you describe him?"

Garrett squinted into the sky for a moment, then replied, "Sandy, curly hair. Not too big a fellow. Around five foot five, I'd judge. Rode all stooped over. Liked to fancy himself a gunslinger. He was a queer one. Seemed to me he read too many dime novels, and he believed every damn one of them. We called him Deadwood Dick once and he began to strut. He was a queer one." Garrett shook his head. "Like I said, the governor sure picked himself a poor sort of man to act as his agent."

"Wallace hasn't been in the territory long, Garrett. Doesn't know the country yet. This fellow probably gave him a line and the governor swallowed it."

"Dudley sure was good at that, all right. You say he's disappeared? You ain't found any trace of him yet?"

"That's right," Longarm said, stretching.

Garrett lifted his foot back off his pommel, then shook his head slowly. "The governor's well rid of him, I'd say. That Lew Wallace must be a little like John back there. John's quick to make alliances, but he isn't too wise about those he lines himself up with, and that's a fact. I never did like that range boss of his, or that clerk."

Longarm grinned around his cheroot. "He's allying himself with you, Pat."

Garrett grinned back and pulled his derby down snugly. "Well, hell, Longarm. A man can't be wrong *all* the time."

They started up again, their horses angling off the gentle hummocks that bordered the river. Longarm knew Garrett had a few more things on his mind, but again he told himself to be patient. They were almost to the river when Garrett glanced over at him.

"One more thing, Longarm. I was just trying to keep John from getting into a sweat back there when I told him Billy the Kid was more than likely in Texas."

Longarm pulled up quickly. "You mean you don't think he's still in Texas?"

"The talk in Roswell is that a gang of outlaws led by Billy are right now cutting John's herds to pieces up near the Apache agency."

"Can you give me a better location than that?"

"Chico Wells. There's a stone farmhouse there; that's supposed to be their hideout. It's southwest of here. Follow the Pecos west until you reach the Wolf Creek settlement, then head for the Mescalero agency."

"Thanks, Garrett."

Garrett shrugged. "If you can take care of those hombres, I won't have the bother when I get to be sheriff." He laughed softly. "If, that is, I *do* get elected. Kimball's a good lawman and, like I told John back there, he'll get the Mexican vote."

They forded the river then, and when they reached the other side, Garrett leaned over and shook Longarm's hand warmly in parting. Longarm liked the man's strong grip, the unwavering gleam in his dark eyes, and sat his horse awhile as he watched the fellow ride off.

Then, following Garrett's suggestion, he turned his horse about and nudged it westward, keeping the river in sight as he rode.

Longarm had left Wolf Creek behind an hour earlier. He was in high country now, and would be on Apache land within another hour if he kept to his present course. There was no trail to follow and he was taking his time, allowing the buckskin to pick its way over the dry, rocky ground. Cresting a low ridge, Longarm caught sight of a lone rider at least a half-mile ahead of him.

The rider was going in the same direction as Longarm. At this distance he could not be certain, but he thought he recognized the rider. A ridge followed the trail the rider was using. Longarm cut for it, letting the buckskin out at a full run for the first time that day. He crested the ridge, then rode hard along the far side until he judged that he had passed the other rider. He found a good spot to view the trail beyond the ridge, dismounted, drop-reined the buckskin, and clambered up into a nest of rocks that crowned the ridge.

The rider coming toward him along the trail was Duke Foster, Chisum's accountant. Something about the way the man rode, a hunched wariness, alerted Longarm. The man was up to something, and Longarm decided to follow and find out what. After Duke was past him, he jumped down off the rocks and remounted.

He stayed on the far side of the ridge as he followed Duke, only occasionally riding its crest to check on the horseman.

About four that afternoon, as he rode through a narrow cleft of rocks, his eyes on Duke on the trail below him, he heard a sixgun cock behind him in the rocks. Longarm swore bitterly to himself, ducked low over the buckskin's neck, and reached in under his coat for his Colt. His hand froze on the walnut grips.

A grubby-looking rifleman had stepped out of the rocks just in front of the buckskin, his rifle on his shoulder, the muzzle staring into Longarm's eyes.

No sense in riling the man, Longarm thought. Slowly he straightened in his saddle and withdrew his hand from his Colt. He heard the chink of spurs behind him on the rocky ground, raised both hands over his head, and turned to see what the second man looked like.

This fellow was tall, unshaven, a mite long in the tooth, and had a red gleam in his eye. He didn't look healthy, but he looked mean enough. The Colt Longarm had heard him cock was in his hand, pointing up at him.

"Howdy," this fellow said, his thin lips peeling back off his yellow teeth. "That's a nice horse you got there. Seems to me you ought to have a wallet to go with it."

Highwaymen, Longarm realized. He remembered the reports, then, that had mentioned the fact that Governor Wallace was also concerned about the number of footpads and highwaymen infesting the county. He cursed himself for not having paid more attention to this complaint. If he had, he might not have been caught so easily.

"If you'll just lower that firearm, mister," Longarm drawled, "I'll be glad to show you my wallet."

"Well, I won't lower it, but you'll show it to me jest the same, I reckon." The fellow flashed his yellow teeth at Longarm, glancing swiftly toward his confederate as he did so.

"Watch him good, Petey," said the fellow with the rifle. "He was reaching for a weapon when he saw my rifle."

"Better get down, mister," Petey said. "Slow-like."

As Longarm swung his leg over the cantle, his back to the two men, he drew his revolver in one lightning movement; the instant his feet struck the ground, the Colt was in motion, cutting in a wide, vicious arc. The barrel struck the rifleman flush on the side of the head. The man was driven into Petey, his rifle discharging into the air. Longarm left his feet then and drove into the rifleman, who went down on top of Petey. There was a muffled shot as Petey's gun discharged. The rifleman cried out, bucked painfully, and then collapsed loosely back onto his partner.

Startled, Longarm drew back—and found himself looking down the bore of Petey's Smith & Wesson.

"Drop the iron, mister," Petey said grimly, shrugging himself free of his wounded partner.

Longarm dropped the Colt beside the tumbling body of the rifleman as it struck the face of the boulder, then moved to get out of the way as the wounded highwayman came to rest at his feet, face uplifted, eyes squeezed shut in pain.

"Let me kill 'im, Petey," the fellow gasped.

"Sure, sure, Frank. I'll help you do it. But later. You ain't in no condition now."

"Damn you, Petey! I won't be in no condition later! I'll be dead!"

"You fellows still interested in seeing my wallet?" Longarm asked.

"Reach in nice and slow," Petey said.

Longarm withdrew his wallet from his inside coat pocket and handed it to the man. The fellow took a step back from Longarm and managed to open the wallet with a flick of his left hand. When he saw the badge, he swore softly and looked down at his partner.

"We got us trouble, Frank. This here's a U.S. deputy marshal."

Frank's eyes were open by this time. He grabbed a boulder and pulled himself erect, his face contorted with the effort and the pain from his back wound. "Just hand me my rifle, Petey. He's done killed me, and if you won't take care of him, I will."

"No you won't," said Petey. He grinned, hooked his right foot in behind Frank's, and yanked. Frank's leg went out from under him and he landed heavily on his back on the stony ground. The man gasped and closed his eyes. Longarm thought Frank was going to cry. "I said *later*. We don't want this guy found. It'll be a whole lot better if we jest make him disappear—like that other one. Otherwise we'll have a whole army of federal marshals combing these ridges."

"You didn't have to do that, you bastard."

"Sure I did. You weren't talkin' sense. You ready to head back?"

Frank nodded slightly.

Petey reached down for Longarm's Colt, picked it up, and stuck it into his belt. Then he pocketed Longarm's wallet. "Okay, mister, lift Frank onto your hoss."

Longarm caught the nearly unconscious outlaw under his arms and heaved him up over the saddle. The fellow managed to right himself somehow and grab the reins. Slumped painfully over the saddle horn, he was able to follow behind Longarm and Petey as they trudged deeper into the rocky country. Petey kept his Smith & Wesson trained on Longarm's back. Every now and then, to remind Longarm that he was there, he'd nudge the lawman in the small of the back with the revolver's barrel.

They came to two waiting horses. Longarm mounted one, Petey the other. Again Longarm led them, Petey riding right behind, the wounded and utterly silent Frank behind him. Petey directed Longarm, and in less than an hour they came to a narrow valley with a small adobe *jacale* tucked in close under a sandstone cliff on the other side of a stream. As they rode across the shallow stream, a burly fellow in a black slouch hat appeared in the doorway, a rifle in his hand.

He waited until they had crossed the stream and pulled up in front of him before he shifted the rifle in his hand and spoke to Petey. "Who the hell's this, and what's wrong with Frank now?"

It was Frank who replied. "This sonofabitch did it, MacGregor! Help me down so I can kill him. Petey wouldn't let me."

Petey slipped off his horse, his sixgun pointed at Longarm. He paid no attention to what Frank had told MacGregor. "Get off, mister. And keep your hands in sight. I can just as well kill you here, but that would mean luggin' you a piece to find a spot in this god-forsaken ground where I could bury you. But I will pull this trigger if I have to."

Longarm kept his hands in plain sight as he carefully dismounted.

"You goin' to tell me what this is all about?" asked MacGregor.

"He's a deputy U.S. marshal. Figured we couldn't just drop him where we found him; it'd cause too much of a commotion, what with that new governor and all. Better if the gent just disappears. Ain't that right, MacGregor?"

MacGregor looked Longarm over quickly, sizing him up. A look of grim respect gleamed in his eyes—and pleasure at the prospect of having such a man in his power.

"Goddamn!" he said softly, almost reverently. "A lawman! All to myself." He licked his lips. "Shit, Petey, you done good."

Longarm did not like the sound of that—nor did he like the look or smell of the man. He was wearing a buckskin shirt with no buttons and nothing on underneath it but a filthy, yellowing undershirt. A beartooth necklace hung about his neck. His britches, the legs of which were tucked into the tops of his scruffy boots, were threadbare. The man's face was covered with a thick, black, curly beard. His eyebrows were equally thick. The eyes that peered out at Longarm from behind all that foliage were over-bright. Longarm detected in them a hint of madness, perhaps.

"Take him inside, why don't you?" said Petey. "But be careful. The marshal is full of tricks."

As Petey turned his attention to Frank, who by this time was leaning over onto the buckskin's neck, Mac-Gregor reached out, grabbed Longarm's shoulder, and spun him roughly ahead of him into the adobe hut. Behind him, Longarm could hear Frank alternately weeping and cursing as Petey dragged him out of the saddle. All Frank wanted, it appeared, was for someone to shove a weapon in his hand so he could kill Longarm.

As the cool dimness of the hut closed about Longarm, he reached into his vest pocket for his derringer. With Petey encumbered with the fretful Frank and MacGregor just stepping out of bright sunshine into the dim interior of the place, this moment appeared to be Longarm's best chance. As he palmed the derringer and started to turn, something struck him on the side of his head, just above his temple.

Lights exploded deep within his head. He felt himself falling. Then came the hard-packed earthen floor of the hut. It slammed up at him, numbing the side of his face. The universe tipped violently under his sprawled body. He was still conscious and saw Mac-Gregor looming high above him, a bearded giant with gleaming black eyes. The man had used the stock of his

113

rifle as a club. He still held the rifle with the stock down, ready for another blow. He leaned his head close, noting that Longarm was still barely conscious. Surprised, he shrugged, straightened, and drove the stock down at Longarm a second time. Longarm tried to avoid the onrushing stock, but found himself paralyzed. The blow drove him through the floor into darkness. . . .

When Longarm came to his senses and opened his eyes, he found himself looking into Frank's yellow, unblinking eyes, less than five inches away. The man's cold body was coiled over his own. Longarm was part of a grisly tangle of life and death in the far corner of the adobe hut. When he tried to move, he found that his hands were bound behind him. He could feel the leather thongs cutting deeply into his wrists. There was hardly any feeling left in his hands.

As his senses returned, he realized that he was bootless, and without his vest. With a determined effort, he managed to twist his body over, pulling himself free of the cold limbs holding him. As he did so, he saw Petey stepping out of the gray morning light into the hut. Petey saw Longarm move and walked over. He did not bother to unholster his revolver as he stopped and gazed down at Longarm. Petey smiled. His long yellow teeth gave him the appearance of an old wolf waiting just outside the campfire's ring of light.

"About time you woke up. Got a job for you—a couple of graves to dig. Your own and that of our fellow soldier of fortune, Frank Riley."

MacGregor darkened the doorway behind Petey. "Bring him out. We got to get going. This lawman is stinking up the place."

"I can't move with my hands trussed like this," Longarm told Petey.

"Aw, shit! Ain't that a shame!"

Petey reached down and grabbed Longarm by the hair. He hauled back on it with a ferocity that threatened to lift every hair from Longarm's scalp. Not wishing to die bald, Longarm managed to scramble frantically to his knees and then regain his feet. He blinked with dazed fury at Petey. The scalp treatment had done wonders for his pounding headache.

Petey shoved him out through the doorway. Blinking in the light, Longarm saw MacGregor watching him, a slight smile on his face. He was wearing Longarm's vest and frock coat without a shirt over the filthy undershirt, and had discarded his own boots for Longarm's. They seemed to fit perfectly. On his head he had carefully placed Longarm's snuff-brown Stetson.

"Pretty clever, ain't you?" MacGregor said to Longarm, patting the vest pocket where Longarm kept his derringer. "You was reaching for it when I hit you. And I was just doing it to make me feel good." He chuckled. "I like this watch too."

"It's an Ingersoll. Take good care of it and it'll last you a lifetime," Longarm replied.

Petey, standing behind Longarm, laughed and poked him in the back, sending him stumbling toward one of the horses.

"If you'll untie me," Longarm said, "I might be able to help you with Frank's body."

MacGregor chuckled. "Sure. Then maybe you can get into some mischief, hey?"

"Why not?" said Petey. "He's a big fellow. We could use his help. Let him try anything he wants. Should liven up the trip some."

Without further discussion, MacGregor produced a skinning knife and stepped in close behind Longarm. Longarm felt the blade slice carelessly through the rawhide. He brought his hands up and flexed them. The returning circulation caused his fingers to tingle painfully. He rubbed his hands together vigorously.

"All right, Marshal," Petey said, "go in there and bring out Frank. We'll sling him over this nag here."

Longarm did as he was told. He worked silently and efficiently for the next half-hour, helping the two men pack their gear for the journey onto the Mescalero reservation. They made no bones about it; they had done this once before and they were about to do it again. They were going to leave his body carelessly buried. If it were found, the Indians would have to take the blame. Longarm himself packed the shovels.

By this time, Longarm was fairly certain that he had found the murderers of that clerk from the Bureau of Indian Affairs, Bernstein. What he had to concentrate on now was keeping himself from joining Bernstein.

They had decided to make Longarm walk. Holding the reins of the horse carrying Frank's body, he toiled ahead of them deeper into the rocky fastnesses of the Mescalero reservation. The sun beat down on his unprotected head with a grim mercilessness that baked his eyeballs. Longarm was storing up a hatred for his two captors that he vowed would last him into the next world, if it came to that. But he said nothing, not wanting to give them the satisfaction, and kept climbing, his unshod feet leaving a dark trail of blood behind.

A little before noon, his captors called a halt. Longarm dropped the reins and sank to his knees on the stony soil, without looking down at his ribboned feet.

The two men were looming over him, grinning.

"How's this spot, Marshal?" Petey asked. "Pretty high. Gives you a fine view."

"It's fine," Longarm managed through cracked lips. He felt as dry as a shed rattlesnake skin, and just about as useful.

MacGregor thrust a shovel at Longarm. The handle had been snapped off a little better than halfway up.

He used it as a crutch to haul himself upright. Steadying himself, he squinted painfully in the awesome sunlight and began digging. The ground was hard and rocky and unyielding. The shortened length of the shovel was no help, either. The two men watched idly, their backs leaning against a boulder, Longarm's last remaining cheroots in their mouths. It was this that Longarm resented the most. But he said nothing and kept digging.

"You're not doing so good," Petey said after a while.

"What's the matter?" MacGregor asked. "Ain't you all excited about digging Frank's grave along with your own? Justice, I calls it."

Longarm straightened. "I need help," he said.

"Keep digging."

Longarm faced MacGregor. "I told you, I need help. You want to get this done today, don't you?"

"We got nothing else to do, Marshal. You just keep on workin'. It's a pleasure to see how well a lawman can use a shovel."

"Does my heart good," said Petey.

Longarm went back to work. About an hour or so later, he had managed to scrabble a hole in the ground deep enough for its first occupant. It was Longarm's task to carry Frank from the horse and dump him into his shallow grave. As soon as he had finished covering up the body, he was set to work on his own grave.

This one, surprisingly, seemed to go faster. The spot they had chosen for him had less stones embedded in it, and the soil was somewhat sandier as well. He finished in half the time, then stepped back from his handiwork, his arms resting on the shovel's handle.

"That's just fine," Petey said.

"You think its deep enough?" Longarm asked. "It don't look so to me."

Petey grinned at Longarm. "Like we said before, lawman, that don't matter none to us. If you get dug up out here, it'll be them Mescaleros who'll get the blame."

"Depends on how I'm killed, don't it?"

Petey's long teeth seemed to grow even longer as his grin widened. "Hell, Marshal. We already got that figured."

MacGregor left the boulder and strode closer, his eyes gleaming in anticipation. "We are goin' to scalp you first. We'll do it nice and clean so you won't lose your senses none. Then we'll carve you up a mite with a Mescalero knife I got stashed in my bedroll. We'll do it Apache-style, then leave the knife alongside what's left of you."

"Might work at that," Longarm agreed amiably. "Why did you only shoot that Indian Bureau clerk, then, and not bother to bury him?"

"How the hell was we to know who he was?" Mac-Gregor replied.

Petey said, "Go get that knife, Mac."

MacGregor hustled over to his mount. Longarm tightened his hands around the handle of the shovel. He saw MacGregor pull the knife out of his bedroll and start back to them. When he judged that MacGregor was close enough, Longarm swung the shovel up and around. The blade caught Petey well in under his chin and sliced through both jugulars. The man's head snapped loosely back. Twin geysers of blood shot sky-ward with astonishing force. Through the bloody froth, Petey's long yellow teeth appeared to snarl silently at Longarm.

Longarm stepped past the collapsing body and swung the shovel at MacGregor. The wet blade made a whooshing sound as it cut through the air. Coolly, Mac-Gregor ducked under it. The force with which Long-arm swung the shovel caused his bloody feet to slip on the uneven ground. As he stumbled past MacGregor, the man thrust up with his Apache knife. The blade sank into Longarm's right side and became lodged between two lower ribs. Longarm's forward momentum twisted the knife out of MacGregor's grasp, but the blade remained firmly embedded in Longarm's side. Longarm collapsed carefully onto his left side, his hand closing about the knife's hilt.

Straightening, MacGregor pulled Longarm's Colt out of his own belt and aimed carefully down at the sprawled lawman. "Damn you, mister!" he cried. "You ain't goin' quietly, is you! I sure wish I could take my time!"

Wearily, through a fog of pain, Longarm waited for MacGregor's finger to tighten on the Colt's trigger. The man cursed as his beartooth necklace swung out, obscuring his aim. He thrust it aside with his left hand.

That was the last voluntary movement MacGregor made.

Like tiny black thunderbolts, two Apache arrows sprouted in MacGregor's neck; the sound they made as they plunged out of the sky was like the whisper of wings. Another arrow plunged deep into MacGregor's right eye. The man peeled violently backward, the Colt clattering on the rocky ground.

Holding the knife steady in his side, Longarm struggled to a sitting position, then dragged himself along the ground to a boulder, against which he leaned as he tried to reach out for his Colt. Before his hand could close on the grips, an Apache moccasin kicked the revolver away.

Longarm glanced up. Toklani was standing over him, his left hand holding a bow, his right hand, wrapped in strips of cloth, at his side. His broad, impassive face regarded Longarm curiously. The Apache was evidently trying to come to a decision as to what to do with Longarm.

Longarm let his hand drop away from the knife. He was too weak to hold it in place any longer. At once the Apache uttered a guttural exclamation, stooped swiftly, and plucked the knife from Longarm's side. The shock of the knife's passage back through Longarm's inflamed ligaments and muscles was so great that he almost passed out. He shut his eyes tightly and hung on, aware of the Apaches talking quickly among themselves.

He opened his eyes. Toklani and two other Apaches were bent over MacGregor. For a moment, Longarm had difficulty understanding what it was they were doing to MacGregor. If they were scalping him, they were doing it in a very clumsy way. And then Longarm saw Toklani straighten. In his bandaged right hand he held MacGregor's beartooth necklace. He lifted it skyward and began to wail. The sound of Toklani's wailing was inexpressibly sad. Despite his own discomfort, he found himself touched by the obvious depth of the Indian's grief. He tried to understand what this had to do with MacGregor's necklace, but the effort seemed to drain his remaining reserves of energy. He felt his head lolling forward. The pain in his side faded. The sky and the rocks spun sickeningly about him.

Chapter 7

Longarm had nightmares. Dark faces leaned close,
their eyes blazing. Hot, searing towels of pain were
wrapped about his body. Every inhalation, every movement—every thought, even—brought the spiderweb of
pain in which he was ensnared to quivering life. Dark
shapes moved about him, every sound they made in-
creasing his level of pain. Worms crawled on him, fed
on him, burrowed into his brain. He was a little boy
again, running from the deranged shapes that pursued
him, his screams lost in the immensity of the soundless
maw into which he fled. . . .

He opened his eyes and saw Nalin leaning close.

"I'm cold," he said.

"That is good," she said, her bright blue eyes glowing in her dark face. It was as if she had accomplished
a great feat. "Your fever has broken. The infection is
subsiding. You are going to be all right."

"Not if you don't get a blanket over me."

She laughed and sat down beside him on the bed.
"You see? You are arguing with me already."

"Is that a change?"

She sobered instantly. "Yes," she said. "That is a change."

"I was pretty bad, eh? Almost slipped over this time?"

"Almost. You had a terrible infection from that knife wound. Your whole side . . ." She shuddered at the thought of it.

"What'd you do? Use your Indian magic?"

"Yes," she said matter-of-factly. "That is just what I did." She pulled the covers up under his chin, reached to the foot of the bed, and drew up what looked like a buffalo blanket. "How's that? When you were feverish, you threw off all your covers."

"A little better. Thanks."

His teeth no longer chattering, he glanced out the window. The sky was bright. Sunlight streamed in through the window, stamping gold rectangles on the floor. He felt elated, as if he had finished a long, hard journey and could now rest. He looked back at Nalin.

"What kind of Indian magic did you use on me?"

She hesitated a moment. "Do you really want to know?"

"Of course."

"We tried spruce balm, but that did no good. So I tried something an old Zuni told me about once—maggots."

"*Maggots!*"

"That's right. Toklani and the other Apaches were astonished. I insisted. You should have seen your wound. It was crawling with them."

"Jesus," Longarm said softly, remembering part of his nightmare.

"But they did the job. Your wound is clean now, and pink. It's closing. You'll be all right."

"Are they . . . still in there?"

"No," she said. "Not since yesterday."

Longarm glanced away from her and out the window at the bright world beyond. "Jesus," he said again, softly this time.

Nalin got up from his bed. "You must be hungry. I'll get you something to eat."

He turned his head and watched her leave the small bedroom. He didn't ask her what she planned to feed him; he was too hungry to want to know. He would just eat it and be grateful.

And pretty soon he would forget about the maggots swarming in his wound.

It was dusk. At Longarm's insistence, he had been allowed to limp out into the front yard. Nalin brought a chair for him, and he sat in it and watched the Indian encampment, the leggy brown children mostly. They never stopped running. Or shouting. A favorite game was to send hoops rolling over the ground ahead of them while they whacked at them with sticks to keep them going. Longarm couldn't figure out what the purpose of the game was, aside from the sheer pleasure of running after the damn things. The women seemed forever busy, while the Apache men seemed to have nothing better to do than hang around in groups, smoking and gambling with limp, dirty playing cards. They played impassively for the most part, only occasionally breaking into sudden whoops. In a few cases, Longarm saw an Apache rise to his feet in disgust, hurl the cards to the blanket, and stalk off. The sense of impending violence at such times hung heavily over the players.

Just before dark, Nalin joined Longarm to place a blanket over his lap. Then she brought out a chair for herself and sat down beside him.

He turned to her and said, "I've got the feeling I'm being allowed to watch something . . . rare."

"You are," Nalin replied. "An Apache village on a quiet midsummer evening. Not very frightening, is it?"

"Hell, it's peaceful. 'Cept the women never seem to stop working."

"Isn't it the same with the White Eyes' women? Remember, I was brought up in Texas."

"I forgot," Longarm admitted with a smile.

"Has Toklani asked for your hand in marriage yet?"

"Yes."

He looked at her. Her round, dark face was impassive for the moment. He could not tell if that was pride he heard in her voice or not.

"When's the big day?"

"I refused him. I felt very honored; I made that as clear as I could. But I refused firmly."

"Why?"

"The school. I love these children. And they need me, Longarm. I can help them in so many ways. But there would be no way, as the wife of Toklani, that I would be allowed to continue teaching. And there are many other things I can do for my people now, that I could not do as Toklani's wife. I was very careful to explain this to him, and he understood. And another thing, though I did not try to explain it: I am of his people, but I am not one of them." She looked at Longarm. "Do you understand what I mean?"

"Sure. But it must get pretty lonely, living in between like that." Longarm looked away from Nalin then, and saw Toklani, with two other Apaches, approaching them through the junipers. "Speak of the devil," he said.

"Toklani came by often while you were feverish. He has something he wants to tell you. It is very important to him that he has this chance to speak." She got to her feet as Toklani came closer.

"Stay here," Longarm said, laying a gently restraining hand on her arm. "I think I'm going to need an interpreter."

"I had no intention of leaving you."

Toklani came to a halt just in front of the lawman, his two companions just behind him. Longarm struggled to his feet. Using the back of the chair for support, he managed to stay upright. He knew, somehow, that this was important.

Toklani's white teeth flashed in his dark face. He spoke quickly to Nalin, his dark eyes regarding Longarm all the while with an emotion bordering surprisingly on affection. Nalin turned to Longarm.

"Shall I address you by your Apache name?" she asked.

"And what might that be?"

"To-ha-desti-na."

Longarm repeated the syllables softly and carefully.

"It means, Tall Tree Who Refuses to Fall," she explained.

"Shorten it to Tall Tree," Longarm said, smiling warmly.

Nalin laughed and spoke to Toklani. The Apache nodded solemnly. It would be as Longarm wished. Tall Tree. Nalin looked back at Longarm.

"Toklani salutes you," she said. "He saw you decapitate that fellow." Nalin winced a bit as she said this. "He saw how fiercely you fought, and with what courage you awaited the final bullet from your enemy. You did not cry out or plead for your life. You have a brave soul for a White Eyes. Toklani is proud that he has given you two fingers in battle, just as he is ashamed that, in his terrible grief, he accused you of killing his woman."

"Tell him I understand about that. And thank him for his compliment. He is a brave and fierce warrior of the Apaches, and I am honored that he salutes me. Also tell him I would like to know how he happened along when he did."

"Oh, I know that," Nalin said. "But I'll let him tell you."

She spoke for a long time, her voice transforming the deep, guttural language of the Mescalero Apache into something almost approaching music. As she relayed Longarm's compliments, Toklani nodded slightly to Longarm in acknowledgement. In his reply to Longarm's query, he turned to one of the Apaches behind him and let him speak, then joined in to complete the telling.

At last, Nalin turned back to Longarm with her account. "Toklani's friend, White Wolf—the brave on Toklani's right—saw the three of you entering the Apache territory. He stole close enough to see the bracelet on the neck of one of them. It had belonged to Toklani's wife. He returned to camp at once to summon Toklani, who joined him with this other brave. By the time they got back, you had already dug the graves. As they approached still closer, you began your attack with the shovel. When they saw that you were not going to prevail, Toklani sent the first arrow into the killer of his woman. Then the others added their own arrows." She paused a moment before finishing. What she had to tell Longarm was a mite grisly. "The two White Eyes were stripped naked and staked out on the ground. The vultures are already feeding on their carcasses. Soon their white bones will shine in the sunlight and their spirits will wander without rest over the rocky land."

Longarm nodded toward Toklani. "Tell him I am happy he came along when he did. Tell him I am sorry about his wife. And tell him also that I think what he did to those two men was fitting."

Nalin translated. Toklani stepped forward and, with his mutilated right hand, slipped a knife from his belt. He spoke directly to Longarm as he did so, while Nalin translated rapidly.

"This knife belonged to his woman, Azul," Nalin said. "It is the same knife Toklani pulled from your side. He now returns it to you as a gift—from him and from the spirit of Azul."

Longarm took the knife and nodded his thanks to Toklani. "Tell him I am honored."

Toklani did not smile, but his eyes revealed the pleasure he felt. Typical of most Apaches, Toklani was considerably shorter than Longarm. Yet he was a magnificent physical specimen without a scrap of tallow on his broad-shouldered, narrow-waisted body. A great shock of black hair reached to his shoulders. A clean white headband kept it in place. His hooded eyes peered out at Longarm from a broad, flat face that was tanned to a rich chocolate brown. He wore a buckskin shirt and a breechclout. The tops of his moccasins were folded down. Longarm was pleased that this magnificent warrior was no longer his enemy.

Toklani spoke then to Nalin—a few words only—after which he turned and walked back with his companions toward the encampment. Nalin laughed.

"He told me I have done well to save the Tall Tree," she said. "My medicine is good. Now I should give you still more medicine."

"Is that so?"

She looked at Longarm with cool, appraising eyes. "But of course he has more confidence in your powers of recuperation than I have."

"I think he should be an excellent judge of stamina."

"He did not sit by your side for close to three days and nights."

"Did you?"

"I did."

"I'm grateful to you, Nalin. More than likely you saved my life. You and them maggots."

"I shouldn't have told you about them."

"I can handle it. But I'm getting kind of chilled standing here by this chair. You want to help me in?"

"Of course."

When they were inside, Longarm moved carefully over to the bed and eased himself down onto it. Nalin stayed close beside him. Night had fallen rapidly. He could see some fires winking in the night from in front of the wickiups on the other side of the junipers. The Apache children were still playing games, despite the darkness. Their shouts came clearly to them through the windowpane.

"How do you feel?" Nalin asked.

He looked back up at her round, concerned face, with its bright, incredibly blue eyes. "I'm still a mite chilly." Then he reached up and pulled her down beside him on the bed. "Maybe we ought to try Toklani's suggestion. By the way, he seems to've recovered right nicely from his disappointment at being turned down by you."

"He has two other wives to console him. And perhaps we might try his suggestion." She got up from the bed. "I have things to do. I will be back. Rest now."

"You're hoping I will go to sleep."

"If you do, it will be good for you." She smiled. "But either way, I will see to it that you sleep well tonight."

He watched her leave the bedroom, then he undressed and crawled in under the rough blanket. He lay on his back, listening to her in the kitchen. The sound of the Apache children ceased. Longarm's eyes closed. He opened them quickly, startled at the speed with which sleep was claiming him. But his eyelids were as heavy as anvils. The next time they closed, sleep came with a rush.

When he opened his eyes again, it was still night and a delicious warmth was stealing over him. He became aware of Nalin's presence under the blanket beside him. He turned and saw her face mere inches from his.

She laughed softly, leaned still closer to him, and kissed him softly on the lips.

He reached over to pull her closer.

"No," she whispered. "Lie still."

He did as she bid him. Slowly she pressed him back, her lips on his, her hand gliding swiftly down his flat stomach to his groin. Fire seemed to trail from her fingers. Her lips still locked on his, her fingers closed about him gently. Though still half asleep, he felt his erection growing under her gentle ministrations. Her other arm was around his neck by this time, holding his lips tightly against hers. Her tongue was alive, darting with an impudent recklessness that caused his head to swim. Her lips released his. She leaned back, smiled down at him, then kissed him lightly on the forehead.

Gently, effortlessly, she eased her body onto his. He felt her lift for a moment, then drop lightly upon him, her vagina closing hungrily about his shaft. The warmth of it sent ripples of heat pulsing up his torso. She leaned forward. Her cheek rested on his chest. With her arms clasped about his torso, she began to rock slowly.

Longarm closed his eyes and leaned back. He lost track of time, of how long it took them to climax. When at last they shuddered convulsively in unison, he felt only an aching delight mingled with an inexpressible sadness that it should have had to end. For a while he had passed over into another country. He felt her lips kissing away the perspiration on his chest and face. Abruptly, her body lifted from him. He heard her light steps on the floor, and she was gone.

He felt himself drifting off into a deep, dreamless sleep. As Nalin had promised, she had seen to it that he would sleep well that night.

Two days later, Nalin and Longarm were breakfasting on the back porch when Nalin cleared her throat tentatively. Earlier, Longarm had announced his intention of riding out, and Nalin had grown thoughtful as she joined him at the table. Longarm looked at her, his eyebrows raised.

"What is it, Nalin?"

She picked up the blue graniteware coffeepot and filled Longarm's cup. "I lied to you before—about William Bonney."

"You said you didn't know him. Do you?"

"I thought I did. I thought he was a friend to the Apache, as it is said he has always been a friend to the Mexican settlers, those who owned this land for so long before the Anglos came. But it seems he has turned on us."

"How?"

"He is stealing our horses."

"Go on."

"While you were sick, White Wolf saw Billy and four other riders driving off some of our horses that were grazing near the pass. He was alone and mounted on a winded horse. Bonney and his men drove him off with their rifles, and then easily outdistanced White Wolf. The agent says he can do nothing."

"I'm surprised that drunk can even sit a horse."

"He hasn't been able to for the last week. I have written a letter to Washington."

"That ought to do a whole hell of a lot of good," Longarm muttered cynically.

"Meanwhile, Longarm, the agency police approached Toklani with a suggestion."

The way she looked at him, Longarm thought he knew what she was about to say. "Out with it," he said. "I'll listen, I promise."

"You are a lawman, Longarm; perhaps you could help us. The Apaches have been losing much of their best stock. It is their only wealth. You must help."

130

"Is this the only rustling the Kid has had a hand in?"

She shook her head. Her eyes evaded his for a moment. "He has been rustling cattle too."

"Whose?"

"Chisum's Jingle-Bob brand, mostly."

"The Apaches didn't think that was worth mentioning, eh? But now Billy is stinging the Apaches too, so you want help."

She looked at him with some defiance. "John Chisum owns most of New Mexico, or thinks he does. He has more cattle than he can count. His riders are a law unto themselves. Heaven help the Apache who finds himself alone with a band of Chisum's men. They are not kind, Longarm."

Longarm was silent as he gazed into the pungent black depths of his coffee cup.

She sighed deeply, her round face lifting to his, a small, bitter smile on her face. "Say it, why don't you? 'Now the shoe is on the other foot.'"

Longarm grinned. "I don't have to; you just said it for me."

"Well, will you help?"

He grimaced slightly, as he leaned back and rubbed the back of his neck. "What can I do?"

"White Wolf thinks he knows where Bonney and his gang are holed up. But it is off the reservation, and the agency police do not dare leave the reservation to attack any White Eyes, even if those White Eyes are Billy and his band."

"I can understand that."

"But with you, it might be different."

"I could sort of deputize them, you mean."

"Yes."

"And where would this gang be?"

"I'll let White Wolf tell you. He speaks English very

well for an Apache." She smiled proudly. "He has attended many of my classes with his son."

Longarm finished his coffee and stood up.

Nalin leaned back in her chair and smiled up at him. "You'll do it then?"

"It's better than riding back to Paso Robles with nothing but a dimple in my side to show for all this aggravation."

Nalin got to her feet. "I'll send one of the children for the agency police."

"You do that," Longarm said, snugging down his Stetson and stepping off the porch. "I'll go see if I can scare up White Wolf."

Longarm started across the yard, heading for the Indian settlement beyond the trees. It felt kind of spooky to be going after the likes of Billy the Kid. The Kid's reputation seemed to fill this parched, lawless land, to hang almost palpably in the air. Already, Billy the Kid's reputation had reached the East. His lurid exploits, magnified tenfold, were being trumpeted on the covers and within the pages of Beadle's dime novels. The Kid would soon rival Deadwood Dick in popularity.

Trouble was, Billy the Kid was real. Deadwood Dick would be a hell of a lot easier to bring down than the Kid.

Chapter 8

Longarm reined in his buckskin. White Wolf pulled to a halt on his right. Toklani and the three agency policemen closed in on Longarm's left. Below them, tucked in under a cover of cottonwoods, was the stone farmhouse White Wolf had described to him. Longarm had come to attention at once when White Wolf had mentioned the place; indeed, from that moment on, Longarm was certain the Apache was on to something.

It was late afternoon. The sun was still blistering the landscape. The rock faces on all sides were shimmering in the heat. The sun's rays rested like a hot brand on Longarm's shoulders. The only living things, besides themselves, that they could see moving through this hellish landscape were the vultures drifting in the brassy sky overhead.

Pulling his hatbrim down further to shade his eyes, Longarm studied the farmhouse carefully. It was a one-story structure, low and solid. The roof was of tiles, many of which were broken. In places the roof was bare, and weeds had sprouted in spots along the edges. Behind the building was a corral and a privy.

The barn was in need of repair, but was still upright and had most of its roof intact. The well was in the front yard. Four saddled horses were tied up in the cottonwoods, and twelve fine-blooded, unsaddled horses were crowded together in that section of the corral closest to the shade of the cottonwoods. A saddled horse was tied to a broken hitch rail in front of the farmhouse. Squinting through the glare, Longarm thought he could see Chisum's "rail" brand on the animal—a single long line extending from the horse's shoulder all the way to its hip.

Longarm straightened in his saddle. He did not have a warrant; on what pretext could he approach whoever was inside that farmhouse? And how could he be sure the Kid was in there?

Longarm heard an angry mutter from Toklani. The Apache was leaning well over his mount's neck, shading his eyes with his forearm. Longarm heard White Wolf query him. Toklani replied quickly, angrily.

White Wolf turned to Longarm. "Toklani see the horse of Crooked Fox in the corral!"

Longarm smiled. He had his excuse.

The farmhouse door opened. Longarm was not surprised to see Chisum's trusted clerk, Duke Foster, turn in the doorway for a few parting words with someone standing in the darkness of the doorway, then leave the farmhouse and mount up.

He watched as Foster rode off. Too bad. But Longarm knew where to find him again. Garrett's suspicions had been justified, it seemed. This was where Foster had been heading that day when Longarm had met up with Petey and Frank. Glancing back at the farmhouse door, Longarm saw that it was closed again. The men inside were staying where they were—out of the heat.

The farmhouse was a fortress. A frontal attack would accomplish little. Surrounding the place and announcing their presence would only cause those inside to hole up until dark and then make a break for it. The Kid had already proven himself a master of that tactic when he had escaped from Alexander McSween's blazing house under cover of darkness, killing one of L. G. Murphy's men and wounding two others in the process. As Longarm considered his options, he was aware of the five Apaches sitting their horses impatiently on both sides of him.

He turned to White Wolf. "Tell the others we'll wait until dark. If those inside don't leave the farmhouse then, we'll break in and surprise them. And you better choose someone to keep a lookout. The rest of us will get out of this sun and find water."

As White Wolf relayed Longarm's instructions, Longarm pulled his horse around and angled back down off the ridge. The long ride in the sun had left him lightheaded. The alkali dust had dried out his nostrils and caked the inside of his mouth. Not far back, he had caught a glimpse of a patch of green along the bottom of an arroyo. He headed for that.

Lying in the shade of a boulder, his head leaning back against his saddle where it lay on the dry ground, a sopping wet bandanna wrapped about his head, Longarm studied his Apache posse. He knew he could trust them. They took his directions without murmur. One of the agency policemen was back there on the ridge watching the farmhouse. He and the two others wore campaign hats, cavalry jackets, buckskin pants, and army boots. They had slung heavy bandoliers over their shoulders and were armed with Winchesters and Colts. Toklani and White Wolf wore buckskin shirts and breechclouts. Instead of army boots, they wore the traditional Apache moccasins, and the only protection for their heads was their heavy black hair. Both carried Winchesters. In addition they carried bows, and quivers stocked with black arrows. Longarm tended to regard Toklani and White Wolf as more deadly than the others. But he was quite willing to let events decide whether he was right or not.

Longarm knew that not too many years before, a feared Apache chief—Charley Pan—had surrendered all of his 2,300 followers to General Crook—but not because he feared the American cavalry. It was his own people, the Apache scouts Crook was using against him, that had driven his people to despair. With the Apache scouts on their trail, they could not sleep because they were afraid of a dawn attack. They could not cook because they knew the fires would betray their whereabouts. They could not remain in the valleys and they could not find refuge in the peaks. It was difficult for Longarm to understand how Apache warriors could turn against and hunt their own kind. Undoubtedly it was partly because the hunt itself mattered so much to them. During this particular hunt, Longarm was glad these Apaches were on his side.

The sun sank below the horizon. A fresh breeze brushed through the arroyo. He glanced up, his gaze following the almost perpendicular rock face. The sky was still bright. He got to his feet. Wringing out the bandanna, he put his hat back on. The Apaches came alive as well. They had long since been told by Longarm how they would flush the Kid and his men. The only response Longarm had noticed as White Wolf relayed his words to the Apaches was the gleam in their eyes. He had taken that for approval of his plan.

In a moment they had saddled up and were picking their way across the narrow stream on their way back to the ridge. When they got there, White Wolf spoke briefly to the Apache on lookout. The Apache replied and went for his horse. White Wolf turned to Longarm. No one had yet left the farmhouse.

Longarm nodded and led the party off the ridge, following a precipitous trail that lead down to a tall cluster of rocks out of sight of the farmhouse on the valley floor. By the time they reached the rocks, it was completely dark. They left their horses and moved cautiously through the darkness toward the farmhouse.

Longarm, just ahead of Toklani and White Wolf, moved into the cottonwoods while the three agency policemen kept on to the farmhouse. Longarm paused beside the saddled horses and watched as one of the Apaches stationed himself at one of the corners of the farmhouse and the other two disappeared to the rear. He lifted his Colt from its holster as he heard Toklani and White Wolf, on the other side of the horses, lever fresh cartridges into their Winchesters. Pale yellow light gleamed through the window. Occasionally the sound of men moving about inside the farmhouse reached across the yard to the cottonwoods.

The horses stomped impatiently and shook their heads. One of them blew heartily through its nostrils, its fancy Spanish bit jingling.

The shot from the rear of the farmhouse echoed sharply in the young night. It was followed immediately by the tinkle of a window breaking. Another shot followed the first, and this time, answering fire came from within the farmhouse. Another shot came from outside at the rear. A second windowpane shattered. Longarm saw an Apache crouching at the corner of the farmhouse. He was just in time. The farmhouse door was flung open and two men spilled out into the night, heading for the cottonwoods.

They were halfway across the yard when the rustler in front was brought down by the Apache fire from behind them. The second man grabbed his companion under the arms and began to drag him across the ground toward the cottonwoods, until an Apache bullet knocked off his hat. Alarmed, the rustler went down on one knee and turned around to return the fire.

Two more men broke from the cabin. Each one went

for an Apache at one of the corners of the building. One Apache caught a slug and spun to the ground. The other Apache ducked back around the corner of the house. This took the heat off the kneeling rustler. He jumped up and dragged his wounded companion into the cottonwoods. The last two men out of the farmhouse were now racing for the cottonwoods, while the first one—crouched behind the trunk of a tree—was covering their run with a rapid, deadly fire.

Longarm stole swiftly around the restless horses toward the man. The fellow was so intent on providing cover-fire that he did not hear a thing as Longarm crept up behind him and rested the muzzle of his six-gun snugly against the back of his neck.

"Drop the gun," Longarm advised him softly. "Now!"

But this one was a hero. He did not want to drop his gun. Instead, he began to turn about, swinging up his weapon as he did so. Longarm clubbed him swiftly with the barrel of his Colt coming down hard on the crown of his head. The man sagged almost soundlessly to the ground.

By this time his two companions were nearing the cottonwoods, stopping every now and then to send a burst of gunfire back at the Apaches. The return fire from the farmhouse was just as heavy. Bullets were whining into the cottonwoods like insane insects, snapping off boughs, plowing into trunks.

Crouching for cover behind the unconscious rustler, Longarm felt a round whisper dangerously close to his right cheekbone. Abruptly, one of the horses whinnied in pain and surprise. It reared, its forelegs striking out savagely at the air in front of it, then fell back upon the other horses, who began to thrash wildly about, whinnying in terror. A flying hoof caught Longarm in the small of the back and sent him sprawling forward onto the ground. He crawled away from the plunging horses and looked back.

In the confusing darkness, he could barely make out Toklani and White Wolf, caught in the midst of the terrified animals, reaching up frantically for the bridles in an effort to haul down the leaping, plunging horses. Scrambling to his feet, Longarm saw the two men charging toward him through the trees. It was clear that they did not see him and were intent only on making it to their horses. The fellow in front was a tall, skinny jasper; his companion, smaller and slighter in build, was still firing back at the Apaches. He held his weapon in his left hand. Billy the Kid.

Longarm yelled out, "Hold it! Both of you!"

The tall one did not do as he was told. Furious, he kept coming at Longarm, his sixgun blasting. Muzzleflashes lanced twice through the darkness. Then Longarm heard the snap of a hammer falling on an empty chamber. He was already swinging up his own Colt. It bucked in his hand. The fellow caught the slug in his midsection, but his momentum kept him coming. He plowed into Longarm, driving him backward onto the ground.

The pall of smoke added to the night's confusion. The flopping body on top of him and the sound of the still-maddened horses rearing just behind him in an ecstasy of terror—all this reminded Longarm that he was in the midst of a nightmare over which he had no control. As he struggled out from under the wounded man, he was knocked brutally to one side as the Kid swept past him. His head struck the trunk of a tree. Dazed, his gun falling to the grass mere inches from his nerveless fingers, he watched the Kid yank one of the horses around and leap aboard. The snapping of its reins came to Longarm clearly as the Kid dug his spurs into the horse's flanks, bent low over the horse's neck, and rode out through the cotton-woods.

Toklani was the first to reach Longarm. There was a gash on the Apache's cheekbone where a hoof had caught him. But the Apache seemed unaware of it as he helped Longarm to his feet. The agency policemen raced into the cottonwoods. Two of them had minor wounds. White Wolf, limping noticeably but impassively, joined Toklani. The wounded rustlers were sprawled about them in the darkness. Only one was still conscious. The horse that had been struck by a stray bullet was on the ground, still thrashing feebly; the remaining two animals, blowing fretfully, had calmed down somewhat, but their flanks were rippling continuously, their tails whisking.

Longarm bent for his Colt and hat. "Take care of these fellows," he told White Wolf, "and wait here for me. I'll bring the Kid back."

He turned then, and moved swiftly across the yard to the rocks where his buckskin was waiting.

I'll bring the Kid back.

As Longarm pounded along the trail through the morning light, he remembered that vow with some misgiving. He had better come back with Billy. If he did not, his Apache allies were going to be laughing about him around council fires for generations to come.

A little after midday, Longarm caught a glimpse of the Kid cresting a ridge less than a mile ahead. From then on, he had little difficulty staying with him. A stream gleamed off the trail along about midafternoon. It was flanked by cottonwoods and scrub juniper. He decided he had better take the time to water his horse and let it rest up some. It was either that or lose his mount. The Kid was not too far ahead of him, and was driving his mount hard. If he wasn't thinking of his horse at this moment, maybe he should be.

Longarm dismounted just before he reached the stream, and moistened the buckskin's nose with a wet handkerchief. Then he filled his hat with water and gave the animal a drink, being careful not to let him bolt it. At last, satisfied that the horse had as much sense as he had, he loosened the cinch and lifted the saddle blanket. With a gentle, probing hand he felt for saddlesores and any wrinkles in the blanket. Finding neither, he saw finally to his own needs.

Hunkering down beside the stream, he cupped his hands and drank. The cold water dribbled off his chin and down inside the front of his shirt. The probing tendrils of icy water sent delighted shivers up from his belly. He went down on his knees and ducked his bared head under the water, thrashing it back and forth like a large spaniel. Emerging thoroughly refreshed, he stood up and flung his hair back. Watching him, the buckskin bobbed its head a couple of times, as if to compliment Longarm on his good sense.

Longarm snugged down his wet hat. Then he tightened the cinch carefully, eased himself up into the saddle, and returned to the trail. He had taken his time. It was as if he were deliberately delaying the inevitable. Perhaps, he mused, he just wasn't all that anxious to bring in Billy the Kid. It might even be a shame to end all the wonderful speculation growing up around this gunslick's career.

As soon as the trail got reasonably fresh again, Longarm began to push the buckskin. The animal responded, and by late that afternoon the Kid was in constant sight, less than a quarter of a mile ahead. But now they were entering a stretch of badlands that would soon offer the Kid ideal cover. Longarm spurred his mount in hopes of bringing the Kid within range of his Winchester. The buckskin responded to the limit of his magnificant heart. But it was no use. The Kid booted his horse on into a narrow, twisting arroyo—and vanished.

Longarm followed. The Kid's sign led down a rocky defile that wound from the arroyo down into a steep-walled canyon. A half-mile later, the canyon's walls fell away. The trail broadened out onto a brushy flat. Longarm smelled sage. The Kid's trail led across the flat and was so recent that no sand had yet blown into the hoofprints. The flat led to a steep, rain-scoured gully. Longarm settled into a rocking, downhill lope. Soon he was moving into wilder, more rugged country. The red earth was slashed by winding, sheer-walled draws. Flat-topped buttes towered on all sides. The Kid's tracks—fresher now with each passing moment— led through gravelly arroyos and on into deep, rain-washed gullies. Longarm's eyes were sore and grainy. The hours of steady riding had left him muscle-racked, his inner thighs aflame with saddle gall. His only consolation was that the Kid could not be feeling much better.

The trail turned into another draw and wound down between massive shoals of red rock. The canyon's walls closed in on him. The trail snaked in endless loops, as the canyon cut deeper and deeper into the massive rocks shouldering high on both sides. Guiding his mount carefully around a bend, Longarm reined in suddenly.

The Kid's horse was in the trail, abandoned.

The animal was lying on its side. At sight of Longarm, it made a valiant effort to lift its head. But it was no use. It fell back, its great eyes bulging, its lathered mouth gaping. Broad, slashing streaks of lather had dried on its flanks and the Kid had not even taken the time to loosen the cinch, let alone remove the saddle in case the animal should recover. Swiftly, Longarm dismounted and began to remove the saddle.

The shot came as he lifted the saddle free. The slug whined so close that Longarm almost dropped the saddle on the horse. He spun, flung the saddle to the ground, and flattened himself against the face of a boulder, swearing. He should have been expecting something like that. He drew his Colt and glanced up the rock face.

He smiled thinly and shook his head. He wasn't going up there, not after the Kid. He had something the Kid needed down here—a healthy mount. Longarm ducked close in under the cliff, took off his hat, and poked it slowly out away from the wall. The shot came almost instantly, the round missing the hat by inches and ricocheting off the wall beside him. Longarm let out a sharp, painful cry, then flung himself heavily down along the base of the cliff. He was careful to let his hat and Colt fall to the ground in plain view. Groaning softly now, he drew both hands in under his stomach, then stiffened, clutching his derringer in his right hand.

He waited. To keep himself alert, he began to count to himself. He kept counting as the silence in the narrow canyon deepened. He heard tiny pebbles bouncing down the rock face from directly above. He controlled his breathing so that there was no telltale rising and falling of his chest. Sweat dripped soundlessly off his forehead onto the bedrock under his left cheek. Tendrils of salt perspiration collected in his brows and trickled down into the corners of his eyes. They stung persistently. Longarm tried to blink his eyes clear, but the sweat just burrowed deeper. The discomfort became maddening, but he kept himself as still as death.

Larger rocks were tumbling down from above. Some struck his outstretched leg; others bounced on the rocky ground beside him. Longarm heard the sound of two boots landing heavily on the hard ground. Then came the chink of spurs as Billy the Kid moved cautiously closer and peered down at his latest victim. He could hear the Kid's steady breathing and smell his sweaty shirt, the stink of his old riding boots.

The cold muzzle of a gun barrel was pressed suddenly against Longarm's right temple.

He tensed himself and prepared to roll over swiftly. Abruptly, the Kid pulled the muzzle away. Longarm felt the Kid poke a foot under his side and lift, flinging Longarm over onto his back. As he flopped over, he swung up his twin-barreled derringer. It was already cocked. The Kid had lowered his gun to his side when he rolled Longarm over. Looking down into the twin bores of Longarm's derringer discouraged the Kid immediately. He lost heart.

He took a step back and let his Colt drop to the trail. "Shit," he said bitterly.

Longarm got to his feet and, pocketing the derringer, picked up his own Colt, kicked the Kid's weapon away, then advanced on the Kid, peering at him intently. He was sure of it now—absolutely positive, in fact.

"You ain't Billy the Kid," Longarm said, pulling up in front of the man. "Who the hell are you?"

"Yes I am," the fellow insisted, his voice high, nervous. "I'm Billy the Kid."

"That so?"

"Sure." The fellow tried to straighten himself, thrusting his narrow shoulders back. "I'm Billy the Kid, all right. You can take me back if you want, but there ain't no jail goin' to hold the Kid."

Longarm almost laughed. If this was the Terror of the Southwest, the romantic hero of the very latest dime novels on sale in Denver, then Longarm was Alexander the Great, weeping for worlds to conquer.

Longarm holstered his Colt and took a step back. "You can tell me," he said, grinning. "I won't snitch on you. You got the floppy hat and all, and you're a left-handed gun. But if you're Billy, I'll eat them boots of yours, smelly as they are."

"I'm Billy the Kid," the fellow insisted, a little desperately this time.

"Who you working for? Who put you up to this?"

"What do you mean? Nobody put me up to nothing. I'm Billy the Kid and I got me a band of outlaws. We been tearin' up this territory."

"Sure. And you're the daddy of all the badmen that ever come from Buzzard Hole. You was nursed on whiskey, you cut your teeth on a circular saw, and rattlesnakes was your playmates. You're so hard you kick fire outa flint with your bare toes." Longarm put his head back and laughed.

Furious, the fellow whirled, sprinted to Longarm's buckskin, and hauled the Winchester from its sling. As he levered a cartridge into the chamber, Longarm drew his Colt. Both men fired, Longarm's shot coming a split-second sooner. The bullet caught the fellow who called himself Billy the Kid belt-high, jackknifing him abruptly, sending him reeling backwards. The Winchester's shot went high. Longarm heard it ricocheting harmlessly off the rock walls behind him as he crouched, ready to fire a second time.

Twisting slowly on his side, the fellow tried gamely to lever a fresh cartridge into the Winchester's chamber. Longarm walked over, took the rifle out of his hands, then knelt beside the wounded man. The fellow glared up at Longarm, his face set in a bone-white, painful grimace.

"Damn you," he managed. "Damn you to hell."

Longarm holstered his Colt. "I am sorry," he said. "I shouldn't have deviled you like that." He pulled the man's hands away from his wound and winced.

A mass of glistening, blood-flecked entrails was bulging out of the hole in his gut. Each labored breath brought more. A steady rivulet of greenish bile flowed steadily from the gaping rent. Longarm let the man's hands return to the wound. The poor fellow attempted to tuck his bloody entrails back inside his belly. He didn't do a very good job.

"Oh, Jesus!" the man cried weakly. "I'm coming apart. You done me in, mister. Who the hell are you?"

"Custis Long, a deputy U.S. marshal. You going to tell me who *you* are now?"

The man coughed. He seemed to be strangling on something, the paroxysm causing him to pull his hands away from his wound. "McBride," he gasped. "Dudley McBride."

"You'll be pleased to know," said Longarm, "that the governor was worried about you. When you disappeared, he sent me to find you."

"The old fool!"

"He must have been, to make *you* his agent."

The fellow started to say something. Longarm stood up and watched the painful struggle. Beads of sweat stood out on McBride's gray face. Suddenly his eyes bugged, his head dropped to the canyon floor, and his hands fell away from his wound. Still at last, his entrails rested on the rocky ground.

Longarm looked away. That he did not get sick was a tribute to his stomach, not to the way he felt.

Chapter 9

Longarm buried Dudley McBride in a shallow grave,
onto which he piled a clumsy mound of small boulders.
It was not too pretty a job, but it was done well enough
to discourage coyotes and vultures. He fastened a cross
out of two sun-bleached juniper branches, tying the
crosspieces together with what was left of the reins
from McBride's dead horse. Spurring the mount out of
the cottonwoods, McBride had broken off the reins,
forcing him to lean far out over the animal's neck in
order to guide him. This was the reason he had not
been able to outdistance Longarm during the night.

The next day, Longarm arrived back at the stone
farmhouse and presented McBride's boots, weapon,
and hat to the Apaches as proof that the Man Who
Wanted To Be Billy The Kid would never again lead
his band against their horse herds. The Apaches were
satisfied. Longarm saw no trace of the captured
rustlers, but the Apaches volunteered no explanation
for their absence and Longarm decided it would be
simpler to ask no questions.

He took leave of the Apaches then, and set out for

John Chisum's Jingle Bob spread, arriving the next day a little before noon. This time his escort into the compound was more polite, if not less suspicious. Chisum was standing on the porch of the Long House, waiting to greet Longarm.

"Good to see you again, Longarm," the tall rancher said. "Light a spell. We've got plenty of coffee and more than enough room."

"I'd appreciate that, John," Longarm replied.

He dismounted and handed the buckskin's reins to a cowpoke who had hustled over from one of the horse barns, then mounted the porch and followed his host inside. Sallie, looking as cool as a daisy and just as pretty in a soft blue, ankle-length dress, was waiting in the big living room to greet Longarm. After the pleasantries, her uncle asked her please to have the coffee brought in.

As Sallie left the room, Chisum turned to Longarm. "Sit down, Longarm. You look done in."

As Chisum sat on the sofa, Longarm slacked gratefully into an upholstered chair. "I been in the saddle or sleeping in a soogan for longer than I care to recall," he admitted, taking a cigar from the box that Chisum proffered.

"Want to tell me about it?"

"That's why I'm here."

At that moment, Rosita hurried in with the coffee and whiskey. As she set the large tray deftly on a low table in front of Longarm, he lifted his eyes to hers and caught the sly delight at his presence that gleamed in them.

"You've been busy, then," Chisum said.

"Busy enough," Longarm agreed, mixing the whiskey and coffee, then sipping it. "Caught that Billy the Kid who's been rustling your stock."

"The devil you did!" The man was astounded. And delighted. He almost jumped to his feet.

148

"Trouble is, it wasn't the right one."

Chisum frowned impatiently. "You want to try that on me again, Longarm?"

"The fellow I caught was rustling your stock all right—along with some Apache stock as well—and he was pleased to style himself as the original Billy the Kid. He had his own small band operating from a stone farmhouse south of here and close to the Apache agency. He's got a blanket of New Mexican earth over his carcass now, and he's sleeping sound as a stone. But he wasn't Billy the Kid, he was the jasper Governor Wallace sent me out here to find, that agent of his, Dudley McBride."

"But you nailed him."

"I nailed him."

"Well, that's all that matters. I guess Garrett was right. The Kid's in Texas with Bowdre."

"Maybe," Longarm said, as an errant thought picked away at the corner of his mind.

"You don't think so?"

"I don't know." Longarm shook his head. "Thing is, this fellow did everything he could to make himself look like the Kid, even down to the hat he wore. And he was a left-handed gun, like the Kid."

"What are you driving at?"

"Somebody put him up to it, I'm figuring. Pretty slick too. This jasper was really getting to believe he *was* the Kid."

"You got any ideas who might have been behind this?"

"Yup."

"Who?"

"You ain't going to like this, John."

"Damn it, Longarm! Stop this cat and mouse! Who you got in mind? Tell me!"

Longarm took the cigar out of his mouth. "How long has Duke Foster been with you?"

"Duke? Why, he was with me in Texas. He goes back a long ways, Longarm. He's pretty close to kin. You aren't going to tell me you suspect *him,* are you?"

"I'm afraid I am."

Chisum was astounded—and angry. He got slowly to his feet and glared somberly down at Longarm. "You are a guest in my house, so I will not ask that you leave. But I want you to understand here and now that what you have just said makes it your word against Duke's. And I stand by my friends."

"Bring him in here and let him deny it himself."

"I'll do just that!"

Chisum stalked into the kitchen. Longarm heard him tell Sallie to go for Duke Foster, that he was in the ranch office. Then Chisum returned to the living room and, still standing, waited for Duke Foster to arrive.

Longarm puffed on his cigar and sipped his coffee. Presently he heard footsteps on the front porch, and a moment later, Duke Foster entered the living room. Longarm watched him carefully. The man appeared cool enough. When he saw Longarm, he nodded curtly. It was his usual manner; there was nothing vindictive in it.

"Longarm has something to tell you," Chisum said, his lean face flushing in concern and embarrassment.

Foster frowned and looked with somewhat more focused attention at Longarm. He had obviously caught the nervous concern in Chisum's voice. "What is it now, Longarm?"

"I apprehended that jasper who's been going around calling himself Billy the Kid," Longarm said amiably. He smiled. "Dudley McBride. He did some talking before he died."

Foster whirled on Chisum, his face slack with shock. "John! You ain't gonna believe what this fool lawman says, are you? Dudley was lying! I ain't had nothing to do with him!"

150

Chisum was so upset at Duke Foster's response that he sat down limply on the sofa, pain etched clearly in every line of his face. He looked without a word at Longarm. Longarm looked away from the stunned rancher and up at Foster.

"Glad to hear that, Foster," Longarm said softly and clearly. "What I want to know is, how the hell did you know what Dudley would tell me before he died?"

Foster backed up in sudden dismay, aware that his own words had just damned him. He looked frantically around at Chisum. He did not wear a sidearm, but at that moment he looked desperate enough to use one.

"John!" he cried. "You got to believe *me*, not that no-account drifter, McBride!"

Longarm looked over at Chisum. "Has Duke, here, been gone from the ranch for long stretches every now and then?"

Chisum, his color returning, nodded.

"And not long after, your boys report another raid on your stock, or another bunch of cows missing, right?"

"Yes," Chisum said dully, looking miserably over at Foster. "That's right." Chisum got back up onto his feet and took a step toward Foster. "You sonofabitch!" he said evenly. "It's been *you* all along!"

Foster took a step back, glanced over at Longarm, then turned and bolted from the room. His heavy boots sounded in the hall, then he was through the door. The two men could hear his running feet crossing the yard, heading toward one of the stables.

"Let him go," said Chisum wearily, sinking back onto the sofa. "Let the poor sonofabitch go."

Longarm reached for his coffee, lifted it to his mouth, and finished it. Then he stood up, stuck his cigar back into his mouth, and went to the window. "Sure. I'll let him go, John. But I want to see where he goes to."

"You mean he's not in this alone?"

"Duke Foster doesn't appear to me to be the kind of man who'd have the grit or the brains to cook up a scheme like this all by his own self, if you'll pardon me for judging him that harshly, John. Someone put him up to it just as sure as roadapples."

It didn't take long. Foster appeared in a stable doorway, pulling a horse behind him. The man mounted up swiftly, glanced toward the Long House, then spurred the horse furiously as he galloped out of the compound. The sound of his horse's hooves echoed all the way into the long, cool living room.

Chisum looked up. "Is that him?"

"He's on his way."

Chisum shook his head sadly. "Been with me since Texas. He was almost kin, Longarm. Kin!"

"I've seen some pretty nasty feuds among kinfolks, John."

"Sure, but . . ." The man was at a loss. He looked over at Longarm. "He was the one who kept telling me he was sure it was Billy the Kid stealing our cattle."

"How did he take to your idea of pushing Pat Garrett for sheriff?"

Chisum grew suddenly alert. "Now that you mention it, he was against it. All the way. Said our boys could handle the rustling." Chisum looked with sudden alarm at Longarm. "Jim! Jim Highsaw! You don't think *Jim* could be—"

The man couldn't finish it. He left the unspoken question hanging in the silent room. Longarm clamped his jaw down on his cigar and turned from the window. "You'll have to figure that one out for yourself, John. I'm going to need my horse again. Duke Foster seemed frightened enough to go straight to wherever he's bound for, but he just might get a little crafty. I'll want to hang onto his tail pretty close."

"Will you need a fresh mount?"

"Thank you, John, I'd appreciate that. And canteens of water, if you have them."

"I have them. Army canteens, big canvas-covered ones." He got to his feet. "When you find out who's in this with him, what are you going to do to him, Longarm?"

"Hold him for trial, if you'll press charges."

"I won't do that, Longarm. You just tell him to get out of New Mexico, that if he comes back, I'll personally hang him from that cottonwood out front."

Longarm nodded and started from the room, unwilling to leave its coolness for the hot sun and saddle, the bone-rattling grind of another long chase—until he thought of Marshal Billy Vail, growing flabbier and slower with each passing day as he sat behind that desk in Denver. With an inward sigh of resignation, Longarm snugged down his Stetson and waved to Chisum.

"I'll be in one of the barns, picking out a mount."

"I'll go with you, Longarm," Chisum said. "I'll help you pick out what you need. And we'll get those canteens for you as well."

The two left the room together and, a moment later, stepped out into the blazing New Mexico sun and started across the hard-packed yard. Longarm glanced at Chisum as he strode beside him. The fellow was holding up well enough, but he looked like he had been kicked in his nether regions not too long before and was still a mite shaky. Longarm felt sorry for the man. As Garrett had said, Chisum was a poor judge of men. And Longarm did not envy the big rancher his current dilemma—checking out his range foreman to see if maybe he had been in league with Foster. Highsaw and Foster had seemed pretty chummy that evening when they joined Garrett and Longarm at dinner with Chisum and his niece, but that didn't necessarily mean the two were feeding at the same trough.

Foster had been close to Chisum, too—close enough

to fool the man completely. He could just as easily have pulled the wool over Highsaw's eyes.

It became apparent by late afternoon where Duke Foster was heading. Longarm pulled back some and eased up on the powerful chestnut Chisum had selected for him. Paso Robles was just over the next couple of hills. Already the bright green of the grassy slopes that fanned out from both shores of the river were in sight. Soon he was riding through the lush pastureland, marveling that in this hot land such growth could sustain itself.

He was within sight of the church's bell tower in Paso Robles when he caught sight of Hank hazing a small herd of horses toward Maria Antonia Lugo's hacienda. Longarm hailed the young hostler, who reined in his mount to wait for him.

Squinting through the sunlight at him, Hank smiled. "Welcome back to Paso Robles, Mr. Long. What happened to that nice buckskin you was ridin'?"

"He got plumb wore out, Hank."

"That chestnut's a fine-lookin' animal. Chisum stock, ain't it?"

"You can read the brand as well as I can."

"Yup. Fine stock. Looks like you got powerful friends, Mr. Long."

Hank turned back to his job then, lifting his coil of rope and turning his mount swiftly to cut off a frisky yearling that had hopes of bolting back to the sweetgrass they were leaving. Once Hank had the herd moving back toward the river, Longarm settled into an easy lope beside him and examined the fellow closely. Once before, he'd had a notion about this friendly young man, only to dismiss it when he began to pick up sign that Billy the Kid was far from Paso Robles, raising hell and rustling cattle. At once he had relaxed around Hank, sure his uncertainty about the young man was only the fool ticking of his overly suspicious nature. But now, having discovered that the Kid he had been hearing about was an imposter, Longarm found himself regarding Hank a mite more closely.

They were almost to the river. Hank and Longarm had pulled back a bit. The horses, smelling the water, needed no urging to go on. Hank had been holding the coil of rope in his left hand. Now, as he hung back to let the horses have their run at the river, Hank glanced almost slyly at Longarm—as if he were well aware of Longarm's troubled speculation concerning him.

Abruptly, Longarm came to a decision. He pulled up, steadied the chestnut, then called softly to Hank. Hank reined in his mount and turned in his saddle to watch Longarm warily, the ghost of a smile on his narrow face.

"What's the trouble, Mr. Long?" he inquired.

Without warning, Longarm drew his Colt on Hank. His draw—as usual—was lightning-fast. The barrel was clear of its waxed holster and the muzzle steadying on Hank's chest before Hank had lifted his own heavy Colt clear of its holster. Hank smiled, his sixgun frozen in mid-draw. Hank was fast, very fast, Longarm noted —but not fast enough. And he drew with his right hand easily, naturally. Hank was not a lefty trying to pose as someone who was right-handed.

Longarm smiled back at Hank and returned his Colt to his holster. "Thought I saw something, Hank. Guess it was just my imagination."

Still smiling, Hank let his weapon drop back into its holster. "You sure it was just your imagination now?"

"Yep. I'm sure. Let's get after them horses. I wouldn't want you to lose your job. Here comes Maria now."

The two men rode after the horses. As they got closer to the cottonwoods lining the bank of the river, Maria Antonia Lugo, riding a tall, spirited black, splashed across the shallow ford, then loped through the trees toward them. Both riders pulled up. Maria was dressed to match her mount. She wore a black sombrero, a black velvet vest trimmed in silver, and black trousers tucked into the tops of her black, finely tooled riding boots. The silk blouse under her vest was a sparkling white in contrast. Though she was dressed entirely in men's clothing, Longarm thought that few women he had ever seen looked more feminine as she pulled her mount to a halt between them.

"I saw that, Mr. Long," she snapped. "You pulled your weapon on Hank." She was breathing heavily, her copper face flushed darkly, her deep brown eyes flashing. "Does that mean you're arresting my wrangler?"

"As I explained to Hank," Longarm replied, "I thought I saw something."

"A snake in the grass, maybe," Hank suggested lightly.

"It's all right then?" Maria said, turning to face Hank.

Hank nodded. "I guess so. But you'll have to ask Mr. Long. Maybe that wasn't no snake he saw in the grass."

"All right, Hank. Take care of those horses."

Hank touched his hatbrim to her and spurred his mount toward the crowd of horses that were now nudging each other and milling at the water's edge. Longarm could see *vaqueros* on the far side of the river, opening the corral gates to receive the horses, while others rode down to the river to help Hank. Longarm looked back at Maria.

The woman's patrician beauty still impressed him. Perhaps it was her strong, thick eyebrows, her broad brow, her high cheekbones. Breeding, he thought to himself. This woman had it, and it gave her backbone.

Enough sand, in fact, to go against a federal lawman to protect a wrangler and stablehand. *But from what?*

Longarm wondered. What was Maria protecting Hank from?

"I am sorry, Mr. Long," Maria said, "for my rudeness."

"Call me Longarm. And you're forgiven."

She nodded curtly and took up her reins. She was in the act of pulling the black around when Longarm spoke out: "I would like to talk to you, Maria. Just you and Father Chaves, if you don't mind."

She quieted her horse with a gentle pat on its neck and glanced back at him, a slight frown on her face. "Now?"

"At your hacienda, if you reckon you could spare me the time."

The challenge to her hospitality brought the color back to her cheeks. "You are welcome, of course," she snapped. "Come along!"

She pulled her horse around then, swiftly yet without cruelty, and reached the river well before Longarm. He made no effort to catch up to her. It was best, he thought, to give her a chance to alert the servants.

While they waited in the living room for Father Chaves, Longarm complimented her on her command of English. She told him she had been taught the language in a St. Louis convent. Then he asked about her husband. She looked at him a long while before answering, as if she were wondering if she dared.

"He is dead," she said suddenly, looking away from Longarm. She was sitting on the edge of her couch, her hands folded in her lap. Her long white fingers plucked at the crease in her dark trousers.

"I'm sorry," Longarm said softly.

"He was killed by one of Sheriff Brady's hired assassins, with Brady looking on. The man found it amusing, I believe, to watch a greaser twist on the end of a rope."

"He was hanged?"

"He was herding some cattle, which he had purchased in Texas, past Lincoln. Brady and his men rode out for a little diversion. When they asked for the bill of sale and my husband passed it to Brady, he tore it up, proclaimed my husband a rustler, and handed a rope to one of his men. It was difficult for the men to hang my husband. They were very drunk, you see."

"How did you hear about this?"

"I saw it with my own eyes, Mr. Long. I was there. My husband had seen the sheriff and his men approaching, and had given orders to our *vaqueros* to ride off with me, to protect me at all costs. They protected me well. From a safe distance we watched. There were tears in the eyes of every man with me."

"But not in yours."

"My heart turned to stone, Mr. Long. It remains that way now. And it is good. I can never be hurt like that again. Of course, Brady is dead now."

Longarm nodded. "Killed by Billy the Kid."

A cold smile lit her face.

"I am sorry—very sorry—about the tragic death of your husband, Maria. But you mustn't think all lawmen are as rotten as Sheriff Brady."

"I am not a fool, Mr. Long. I know that."

Longarm smiled. "Then call me Longarm."

"I will call you what I please. And you will accept it as the gentleman you profess to be would accept it, without protest."

They were silent, then, until Father Chaves entered the room. Longarm stood and shook the padre's hand. The priest seemed pleased to see him again. "You are well, praise be to God," he said, smiling broadly. He sat down beside Maria.

"It *is* a wonder," Longarm agreed. "This here Lincoln County resembles a nest of unhappy rattlers, I'm beginning to think." Longarm sat back down.

"Why did you wish to see us, Mr. Long?" Maria

asked. She did not bother to disguise her impatience. It was obvious she felt she had more important things to do than entertain Longarm and the local priest.

"I want you to tell me what you know about Charles Kilrain."

The priest looked in astonishment at Maria, then back at Longarm. "But what is there to tell? He is a man of God!"

"Why do you say that? He hasn't won the election for mayor yet, has he?"

"Do not joke, *señor!*"

"Kilrain has been very generous to the church," Maria explained impatiently. "Unlike most Anglos, he seems to harbor no contempt for people of Spanish parentage—those of us whose ancestors watered this ground with their blood for three hundred years before the Americans came. He does not exclude Mexicans from his saloons. He is a gentleman. He wants to be mayor of Paso Robles. I see no harm in that."

Longarm smiled ironically. "And of course he'll see to it that his friends or lackeys will sit on every important council. He'll appoint town councilors, local police. You are putting yourselves and this entire town into the hands of a man you know very little about."

"Ah!" said Father Chaves. "What more do we need to know but that he is generous to the church and honest and fair to all men, regardless of the color of their skin? The man is open and warm hearted without guile."

"Unlike most Anglos," Longarm prompted.

The priest shrugged, as if to say, *You said it, I didn't.*

"It is true, Mr. Long," Maria said. "We know very little about him and I would like to know more. Admittedly, it would have been better if Gonzales Torrios were still here. He was also running for mayor and he had a strong following among the small ranchers and most of the parishioners."

"What happened to him?"

"He has disappeared."

"Interesting."

"It is not as you might think. He went south to Texas to purchase a herd. If he could not get what he wanted in Texas, he had considered going still farther south to Mexico. If he did, then I fear for his safety. The situation in Mexico now is very unsettled and dangerous. I am sure you are aware of this."

"I am. But I've sure found sunny New Mexico a mite troublesome as well. Have there been any other disappearances of people who might have decided to take a stand against Kilrain's takeover of Paso Robles?"

Father Chaves looked troubled. "You say, 'takeover.' I do not think that is fair. This town's businesses were being run by men who would never deal fairly with our poor, with any native New Mexicans."

"You mean no credit."

"Worse than that. Credit, but on terms that were impossible, confiscatory. Only the Anglos could get decent credit. Only the Anglos could walk unmolested into any store in town."

"Under Kilrain, all that's changed?"

"Yes."

"You have no idea, my son," said the padre, "how humiliating that treatment was for those of us whose ancestors settled this land, who fought the Apache alone for hundreds of years. Kilrain's bank now extends credit to all inhabitants of Paso Robles and the surrounding country, without regard to the color of one's skin. If this man is the devil, as you are trying to suggest, I, for one, see no sign of it."

"Isn't the devil also called the tempter, Father?"

The man threw up his hands in exasperation at Longarm's remark and looked to Maria for support. She had been listening carefully. Her intelligent eyes were now somewhat troubled. She looked away from Chaves and over to Longarm.

"There was one other disappearance," she admitted, "of someone who opposed Kilrain. He owned the general store and had a controlling interest in the bank. He did not want to sell to Kilrain, even though other stockholders in the bank were willing."

"What was his name?"

"Barker. He got very drunk one night and marched into the Dry Gulch, announcing that he was ready for Kilrain." She paused unhappily at the recollection of what had followed.

"Go on, Maria."

"It's not clear what happened. The reports that came back to me were that Barker was abusive to Kilrain, but that Kilrain refused to be provoked. It was when Barker turned on one of Kilrain's men that real trouble started." She frowned. "His gun was taken from him and he was beaten severely. Some say he managed to get on his horse and ride out, but others are not sure. The fact remains, however, that Barker was . . . never seen again in Paso Robles."

"Not after that night."

She nodded.

"My son," Father Chaves suggested gently, "it was you, yourself, who saw to the . . . disappearance of another of Kilrain's rivals."

"Fred Bushnell."

"Yes, my son. Is not his blood on your hands?"

"No, Father. It is not."

Maria frowned, her strong eyebrows knitting. "But we all heard. You brought in Bushnell's body yourself."

"But I did not kill him." He smiled. "It's a trifle complicated, I admit."

"My son," Father Chaves said, "however you wish

to explain it, Death has ridden beside you since the moment you entered this town. Is that not so?"

Longarm rose to his feet. "Thank you," he said. "Both of you have been of some help. Could be you're right. Maybe Kilrain isn't the devil. Maybe he's just a smart businessman who likes Paso Robles and wants to be its mayor. Maybe he's just a big frog who's been looking for this kind of a small pond to hop around in. I don't suspicion there's any law against that. Thing is, Maria—and you too, Father—maybe you should look into this fellow's operation a little deeper, ask a few more questions, before you swallow him entirely."

Neither of them offered any response. Longarm put his hat back on and started for the hallway. Without a word, Maria left the room with him and opened the outside door. As she stepped back to let him out, Longarm looked at her.

"I hope I haven't upset you, Maria."

"Of course you have," she snapped. "Wasn't that your intention?"

"I need information. And, too, if this jasper Kilrain is a rotten apple, I think you ought to be warned."

The woman smiled, her imperious features softening just a little. "Perhaps I am not being fair to you, Longarm. You are, after all, only doing your job. But Father Chaves is right, you see. The stench of Death hangs over you."

"And over this territory, Maria—and this town."

He nodded curtly and left Maria standing in the back doorway as he headed for her stables where he had left his horse.

Chapter 10

As Longarm rode past the Dry Gulch, he noticed a large banner draped over the saloon's high false front. VOTE FOR CHARLIE KILRAIN—YOUR NEXT MAYOR. It was clumsily printed and one corner of the banner had come loose; but there it hung, an appeal to the voters. The election was on. Next week Paso Robles would have its new mayor, and there didn't seem to be any reason in the world why Charlie Kilrain would not be it.

There were other, smaller banners, announcing many fandangos, all in celebration of Kilrain's upcoming victory at the polls. Some of the banners over the general store and the bank were in Spanish. A clever move. Well, this Kilrain *was* clever, Longarm saw no sense in denying that.

He was almost to the livery stable when he noticed something else—a dimension that had been added to Paso Robles during his absence. He had no doubt that Kilrain was responsible, and at once Longarm wondered if this might be the one mistake he had been waiting for Kilrain to make. The narrow streets were aswarm with gunslicks. There was little doubt in Longarm's mind who must have brought them in.

He had encountered this species often enough in the alleys and saloons of uncountable border and trail towns of the West. Sometimes Longarm was convinced they had all crawled from a single nest, where they had been stamped out of the same dirty piece of rawhide. For the most part, they cared little about cleanliness or clothes; only their guns, holstered and slung in various odd ways to suit their tastes, gleamed brightly, cleanly in the harsh sun.

Their eyes held no humor, no joy, only cynicism and suspicion. They were men who could laugh loud and long—but smile no more. Death, for them, was a part of living. What belonged to someone else was theirs, if the inclination so moved them. They cared for nothing, since only the moment through which they slouched had any value; they had no past that wanted recalling and no future that meant anything to them. They were human buzzards come to a feast. Only the meal before them was of any importance.

As these men, singly or in groups of two or three, moved restlessly along the sidewalks or burst in and out of both saloons, Longarm saw the barely concealed contempt in their faces as they brushed past the Spanish-speaking natives. They were obviously keeping their natural meanness under tight rein, but that could not last long. On all sides of them they saw potential victims—greasers, raw material for whatever crude amusements might occur to these men when boredom settled too heavily upon them.

Kilrain had shown his hand too soon. Bringing in these gunslicks was a mistake. But his victory was a foregone conclusion. He simply no longer saw any necessity for being careful. And if he could keep these gunslicks on a tight enough rein, it would be all over but the shouting after next week's election.

Longarm dismounted in front of the livery stable and led his horse inside. Hank had just finished stabling the fresh horses he had rounded up that morning, and was busy forking fresh hay into an empty stall.

"I see you've got some new citizens in town," Longarm remarked as the hostler straightened up and rested his pitchfork against the side of a stall.

Hank nodded. "Seems like it, Mr. Long."

"How many, would you say?"

"Close to a dozen now. They been drifting in steady for the past week."

"Been minding their business, have they?"

"They've been awful careful, that's for sure. It's hurtin' them, though. One of these nights they're gonna be cuttin' their wolves loose. It's unnatural to see grown killers like that acting polite and sayin' yes sir and no sir." Hank smiled then, as if he understood perfectly the dilemma these newcomers faced.

"Kilrain brought them in, didn't he?"

"They don't *say* that, but I guess it ain't no deep secret."

Hank whistled sharply and a small, towheaded stableboy came out of the feed room on the run and took Longarm's mount. As soon as he was gone, Longarm said, "I'm looking for a man who might have rode in here earlier, riding another Jingle Bob horse."

"I wasn't here then," said Hank. "But Jimmy took the horse. He's over in that stall." He indicated the mount with a nod of his head. "I don't know the man or where he might be now." Hank smiled. "You'll have to do your own snooping today, Mr. Long."

"Reckon so," Longarm said. "But I aim to get me a bath and a shave first."

"Good idea," Hank said, picking up the pitchfork. "You appear to need both—if you're fixin' to see Kate Ballard."

"Now, how'd you know that?"

"She ain't my woman, but that ain't because she's not pretty enough. She's been real nice to me. You be nice to her."

Longarm had been in the act of stepping through the open stable doorway. He pulled up in surprise and looked back at Hank. He smiled. "Hank, don't you ever tell me how to handle a woman again. Do you hear me clear? Never."

Hank didn't let himself take offense at Longarm's tone. He simply straightened and met the marshal's steady gaze. "You're a lawman," he explained. "You got a job to do. I guess you got yourself set on nailing Kilrain, or whoever it is you're after. Seems to me Kate Ballard might end up getting in the middle. If she got hurt, I wouldn't like that."

Longarm relaxed. "Hellfire, Hank. I wouldn't like that either. I'll do my best—and that's a promise."

Hank frowned and looked away. "Well, I guess that'll have to do."

"Yes, Hank," Longarm agreed, turning and striding into the street. "That will just have to do."

The barbershop was located between the Dry Gulch and Kilrain's general store. The bathhouse was in back. In the alley behind it, two dark-skinned Mexicans were tending the fire that kept a huge kettle of water boiling. Wooden stairs had been placed alongside it, and up those stairs the washroom attendant would climb, dip his bucket down into the steaming water, and hasten back into the washroom to dump the bucket's contents into the various bathtubs. Unlike most public bathhouses in the West, there were thin sheets hanging between the bathtubs, acting as partitions. The air was damp with steam, and the smell of strong soap was a pleasant one for Longarm as he found himself an empty bathtub, tipped the attendant, a Mexican, and began to strip.

The single attendant had to run himself ragged to fill the bathtubs, and once he almost scalded Longarm when he slipped on the soapy floor and momentarily lost control of the flow from his bucket. He smiled apologetically.

"Never mind, *amigo*," Longarm told him. "It's all right. Just keep it coming. I like it good and hot. It boils out the poison!"

"*Si!*" the fellow replied, smiling quickly, then hurrying off in answer to a burly shout for more hot water coming from the far end of the room.

Longarm had already lit a cheroot. Now he leaned back in the steaming water and closed his eyes. He had some thinking to do. Hank was right, of course. Kate was in the middle; she knew a whole hell of a lot more than she had let on. From the very beginning, she had been the decoy and Longarm the target. If it had not been for Hank, it would have worked. And then it had been poor Bushnell's turn to become the bait, with Murales pulling the trigger for Kilrain. Even that old-timer who had identified Murales as a Jingle Bob rider was probably acting on Kilrain's orders. That was why Kilrain had killed Murales. In another minute or so, Murales would have spilled his guts to Longarm.

And Kate. Poor Kate. She had prevented Murales from killing him. Kilrain could not have liked that. Yes, Hank was right: Kate was squarely in the middle, and it was her heart that had put her there.

Longarm began to splash around for the long-handled brush and the bar of soap. He had promised Kate a ride in the country and maybe even a picnic when he got back. It was a promise he meant to keep.

Longarm was stepping out of the bathtub, feeling ten pounds lighter, when he heard the Mexican attendant scream. That a grown man should utter a howl of pain and terror with such an undertone of pure, abject despair made the short hair on the back of the lawman's neck prickle. He stepped into his britches without bothering to dry his long legs, snatched his Colt from its holster, and pushed through the hanging sheets.

He found himself in the doorway at the rear of the bathhouse. Two of Kilrain's bully boys had come loose at the hinges. They were holding the attendant over the big kettle and were in the process of dunking the man headfirst into the boiling water. They had already dunked him once, it appeared. The attendant's face looked like a side of raw beef. He was blinking wildly, obviously blinded, screaming at the top of his lungs. Two more of Kilrain's men were standing naked in the doorway beside Longarm, roaring with laughter.

"Burn the greaser!" one of them yelled. "Go to it, Amos! Grill the sonofabitch!"

Longarm stepped roughly past the two in the doorway, raised his gun, and fired into the air. The detonation was close enough behind the two men that they almost dropped the attendant.

"Put him down!" Longarm told them. "Now!"

The two men turned, astonished. Both were as naked as their friends, their powerful, hairy torsos still begrimed, their faces unshaven, their eyes red-rimmed with drink. Longarm lowered the Colt's muzzle. As the two men found themselves peering into its bore, they stepped back from the kettle, lowering their victim somewhat.

The shot had silenced the attendant. He was just whimpering in pain now, calling to Jesus and to the Blessed Virgin Mary to restore his sight. The two men hesitated.

"Hey," one of them said. "We got to teach this greaser a lesson. He scalded Amos here when he was pouring the water."

"Sure," said the other. "He did it on purpose, the dirty greaser."

168

"I said put him down."

The two men glanced at their companions standing in the doorway. Then they both smiled at Longarm. "Sure," one of them said.

They let the attendant fall. The fellow landed feet first. His legs crumpled under him, and he lay moaning softly on the ground. The two other Mexicans who had been tending the fire under the kettle dragged him quickly away and flattened themselves against the wall of the building. They were frightened at their audacity, however, and did nothing more for the attendant.

Longarm turned back to the doorway. The two other naked men were in the process of ducking back inside the bathhouse.

"Hold it!" Longarm shouted. "Get back here, you two apes—or I'll make your assholes a size bigger with a round or two. All I want is an excuse."

They pulled up quickly, turned, and stepped warily out into the yard. The barber, accompanied by a customer with a white sheet tucked into his collar and some fresh lather sticking to the side of his face, appeared now in the doorway. The barber's face was beet-red in outrage, and the straight razor he held in his hand trembled.

"What in blazes are you doing there, mister?" the barber demanded. "You better put down that gun before I call Charlie Kilrain over here."

Longarm smiled. "You just go and do that, you hear me?"

Longarm swung the Colt toward the barber. With a cry of dismay, the fellow vanished from the doorway. Longarm could hear him racing back through the bathhouse for help. He turned his attention back to the two bully boys who had been standing in the doorway. Without their weapons they were truly naked—and acted it.

"You two," Longarm said. "Each one of you pick

up one of your buddies here and sling him over your shoulder."

They each took a step toward the two other men, then pulled up in confusion and looked back at Longarm as it came to them just what he had in mind.

"You heard me," Longarm said.

"Shit on you, mister," one of them said. "You better put that weapon down and ride out of town fast, while you still got all your hide on."

Longarm smiled, lifted his Colt so that he could sight along its barrel, aimed carefully, and fired. A portion of the fellow's ear flew off and a sudden streamer of wine-red blood went with it. At once the man's pale, freckled shoulders and chest were ribboned with blood. His hand flew up to clap itself over his torn ear, his eyes bulging in dismay.

"Hey, now!" he cried, backing up. "You just shot me!"

Longarm was still smiling. He trained the Colt on the fellow's companion. This worthy needed no further encouragement. He leaped forward and, with a prodigious heave, managed to sling one of the two men standing by the kettle onto his shoulder. This fellow immediately began to struggle to get down and the other started for Longarm. Longarm stepped forward quickly to meet him, swung his Colt in a murderous, level arc, and caught him on the side of the face. With that swing, Longarm had given vent to all the pent-up fury he had been storing since he had first seen that struggling Mexican hanging above the boiling kettle. The naked gunslick went flying sideways. For a moment, both of his feet were off the ground. He hit and flipped over to lay face up, unconscious, with a swelling, misshapen indentation where his cheekbone should have been.

Crouching, Longarm brought his Colt back and trained it on the plug-ugly who was still holding his companion on his shoulder. "Up those steps there. Go on!"

The big fellow straightened himself, strode purposefully toward the kettle, and quickly mounted the first step. He stopped then, because his burden was crying out and struggling to get free.

"Keep going," Longarm snapped, "or I'll blow off a piece of that fat ass. And when you get to the top, hold the sonofabitch there for a minute. I want him to think about it for a while."

The fellow clapped both powerful arms around his struggling burden and finishing mounting the short flight of steps. The man he was carrying began to moan then, as his face hung out over the boiling water.

"Don't do it!" he cried. "Don't do it, Quince! You'll blind me."

"Dump him!" Longarm said.

Quince hesitated. Longarm fired at him. The round came close enough to singe his shoulder. With a convulsive movement, he dropped the man, head foremost, into the boiling cauldron. The fellow's screams were snuffed out as his head was driven down into the kettle by the weight of his body. His dirty bare feet twitched convulsively above the rim of the kettle for a moment or two.

"Pull him out," Longarm said.

Quince had trouble getting a grip on his friend's ankles. Longarm waggled his gun at the other one.

"Help Quince," he told him.

It was a struggle, but after a moment or two they were able to haul their companion out of the kettle. He was still alive, but his face was puffy and raw, the flesh around his eyes swollen. Even had his eyes remained uninjured, he still would not have been able to see. Except for his feet and ankles, his body was raw. Already, skin was puffing and peeling off. He looked like some large, ungainly snake shedding its skin. He moaned continuously.

"Take him the hell out of here," Longarm told Quince. "And you," he said to the other one, "take care of your friend over there. His face looks like it's been busted up some."

"You bastard," the man said, crossing in front of Longarm to get to his still-unconscious companion.

"What's the matter?" Longarm asked. "Why aren't you laughing? You were howling your head off a minute ago. Hell," Longarm said meanly, "I think it's damn funny when the shoe's on the other foot." He leveled his weapon at the man. "And I expect to hear you laughing! You hear me? Start laughing."

The fellow swallowed as he bent to sling the unconscious man over his shoulder, and began a feeble croak.

"Damn you!" Longarm said, smiling coldly. "That ain't a proper laugh nohow!"

The sheepish gunslick tried to do better as he joined his friend, who was having trouble carrying the burned one back into the bathhouse. They were just getting through the doorway with their burdens when the barber showed up with Kilrain and a few of his friends.

"What's all this?" Kilrain asked almost jovially. "Have we got some trouble here? A few of the boys feeling their oats, were they?"

"Not oats, but that tonsil varnish you been selling these gunslicks."

"Gunslicks, Longarm!" The man was offended. He took the cigar out of his mouth and left the doorway to reason with him. "Why, they've come for the election, for all the fandangos, the pretty women. This is going to be quite a celebration. They are not gunmen."

"They're your guests, are they?"

The tall, lean man glanced quickly about him, aware suddenly that Longarm was more than likely putting

172

him on the spot. "Some of them, yes. I suppose you could say that."

"You still planning to run for mayor in this town, Kilrain?"

"Of course!"

"Then look over there against that wall. That Mexican attendant spilled a little hot water on one of your 'guests,' and the 'guest' and his buddy dunked him in that kettle of boiling water. He's blinded, more than likely. They had a funny way of referring to him as a 'dirty greaser.' That should go over real good with the other Mexicans around here; they might begin to wonder some what kind of friends you're inviting to this here election. They might even begin to wonder about *you*."

The man's lean face paled. He looked with sudden concern at the bathhouse attendant. "That's terrible," he said, "monstrous. I shall have my own personal physician attend to him. We'll do everything we can for him." Kilrain whirled on those crowding the doorway. "Don't just stand there! Run for Father Chaves! And get Doc Cook!"

As two men hustled off in response to Kilrain's order, Kilrain looked back at Longarm. "I see you have suitably punished those responsible."

"I did what seemed fitting, Kilrain. Now I suggest you get them two out of town by sundown. Put them in a buggy and drive them to Lincoln; they've got doctors there. And let their two buddies drive them, the ones who thought it was such a pleasure to watch that poor Mexican get dunked. If you don't do that, Kilrain, I just might have to use a local Mexican's *jacale* for a jailhouse and put some Mexicans over the four of them as guards. I don't think they would like that."

"You—could do that?"

"I'm a deputy U.S. marshal, and this is still a territory under federal law—and usage."

"Of course. Well, then. I'll see to it. I certainly do not want men of that caliber to remain in this town. They have proven themselves unworthy of our hospitality."

"That's the truth of it, Kilrain." Longarm smiled coldly. "You put your finger on it."

Out of pure habit, Kilrain started to hand Longarm a couple of cigars. He caught himself in time, pocketed them, whirled, and strode through the doorway. Everyone except the barber left with him. The barber, still purple in the face, regarded Longarm with amazement.

Longarm walked up to him. "If you finished shaving that other gent, I'm next." As the fellow nodded his head frantically, Longarm poked his porcine belly with the muzzle of his Colt. "But I warn you—one little nick, and this damn thing in my hand just might go off!"

The next day, Longarm rented a surrey from the livery. The hamper Kate brought was almost as large as the back seat. He kidded her about it, asking if she was certain it was going to be enough, then drove out to the river and followed it south until they reached a cottonwood grove nestled in among some hills. The spot they selected for the picnic was on a low bluff that overlooked the river. Behind them, forming a small, natural amphitheater, rose a steep knoll, crowned with short grama grass singed brown by the sun.

Longarm took out a cheroot, leaned his back against the trunk of a cottonwood, and watched as Kate, encumbered with skirt, petticoats, and a bustle—not to mention her French corset—set out the food on the sky-blue blanket she had brought. For a while, it seemed the hamper had no bottom to it.

"You really must be expecting company, Kate," he remarked, chuckling, as she placed the pumpkin pie down on the center of the blanket. There were venison, potato salad, a bowl of parboiled corn, tortillas, enchiladas still warm in a covered dish swimming in chili sauce, thick quarters of cheese, onions cooked in butter, thick black bread that must have been recently baked—and finally, the last to emerge from the incredible hamper, a bottle of Medoc.

As Longarm reached for the Medoc, he saw her looking at him out of the corner of her eye. He was not sure, but he thought he saw tears glistening on her cheeks.

"Why did you say that, Longarm? What did you mean?" she asked as she handed him a corkscrew.

Twisting the corkscrew into the bottle's stopper, he looked at her closely. "Mean by what?"

"That I must be expecting company."

He pulled the cork and reached for one of the glasses. "I was just joshing, Kate."

"No, you weren't. You think I expect trouble—like before, in the hotel."

"Well, I wouldn't blame you if you did. We didn't exactly keep this outing a deep, dark secret, now did we?"

"No. I mean you think I planned it then, and that I'm planning on it now. That this picnic is just a—a trap."

Longarm poured the blood-red wine into a glass and handed it to Kate. She took it. He filled a glass for himself. "Maybe it is a trap, Kate. But it just might be that I'm the jasper settin' it."

"And who might you be setting it for?"

He shrugged. "Kilrain, or a few of his new arrivals."

She looked at him bleakly. "You are so romantic, Longarm."

"Drink up, Kate. No sense in getting all riled. We can still enjoy ourselves. It is a very nice spot, you have to admit." He looked up and saw that she was still glaring at him. "Relax, Kate. I'm a lawman, remember. I can't help that any more than you can help being a very handsome woman and what looks like a hell of a cook."

Kate sighed, then brushed the tears off her cheek with the back of her hand. "Serves me right, I guess."

Longarm got to his feet. "Slice me some of that venison, will you? I want to get something I left in the surrey."

"A rifle and a box of ammunition, I'll bet," Kate said, reaching for a knife.

"How'd you guess?" Longarm replied, moving off.

Longarm had stopped the surrey under a cottonwood close to the crest of the knoll. The two horses were placidly cropping the grass at their feet and barely noticed as Longarm lifted his Winchester from the floor under the front seat. As Kate had predicted, there was a small box of shells sitting there, as well. He dropped the shells into a side pocket. Then, cradling the rifle in his arms, he walked to the crest of the knoll and looked back along the route he had taken.

The river gleamed under the high blue sky. Clumps of Maria's cattle grazed on both sides of the stream. Peering intently into the cottonwoods that lined both banks, he saw nothing suspicious. He glanced skyward. Not a single buzzard was in sight. Perhaps that was a good sign. What the hell, maybe the thing to do was just go ahead and enjoy this picnic. Smiling, he started back down the knoll.

"What? No pesky Apaches on the horizon?" Kate asked.

He was pleased to see she had recovered her good humor. "It ain't Apaches I'm afraid of, Kate."

"I know, I know. Eat up. These enchiladas are getting cold. There's your venison. I hope that's not all you're going to eat."

Longarm slumped down in front of the tree and care-

176

fully leaned the Winchester against the trunk. "If I eat all that, Kilrain won't have to come after me. I'll just sink through this grass like a stone dropping in the river."

"Eat."

For a while, Longarm did as Kate suggested. She *was* an excellent cook; the enchiladas and tortillas warmed him thoroughly. As the sweat stood out on his forehead, he reached for his first piece of pumpkin pie—and groaned. Kate laughed.

"What's so funny?" he asked.

"When you put your heart in it, you can eat to make a woman proud."

"You can set a table to make a man's stomach purr, and that's a fact. But I better not have a second piece of this pie. If we do have visitors, I won't be able to move."

"We won't have visitors, Longarm. It is too lovely a day for trouble. You deserve a rest. And so do I."

"I hope Kilrain is as considerate as the weather."

After finishing the pie, he poured himself another glass of Medoc. He didn't know what the vintage was, but it was a good one. He smiled across the blanket at Kate and took another sip of the wine. Maybe she was right; maybe it was too nice a day for trouble. After all, Kilrain couldn't spend all his time seeing to Longarm—and then he *did* have those fences to mend with the Mexicans as a result of his bully boys' actions at the bathhouse yesterday.

"Are you sure you won't have any more?" Kate asked, holding a knife poised over the pie.

"I'm sure, Kate. My compliments to the cook."

"Thank you." She smiled warmly at him. "Do you know how long it has been since I've had a chance to cook for a man?"

"How long, Kate?"

177

"I won't tell you," she said, beginning to clear off the blanket. "Then you'd know how old I was."

He smiled and got to his feet. Reaching for the rifle, he said, "While you're seeing to the housekeeping, I think I'll take a look around."

"I'll be here when you get back."

She was. But not in the same spot where he had left her. The blanket, neatly folded, had been placed by the tree, the hamper beside it. Kate had removed herself to a spot closer to the edge of the bluff, in a more private green world shaded by a thick cover of berry bushes. Bees hovered in the air, their droning adding to the drowsy appeal of the secluded spot. The sweet smell of the blueberries in the sun hung heavily in the air.

Kate had prepared herself for his return. She had removed her bodice and skirt, her layers of petticoats, and was reclining on the grass, wearing only a frilly chemise, her long hair combed out and cascading down across her shoulders. Longarm glimpsed her corset, thrust well away from her in under the bushes. Once again, as on the day when he had first ridden into Paso Robles, he was impressed by the woman's physical beauty—her thick, luxuriant auburn hair swept cleanly off her forehead, her dark, luminous eyes, her flawless complexion—a little flushed now from the wine—her firm mouth with its sensuous lips, parted slightly at that moment in pouting anticipation.

"Well?" she said. "Any sign of trouble?"

"Nothing yet."

"Well, then."

He thought she seemed awfully certain that he would have found nothing amiss, and he wondered at that.

She reached her arms up to him. He placed his rifle carefully on the ground behind him and dropped beside her. Swiftly, nimbly, her fingers went to work on the buttons of his vest. He helped her. Soon his shirt was peeling back off his shoulders. Her fingers dropped to his fly. Impatiently, he peeled off his britches. They fell to kissing. Their hands moved expertly over each other's bodies.

He reached under her chemise and found her drawers. She giggled and lifted her buttocks, and he pulled off the drawers. They landed behind her head. Longarm glimpsed her pubic hair as she flung back the skirt of her chemise, and lifted her leg to straddle him, pushing him gently onto his back as she did so. She guided him into her hot, throbbing depths and began rocking. She flung her head back, and laughing sobs broke from her taut throat. She came almost at once, collapsing forward onto his hard chest.

"I'm sorry, Longarm," she murmured. "That was too fast, wasn't it? But I've waited so long. And all through that picnic I was thinking of you."

Brushing her long hair back off her shoulder, she smiled at him and he felt her tighten her inner muscles around his shaft. She began to rock once again, but slowly this time, and with a devilish skill that soon brought him to full flower. He waited no longer, but rolled her over swiftly and, in the same unbroken motion, pinned her beneath him, stabbing deeper into her than he had been able to manage on his back. She opened her legs wide to engulf him, her hips rocking in unison with his. He thrust faster, then still faster, anxious to beat her to her orgasm. At last he caught up and pushed hard, holding himself deep within her, pinning her to the ground as he came with thunderous force. She climaxed a moment later, cries breaking from her in a series of hard gasps that ended in a single keening cry. And that only set him off again. He held her, digging in, driving down once more until the wild pulsing ended. His arms went suddenly weak and he collapsed forward onto her warm, sweating breasts, and felt her arms encircle him.

Her legs splayed wide, she cradled him gently, fondly. Longarm could hear her crooning to him. She nibbled gently on his earlobes. The soft murmur of the river and the drone of the bees seemed a part of their lovemaking. After a while, he rolled off and they spent a timeless interlude playing with each other, winding down gently, talking softly, laughing easily—until at last he let her climb on top of him again, and she rode him slowly, without hurry, to her heart's content, his climax following hers like a gentle, sweet wave washing over them both.

He waited until they were in the surrey on the way back before he asked Kate how she could have been so certain that they would not be disturbed on this picnic. She looked sharply at him, the warm flush on her cheeks vanishing in an instant.

"You bastard," she said with feeling.

"That's not nice, Kate."

"*You* are not nice!"

"Sorry, Kate. But remember what I said back there. I'm a lawman."

"How could I ever forget?" She shook her head bitterly. "Well, it's a good thing you waited until now to ask me that question."

"Yes. It would have ruined things, wouldn't it? You see, I do have *some* manners, after all. And that *was* nice back there. It would have been a shame to miss that."

This mollified Kate somewhat. A little of the color returned to her cheeks. She glanced unhappily at him. "It's just so discouraging," she said. "You sometimes seem to know everything. Yes, I knew we wouldn't be disturbed. When Kilrain sent one of his men over to the Lucky Lady to ask us where we were going, I told him

180

·north, to the hills. Pine Creek. We were going to picnic in the pines."

"When was this?"

"While you were pulled up in front of the Lucky Lady, waiting for me to come out with the hamper."

"You could have told me."

"I didn't want you to think that Kilrain could ask me something like that, and I would have to answer."

"Kate, I've suspicioned that for some time. Hank has too, I'm sure. Looks like you got yourself between a rock and a hard place. You kind of favor me, I guess that ain't no secret. But Kilrain's your paymaster."

"I'm in a bind, Longarm, and that's the truth! I never wanted to cross you."

"Like that time in the hotel?"

"When they came to your room and found me there, they asked where you were sleeping. They expected me to tell them. I did, but then I yelled out to warn you."

"You've been partners with Kilrain from the start, haven't you, Kate?" It was phrased as a question, but was not one.

"Yes," Kate admitted, her voice close to despair. "We're both from Texas, Longarm. Kilrain made Bushnell put that ad in the El Paso paper and told me to answer it. That was before he realized what an easy mark Bushnell was. I'm just fronting for him at the Lucky Lady so it won't look like he owns *everything* in town."

"What's he up to, Kate? Why does he want to own Paso Robles?"

"I wish I knew for sure. It's not the town so much; it's the fact that he says it gives him control of the area and the local law."

"For what purpose?"

"He keeps mentioning that control of Paso Robles will give him control of the pass too."

Longarm pondered that. South of the pass, the

Jornado del Muerto led to El Paso, a fine market for beef—rustled or otherwise. That was it, then. Kilrain was a rustler looking for a safe and quick way to get his stolen beeves to market. When Longarm recalled the hardcases now drifting into Paso Robles, he knew he was right. But if Kilrain was a rustler, he was not the usual kind. He would keep his hands clean and strut around as the mayor of a small town, dispensing cigars and patronage, becoming a power in the county and finally in the state, while distant gangs did the dirty work. Hell, after a little while, Kilrain could go legitimate, become a cattle broker. It was neat, very neat.

And there was nothing Longarm could do about it. So far, Kilrain's hands were clean.

"Kate," Longarm said, "I'm looking for a Duke Foster. He rode into Paso Robles yesterday. He's on the run from John Chisum. I suspicion he's been working for Kilrain."

Kate nodded. "I know the man. He's holed up in a feed room back of Kilrain's general store. He's already worn out one of my best girls, and he's raising hell with my whiskey stock. He's a frightened man, all right. Was it you chased him into town?"

"I don't reckon he knew I was on his tail. It's his fear of Chisum that's making him run so scared."

"What's he done?"

Longarm told her briefly about his roundup of the small gang of rustlers led by Dudley McBride, and of Duke Foster's part in it. When he had finished, she was shaking her head in wonder.

"You sure have been busy, Longarm. It's a wonder you're still all in one piece."

"Yes, it is. I am very sore in places, I can tell you."

"You didn't act like it back there."

"A beautiful woman can make a man forget a lot of pain, Kate, and that's a fact."

He glanced at her. She was blushing with pleasure.

He looked back at the horses and rippled the reins across their backs. They picked up their heels, and their tails arched prettily.

"I got to hand it to Kilrain," Longarm said. "Convincing Dudley to throw in with him and impersonate the Kid. It worked pretty well. Chisum was convinced it was the Kid who was rustling his stock. Even the Apaches thought so."

"How could you tell he wasn't the Kid? You said you knew right away, as soon as you collared him."

Longarm shifted his reins into his left hand, lifted his wallet out of his inside coat pocket, and handed it to her. "There's a news clipping folded in there. If you'll take it out, you'll see a picture of Billy the Kid. You can't see the face very clear now, but I been studying that picture. That's how I knew Dudley wasn't the Kid."

She took the clipping from his wallet and unfolded it carefully. She frowned as she looked at it. "He looks so cocky, doesn't he, with his head tipped to one side like that? He's just a boy!"

"That's why they call him Billy the Kid."

She laughed. "What outlandish clothes. That vest he's wearing has got the buttons on the wrong side." She folded the clipping carefully, slipped it into his wallet, then handed it back to Longarm.

As he put the wallet back in his inside pocket, he swore softly.

"What is it, Longarm?"

"Riders, following us on that ridge to your right. I just caught a glimpse of them. Looks like Kilrain's men have finally caught up with us."

Kate gasped. "What are we going to do?"

"Find out how many there are, first. Here. Take the reins."

He handed the reins to her, reached down for his

Winchester, levered a cartridge into the firing chamber, then climbed over the front seat onto the back seat.

"What are you doing?" Kate asked nervously.

"You just keep them horses moving along at a steady pace. I don't want them to know we've spotted them yet."

"It may just be a few riders out for a ride," Kate said.

"Sure, Kate." He chuckled.

"My God! You like this sort of thing!"

"It's what I do best, Kate. And it looks to me like the only way I'm going to get anything solid on this Kilrain is to give him and his boys enough rope."

"With us at the end of it!"

He laughed.

The trail they were on wound along beneath the ridge of a divide that followed the river north past Paso Robles. Peering out the back of the surrey, Longarm counted three riders. They were no longer trying to keep out of sight. The lead rider found a trail off the crest of the divide and started down it, with the other two riders following. Soon the three riders were on the same trail the surrey was taking, gaining steadily.

When they were close enough so Longarm could make out the features of the lead rider, the fellow took out his sixgun and fired at the surrey. At that range he had no chance of hitting them. His buddies fell in beside him and then they too began firing after the surrey. They were gaining steadily, but their firing made no sense at all at that distance.

"Aren't you going to fire back?" Kate called back to him.

"Won't do any good, this far away."

But the firing continued from their pursuers, filling the bright day with gunfire. Longarm turned and looked at Kate. She had her hands full with the team.

The horses were straining mightily. The surrey was rocking dangerously as the wheels caught old ruts.

Kate glanced back at Longarm, panic on her face. "I can't hold the horses, Longarm!" she cried. "I can't hold them!"

He nodded grimly. If course. Kilrain's men were going to make it look like an accident—another unfortunate accident or disappearance. The surrey would be found bottom-up in the river, the two horses still in their traces. Later, their two bodies would be found floating downriver. The cause of the accident would be put down to runaway horses.

The riders were closing swiftly on the surrey, but now they were firing into the air. One of them had a rifle and was making a real fine racket as he levered swiftly. Longarm glanced ahead of the surrey. They were coming to a bend, one that swept to the right around the blade of a butte that had calved from the ridge shouldering over them by this time. He reached over the front seat and grabbed the reins with Kate, hauling in with all his strength. The two horses, their blood up, fought the tugging bits, their necks snapping furiously. But Longarm's strength was remorseless. Gradually the horses slowed.

It was a question, however, of how long he could hold them. They whipped around the bend. Longarm stood up and hauled back with both hands, yanking the reins from Kate's grasp at the same time. The horses whinnied in outrage as the bits tore at their mouths. They scrambled to a halt, then reared in pain and fury, their heads swinging around. Kate was flung forward and almost out of the surrey.

Longarm reached over with his right hand and pulled her back into the surrey, then pushed her unceremoniously down on the floor. "Keep down!" he cried. "Here come our friends!"

The three riders had just rounded the butte and were scrambling to a halt in some confusion. Longarm leapt from the surrey to draw fire away from Kate and raced for the cover of the boulder-strewn slope. He managed to get off one shot at the lead rider as he ran. The fellow's hat lifted as the slug tore through its brim. He reached up for his hat, then grabbed at his reins as his horse, upset by the sudden stop, reared. The other two riders were milling behind the first, trying to get off a clean shot at Longarm.

By the time they had settled their mounts, Longarm was in cover. He rested his rifle on the top of a boulder and drew a bead on the first rider. His first shot was low and caught the fellow in the leg. He levered swiftly, fired a second time, and hit the man shoulder-high. The gunman went peeling backward off his mount. The other two riders dismounted hastily and raced for cover.

Longarm took this opportunity to climb higher. Keeping down, he skirted a huge boulder and found a game trail that led toward the top of the bluff. He raced up the trail until he found he had a clear view of the trail below. He saw a hat poking out behind an embankment, a short gun barrel gleaming just below it. Longarm went down on one knee, aimed carefully, and squeezed off a shot. He heard a muffled cry, and both the hat and the barrel vanished. A moment later, he saw a slack body rolling down a slight incline. The fellow was hatless and without his weapon.

One more to go.

He moved higher on the trail, still peering down the slope. He thought he saw movement beyond a berry bush jutting out of the slope. He paused to look more closely, then left his trail and inched down the steep incline to get a better view. He was easing himself around a boulder half-sunk in the red soil, when he heard a chink of spurs behind him. Whirling and ducking low at the same time, he glimpsed a wild-eyed gunman, his sixgun held out in front of him, about to squeeze off a shot. Without raising the Winchester, Longarm fired from his hip. The slug caught the man in the right thigh and spun him around. He grabbed for the boulder, missed, and slammed to the ground, then began rolling faster and faster down the slope.

Longarm watched him go. When he came to rest at the foot of a boulder, Longarm angled his way carefully down to him. After he reached the quiet body, he was about to put his rifle down so that he could inspect the fellow's wound. He never got the chance. The man scrambled to his feet and lunged for Longarm, wresting the rifle from his grasp. As Longarm ducked backward, he lost his footing on the gravelly slope, and fell. Smiling, the wounded gunslick pumped the Winchester's lever and trained the barrel on Longarm's face. This was Quince, the one who had dunked his companion the day before on Longarm's order. There was a pleased smile on Quince's face as his finger tightened on the Winchester's trigger. Getting even was always a pleasure.

From below on the trail came the sharp crack of a rifle. Quince bucked, then sank to one knee, a dark stain growing on his shirtfront. He tried to raise the rifle, then tumbled face forward. He began to roll. Longarm scrambled to his feet and reached out for him, but missed. He caught hold of a sapling to hold himself back and watched as Quince tumbled down the steep slope. Each time the man turned, the gaping wound in his chest appeared to grow larger.

Where the hell had that shot come from?

He looked along the trail and saw Kate moving from behind a boulder, a rifle in her hand. "You all right, Longarm?" she called up to him.

"Yes, thanks to you. Where'd you learn to shoot like that?"

"I'm a Texas girl, don't forget. I've been shooting as long as I've been riding. Get down here, will you? I think I'm going to get sick."

Chapter 11

Kate had picked up the rifle belonging to the first rider Longarm had brought down. The sound of Longarm's third shot when he wounded the other one had given her the direction he had taken. When, standing below him on the trail, she had looked up and seen Quince behind Longarm, she had been too frightened to cry out a warning. The second time she was ready. All this Kate told Longarm between sobs as they drove back to Paso Robles with a dead man draped over one of the three trailing horses, and two unconscious, severely wounded men slumped behind them in the surrey's back seat.

When they entered Paso Robles, Longarm drove straight to the livery. By the time they reached it, a fairly large crowd had gathered. The Mexicans looked excited and curious, and the Anglos—most of them Kilrain's men—were sullen and not very happy at all. As Longarm helped Kate down from the surrey, he caught sight of one of the young swampers who worked at the Dry Gulch racing up the street toward Kilrain's saloon. He had news for Kilrain.

The fellow Longarm assumed was Doc Cook brushed through the crowd to examine the two men in the surrey. The man stank of whiskey and unwashed clothes, and his little black bag was torn. Longarm stepped back to give the fellow room, thanking the fates, as he did so, that this incompetent had not been the one who had seen to his own earlier wounds.

"Gunshot wounds," the man announced in a piping voice as his dirty fingers lifted aside bloody flaps of clothing. "Most likely fatal. They been bleedin' a lot."

Longarm turned away and led Kate through the crush of wide-eyed spectators toward her saloon. She was still pretty shaken, and leaned on him as he walked. Once inside the Lucky Lady, she greeted Lazarus with a wan smile and ordered a whiskey, neat.

"Just let me get this down, Longarm," she said. "Then I'll be all right."

Lazarus placed the drink in front of her. She snatched it up and downed it in one gulp.

"Again," she said.

As Lazarus took back the empty glass, he looked at Longarm questioningly. Longarm held up a finger. "Whiskey," he said.

Kate took her second drink a little more slowly. As Longarm lifted his shotglass, he saw that the color was beginning to return to Kate's face and she stood a little straighter. He glanced around. The Lucky Lady was deserted, except for the barkeep. All the excitement was outside.

"That's some doctor," Longarm remarked. "Where the hell did he come from?"

"Kilrain just brought him in and set him up down the street in an office. He likes Cook. The fellow dug a bullet out of him many years ago and Kilrain lived. He keeps saying that when the man is sober, he's a fine doctor."

"They deserve each other," Longarm remarked, finishing his whiskey.

At that moment, someone strode through the batwings. Longarm turned. It was Charles Kilrain. He had set his long, severe face into what he supposed was a stern aspect, but Longarm could tell that the man was frustrated at the way his plans had gone awry and was now a little uncertain. He did not know what tack to take with this annoyingly elusive lawman.

"Doc says those two men will likely die, Longarm," Kilrain said, coming to a halt before the bar.

"With that sawbones working on them, I guess I'd have to agree with you, Kilrain." Longarm smiled then. "It's your fault, you know."

The man bristled. "How can you say that?"

"If you'd done what I told you to do, and let Quince and that other fellow drive them two scalded jaspers to Lincoln, Quince wouldn't be draped over a horse out there, and his buddy wouldn't be under Doctor Cook's care. You should have sent them to Lincoln instead of after me."

"After you?"

"Yes, after me. And after Kate here, as well."

"I hope you know what you are saying, Longarm." The man was trying to appear outraged. Instead, he looked as though Longarm had just punctured his balloon. His face was drained of color. Longarm heard Kate gasp. Kilrain flicked a glance in her direction. "Such charges are outrageous."

"No more outrageous than what you're trying here in Paso Robles, Kilrain."

"And just what might that be?"

"I'm tired, Kilrain. And so is Kate. Go see to your boys. You got them into this mess, now see if you can help them."

Longarm's tone was harsh. Kilrain was not used to being dismissed in such a fashion. He stood there irresolutely, glancing nervously from Kate to the barkeep. Moistening his lips, he said, "You're right. I should look after those men, Longarm. But remember, you have no proof, none at all, for your ridiculous charges."

"What charges?" Longarm asked innocently. Then he smiled. "Would you like to tell me what I'm charging you with?"

Kilrain started to say something, then spun on his heel and stalked out of the saloon. As the batwings slowly fluttered to a halt, Longarm heard Kate clearing her throat. And then he felt her hand on his arm. He turned to face her. She did not look very well.

"What is it, Kate?"

"Can we . . . can we go over to that table, Longarm?"

He escorted her gently and helped her into a chair. As soon as he had sat down next to her, she turned her frightened eyes to him. "You said Kilrain was trying to kill me too, this afternoon."

"Yes, Kate, I did. After all, you were a witness. And it looks like Kilrain decided you were expendable. Anything to get me off his back."

"I'm scared, Longarm."

"Don't be. He knows now that I'm onto what he's up to. He knows, too, that if he lays a hand on you, I'll come after him. As long as I'm alive, you're safe."

Kate groaned softly and dropped a cold hand onto his wrist. "For God's sake, Longarm, be careful." Then she smiled weakly at him. "For both our sakes."

Longarm took a deep breath. "I still ain't got enough proof. There's nothing solid I can use to point the finger at Kilrain—nothing I could use in a court of law, at any rate. And pretty soon he'll be the mayor of the town, with his own men installed as town marshals. I need Duke Foster, Kate."

"Foster?"

"I'm going to rescue him this evening and take him

to Lincoln. He'll talk when he gets there, or face John Chisum."

"Rescue him?"

"He doesn't know it, Kate, but just like you, he's now a pure problem for Kilrain."

She shuddered, and he went on, "Tonight, when he sends for another girl, let me know."

"Where will you be?"

"I'll be catnapping over there in the corner, nursing a beer. And Kate, after I've taken Foster, Kilrain will want you to tell him what I'm up to. You be sure and tell him—just don't tell him right away."

"Tell him? But why?"

"So he'll think you're still working for him. And tell him you don't believe what I said about him wanting you dead too. Do that, Kate, so he won't feel he has to worry about you. It's your best protection while I'm gone."

"Oh, Longarm, I'm scared!"

"And stay that way. It'll make you careful."

He got up.

"Where are you going?"

"I have to see to some horses for tonight, for Foster and me. Don't worry, I won't be gone long."

As Longarm shouldered his way through the bat-wings, he could feel Kate's eyes on his back. She was a courageous woman who had just saved his life, but he had spoken with more confidence than he actually felt. He hoped his words would give her the backbone she would need to get through these next crucial hours.

And he hoped his own luck would hold.

Kate's girl, carrying a basket of food with the neck of a bottle sticking out of it, rapped softly on the back door of Kilrain's general store. Longarm moved out of the shadows, his Colt drawn. The girl had her back to him and did not see him. He was close enough to hear her curse softly in Spanish, then rap a second time, more urgently.

There was a soft scraping sound behind the door. A key turned in a lock. The door was opened a crack, sending a narrow beam of yellow light probing into the darkness of the back alley. It narrowly missed Longarm, who swiftly flattened himself against the building.

The girl spoke to whoever was at the door. The conversation was short. Longarm heard a soft explosion of laughter from beyond the door. A chain dropped and the door was pulled open for the girl. Longarm waited until the girl was stepping into the back room before he strode out of the shadows and lowered his shoulder against the door.

The girl gasped as Longarm sent the door swinging wide. The fellow standing in the shadows, Foster's guard most likely, looked up in astonishment at Longarm, who brought the barrel of his Colt down on the man's head. He sighed and, without an outcry, sagged to the floor. Even as he struck the floor, Longarm reached out and clamped a firm hand swiftly over the girl's mouth.

"Shhh!" he whispered to her. "It's all right, *señorita!* Nothing will happen to you if you're quiet. *Comprende?*"

She nodded quickly, and removed his hand. She backed fearfully into a corner, her eyes bright with fear.

There was a door to Longarm's left. He pointed at the door and looked at the girl, raising his eyebrows in a silent query. She nodded quickly.

Longarm rapped softly on the door. He heard someone stirring inside. It sounded like Foster was sleeping on a cot. A sleepy voice called, "Who is it?"

Longarm looked at the girl and pointed to the door, sharply. She ran to the door and leaned against it. "It

194

is Constancia!" she called through the door. "*Señora* Kate, she send me with food."

"About time," Foster growled.

Longarm waggled the barrel of his sixgun at Constancia, indicating that she should get back. She darted into the shadows like a frightened animal. A bolt was drawn on the other side of the door, and the door was pulled open.

Longarm smiled thinly down at the unshaven face of Duke Foster. Before the man could utter an outcry, he found himself staring into the bore of Longarm's Colt. Longarm put a finger to his mouth and said, "You yell, and I'll pull this trigger. Now stand still and listen. Kilrain is going to have to get rid of you soon. I'm offering you a chance to ride with me to Lincoln. If you testify against Kilrain, I'll do what I can to get all other charges against you dropped. I'm even pretty sure I can get Chisum to go along with that. Stay here and you're a dead man. Go with me and you've got a chance."

The fellow swallowed, unable to take his eyes off the gun barrel. Slowly, but decisively, he nodded his head. In a hoarse whisper, he said, "I'll go with you."

Longarm holstered his weapon. "Move out," he said. "Now."

Foster stepped past Longarm and out of the room. Longarm found an empty sugar sack on the floor, stuffed a good piece of it into the mouth of the unconscious guard, then dragged him into the small room. Ripping up a blanket he found on the cot, he bound the fellow's wrists and ankles behind him. Then he closed the door on him and beckoned to the girl.

She stole fearfully out of the shadows, still clinging to her basket.

"Go back to the Lucky Lady," Longarm told her. "Tell Kate nothing. No one will ask you any questions. Tell no one what happened here. *Comprende?*"

She nodded her head vigorously. *"Si!"*

He stepped back and she darted out past Longarm and Foster and ran lightly back down the alley. Longarm turned to Foster. "I've got horses in the alley," he told him. "Let's go."

Keeping to the alleys, Longarm and Foster were able to leave Paso Robles without being spotted by any of Kilrain's men. The night was cool, the stars gleamed, the moon was a bright golden coin hanging over the distant hills. They drove their horses hard for the first hour, then let up.

"Why are you doing this for me, Longarm?" Foster asked as he pulled alongside the lawman. "You don't owe me nothin'."

"I'm doing it for myself. It's my job to get Kilrain, or at least to stop him. And you're the one who can help me do that."

"You're right about one thing."

"What's that?"

"I was in danger from Kilrain. Earlier, when I told him I wanted to get out of that room, he just smiled and told me I wasn't going anywhere. Not anywhere at all." Foster shook his head. "I sure as hell knew what he meant, all right."

Longarm glanced back over his shoulder. The flat, moonlit landscape was empty of horsemen, as far as he could tell. He hoped he had hit that jasper in the back room hard enough to put him to sleep for another hour or so. He turned back around in his saddle. Just ahead of him were the buttes and hills, the fingerlike rock projections of the badlands they would have to traverse if they wanted to reach Lincoln by morning.

The badlands hung before them like a mirage for the next hour or so, seeming to get no closer, until they splashed across a shallow stream, climbed the far bank, and looked up and found the buttes and humpbacked hills of the badlands towering over them. It was downright spooky, as though the damn place had snuck up on them while they were negotiating the stream.

The trail that led through the badlands was not difficult to follow in the moonlight. As they rode along it, they were soon lost in great purple shadows cast by the towering rock formations. A canyon opened before them, with a piece of the golden moon peering like a baleful eye over one lip of it. Before rattling into the canyon, Longarm turned about in his saddle and looked back.

Four—no, five—riders, punishing their horses cruelly, were galloping silently up to the far bank of the river. Longarm turned about and urged the chestnut on into the canyon. Once they were well inside, he heard for the first time the distant, ghostly echo of the pursuing horsemen as their horses splashed through the stream and galloped up the near bank. Longarm glanced at Foster. The man had seen all that Longarm had, and now he heard them as well.

"Let's go!" Longarm cried.

The two men galloped on through the canyon, not sparing their horses. They left the canyon, found themselves on a rocky ridge, traversed it for at least half a mile, then cut down onto a dry riverbed, followed it for another mile or so, then cut into a narrow arroyo. Emerging from this, Longarm found himself facing a series of low hills capped with jagged rimrock.

"Up there!" he told Foster.

The horses bounded gallantly up the steep, talus-littered slope, and kept driving until they were at the top. But that was all the two mounts had left in them. Longarm flung himself from his horse, pulling his Winchester from its boot as he did so. Foster also had a rifle as he dismounted; Longarm had thought to provide him with a long gun for just such an eventuality.

"Pick your emplacement," Longarm told the man.

"They'll be spilling out of that arroyo pretty damn soon."

Foster nodded and angled down the slope well to Longarm's left. Longarm watched as he disappeared among a cluster of rocks, only to emerge, a moment later, still farther down the slope and take a position behind a low, flat-topped boulder. There was a ridge behind Foster, off to his left, but Longarm was reluctant to call out or risk a shout at this stage to warn him. Longarm led the horses back off the ridge, well out of sight behind it and in among some rocks. They were still trembling from the exertion of that last run, but they both looked healthy. As Longarm left them, he saw their heads drop to crop at the sparse grass at their feet.

Longarm had just positioned himself among some rocks that gave him a clear view in almost every direction, when the first of the pursuing riders erupted from the mouth of the arroyo. Longarm tracked him carefully as the fellow rode in a tight circle, his eyes on the hills around him while he waited for his companions to catch up with him. They boiled out of the arroyo soon enough.

As they came together, milling about and doing what they could to settle down their horses, Longarm was able to hear their voices echoing off the stone walls and the clatter of their horses' nervous hooves. They saw Longarm's tracks easily enough in the bright moonlight, and they knew that, more than likely, Longarm and his companion were up there behind the rocks waiting to blast them.

And they were right, Longarm conceded grimly, still tracking that first rider. But he wanted a cleaner shot. He wanted the riders to start up the steep incline. Glancing quickly over at Foster, he hoped this was the reason Foster was holding his fire as well. Abruptly the discussion below them was over, and the lead rider spurred his horse toward the slope. Longarm swore softly as he tucked the stock of his Winchester into his shoulder, sighted carefully, and squeezed off a shot. The round richocheted off a rock close beside the horse. The rider flung himself from his horse, flipped over onto his belly, and began pumping shots up at Longarm. The fire was so rapid that the rocks around Longarm were singing. He poked his head up twice and managed to disturb the ground around the prone gunman, but that was the best he could do. Meanwhile, the other riders had abandoned their mounts and were crawling up the slope toward him, moving from one cover to another with disheartening ease.

Longarm tried to discourage them with occasional shots in their direction, but it did little good. And where, Longarm wondered, was Foster? He was flanking most of them by this time. A bullet whined overhead, struck a rock behind him, and richocheted into the night. Longarm poked his head up and saw someone's ass inching up the slope directly in front of him. He sighted carefully, but before he could get off his shot, Foster fired from his own position. The fellow just below threw up his arms, screamed bloody murder, and began rolling back down the slope.

The gunmen were suddenly discouraged. In disarray, they scrambled back down the slope. Longarm and Foster took turns firing on them. A second gunman was winged, not seriously, since he remained on his feet and only ran faster for cover. But in his haste, he left behind his rifle.

And then all five, including the more seriously wounded gunman, were out of sight.

But they were not out of mischief, that was for damn sure. Longarm took the time to reload his Winchester. As he thumbed the cartridges into the magazine, he glanced up at the moon. It was no longer as bright as it had been, and would most likely set before long. There were four of them still reasonably healthy, and only two men to stand them off. Longarm sighed and continued to load. He shouldn't be worried. After all, his motives were pure and his heart was good.

The moon had long since dipped behind a butte off to Longarm's right, leaving only an eerie glow that raised hell with distances and seemed to cause the grotesque rock-shapes looming over them to hover threateningly.

"Hey, Longarm!" It was Foster.

"Yeah?"

"What's going on?"

"They're sneaking up on us. Keep an itchy trigger finger and fire at anything that moves!"

His advice to Foster had not been given in jest. Longarm figured that the remaining gunmen had separated and were now moving up the slope, some from the front, others from the rear. If they were smart, each would find a good position, wait until daylight, and commence firing.

So why in tarnation was he waiting here for the sun to come up?

Peering down the slope, he saw the darker shadows of the horses moving against the lighter shadow of the canyon wall. Occasionally one of the horses nickered, the sound floating up to him like a ghostly laugh. Kilrain's men had not bothered to picket them.

"Foster!" Longarm whispered. "Work your way back up here."

"That you, Longarm?" Foster's voice was hoarse with fear.

"Who the hell do you think it is?"

Longarm listened for a moment. When he was sure he could hear Foster moving toward him through the darkness, he left his position and hurried back to where he had left the horses. He took their reins in his left hand and led them carefully back to the crest of the ridge.

A shadow loomed up in front of him and he almost fired point-blank before he heard Foster's nervous voice. "That you, Longarm? What the hell you doin' with them horses?"

"Take yours and follow me down there. We're leaving here and taking them jaspers' transportation—if we can get away with it."

Longarm handed Foster the reins to his horse, then led his own mount down the steep slope. The horse was a help as it dug its hooves into the shifting talus and gave support to Longarm as he slipped and slid his way toward the canyon floor. Behind him, Foster was cursing softly as he too struggled on the steep slope and tried to contend with the almost pitch-black darkness. They were almost off the slope when a sharp cry came from halfway up the slope, about a hundred or so yards to Longarm's right.

"They're after the horses!"

A shot followed, and the slug richocheted off a rock just in front of Longarm. He steadied his feet in the shifting ground, swung up his rifle, and levered swiftly. Bracing the rifle against his hip, he squeezed off a volley toward the location of the muzzle-flash. Quite a few of the bullets whined off the slope harmlessly, but Longarm heard also the sound of a gasp and then the metallic clatter of a gun being dropped.

Swiftly, Longarm pulled his horse all the way down the slope, then swung into the saddle, dropping his rifle into its sling. "Mount up," Longarm said to Foster, "and help me drive them horses back through that arroyo!"

"By Jesus!" Foster cried excitedly. "We got 'em now!"

As Longarm rode toward the milling shadows ahead of him, he heard Foster's mount moving up behind him.

"We goin' to stampede them?" Foster cried excitedly as he rode up alongside Longarm.

Longarm could see his sixgun gleaming in the dim light. "Maybe. If they don't mind us," he replied.

They were almost to the horses when fire from two spots high on the ridge broke out. Someone began cursing and shouting at the same time as it became apparent what Longarm was up to. The rounds buzzed dangerously close and one of the horses they were loping toward uttered a high, angry whinny and went down. The whine of richocheting slugs grew louder as they neared the canyon wall. Ahead of them, the four remaining horses were milling frantically.

"Spread out! Drive them into the arroyo!" Longarm cried.

Foster broke to Longarm's left and Longarm went right, still driving forward toward the gaping slash in the canyon wall looming ahead of them. The horses kept milling until Longarm and Foster were almost on them. Then one of them broke for the arroyo and the rest followed.

Behind him, Longarm could hear the sound of men plunging wildly down the steep, talus-littered slope, firing as they came. A slug whispered past his left shoulder. Another ticked the brim of his Stetson. Longarm hunched low over his horse and kept driving for the arroyo. He could see Foster moving up just a bit ahead of him and the horses plunging into the arroyo. The firing behind them was incessant, however. Longarm wondered how it was possible for Kilrain's men to miss such hefty targets. And then all four horses had vanished into the arroyo, with Foster cutting in right behind them.

At that moment Longarm saw Foster stiffen, then slip sideways in his saddle. Foster managed to hang on, but the sudden movement had broken his horse's stride. Longarm galloped up beside him, reached over, and yanked him back onto his saddle. Longarm could not see Foster's face, but his voice was laced with pain as he spoke to Longarm: "It's my back! Jesus, it's all tore up in there. I can hardly swallow!"

"Keep going! We've got to keep these horses moving through here! You'll be all right. Keep going!"

Foster nodded obediently, and Longarm saw the man clap his spurs to his mount's flanks. The horse leaped forward. Longarm hung back, watching. It did not appear that Foster would be able to ride much farther. Damn. The man had proven to be a good sidekick in an emergency. Scared though he was, he had taken instructions well and used his head. It was not so difficult to understand, now, why John Chisum had stuck by this man since Texas. Whatever it is that makes a man throw a wide loop, it usually isn't cowardice. It was just plain stupidity, mostly. And this here Foster in front of him was sure as hell going to pay the full price for his.

Somehow, Foster stayed on his mount for maybe five or six miles. Dawn was beginning to lighten the sky when Foster pulled raggedly back on his reins, looked apologetically at Longarm, then slid slowly off his horse. He left a broad slick of blood on the saddle as he did so. He was clinging to the cinch strap when Longarm dismounted and helped him to the ground. As Longarm placed his hand on his back to guide him, he felt the bullet hole. It was big enough; the bullet must have tumbled before it hit him. A richochet.

"The horses still goin'?" Foster asked.

Longarm glanced up. Yes, they were. Still pounding heavily down the trail, heading back to Paso Robles. "Sure, Foster. We left them bastards without transportation. They'll have to walk back to Paso Robles, if that's where they head for. But I got a feeling those who can walk are not going to try to make it back, not with their tails between their legs."

"That's good," Foster said hoarsely, and began to cough.

Longarm saw a thin stream of blood trail from the corner of Foster's mouth. The coughing fit took hold, and when the paroxysms had finally passed, the man seemed to have shrunken considerably.

"Just let me lie back for a little while, Longarm. It hurts like hell. Jesus. I hope I don't cough like that again." He smiled weakly. "Wages of sin, wouldn't you say, Longarm?"

"Why the hell did you cross Chisum, Foster? Throwing in with a guy like Kilrain makes about as much sense as sleeping with a rattler."

Foster winced and looked away. "Money, Longarm. Hell, do you know how much Chisum pays me? I'd be put out to pasture soon, and what would I have? All these years I been with John, and all I'd've got when I rode off was a firm handshake and a clap on the back. Shit. With the money I was supposed to get helping Dudley whittle John's herds some, I could buy myself a little ranch up in Wyoming." He coughed weakly, then grimaced in pain. "Had the place all picked out, too."

Again Foster began to cough. This time the violence of the spasms caused the man to groan in despair and roll over onto his side and draw his knees up sharply. When he was finished at last, he had coughed up clots of blood and his face was the color of alkali dust, his eyes squinting painfully up at Longarm.

"Leave me here, Longarm. Just ride out."

"No."

"You heard me, damn it! Can't a man have no privacy? I'm goin' to shit my pants soon, and maybe cry a little. That's how bad I feel. The least you can do is leave me be now. They ain't nothin' you can do.

Even a dog gets a chance to crawl off somewhere alone. . . ."

He closed his eyes tightly then, and tried to fight off another coughing fit. Longarm had been down on one knee beside him. He stood up and took a step back.

Foster's eyes flickered open. "That's it," he gasped. "Leave me be, Longarm. Thanks. Hell, this ain't so bad a way to go now, is it? Throwin' a little lead. Maybe I took a few of them bastards with me. . . ." He tried to smile. It was a ghastly parody and didn't work at all. ". . . and maybe that place in Wyoming would've been a bust anyways . . . better off this way. Go 'way now, Longarm . . . please . . . leave me be . . ."

Longarm reached back for the reins of his chestnut, then swung aboard. He kneed the horse over to Foster's mount and snatched up its reins. Trailing the horse behind him, he rode off slowly. He looked back once to see Foster still lying on his side. The man appeared to be coughing again. His head was hanging down and he appeared to shrink with each paroxysm, each shuddering wrench. Longarm turned himself around and rode with his face resolutely forward. He did not look back again.

Chapter 12

Kilrain was standing in front of the Dry Gulch when Longarm rode in that afternoon trailing Foster's riderless horse behind him. Longarm noted the stubborn resolve on Kilrain's long, lean face and the way his jaw had clamped down on his fat cigar. Before Longarm rode past the saloon, Kilrain turned on his heels and pushed through the batwings into the Dry Gulch.

Longarm tied up both horses in front of the Lucky Lady and strode in. Poker players surrounded most of the tables, but the roulette wheel was still, there were only a few men at the bar, and Lazarus was keeping himself busy by polishing glasses. Four of Kate's girls were sitting at a rear table giggling, with tall glasses of beer in front of them.

"You want Kate?" Lazarus asked, as Longarm bellied up to the bar.

"And a beer," Longarm replied.

Lazarus walked down the length of the bar, stuck his head up the stairway, and called Kate's name, then returned to draw Longarm's beer. Longarm hauled the beer over to his favorite table in the corner—one that gave him a clear view of the front door—and slumped wearily into the chair. Tipping the chair on its rear legs back against the wall, he lifted the beer up to his mouth, dipped his snout into the cool suds, and drank greedily.

He was still thinking of Duke Foster back there in the badlands, wanting only to be left alone to die like some old fleabitten hound dog too far gone to keep up with the pack. The thought made Longarm both somber and quietly furious. Kilrain. The man was a pinch of arsenic dropped into a peaceful pool. He was that sneaky. And each one who visited that pool stiffened and died. Foster was only Kilrain's latest victim.

Longarm had come back for Kilrain. He had no choice now. He had needed Foster's testimony. The man would have stood up well in court. Without that proof, Longarm had nothing to bring to Governor Wallace. There was no law against running for mayor of Paso Robles or letting unruly drifters come by to watch the festivities. Still, from the beginning, Longarm had kept in mind the fact that he had two ways he could play this hand. Now that he had tried to play it straight, he would see what a little bluffing would do.

A thought occurred to him then. He put down his glass and slipped out his wallet. He unfolded the picture of Billy the Kid and studied it carefully. Kate had been right; the buttons were sewed on the wrong side, all right. Or *were* they?

Kate appeared on the stairway, spotted him at once, and hurried over to his table, calling over her shoulder to Lazarus to bring her a whiskey. Longarm put the clipping away as Kate slumped wearily into a chair and stared for a moment, puffy-eyed, at him. She had been crying.

"You lovely sonofabitch," she said softly, smiling at last. "You great big lucky sonofabitch. Kilrain sent an army after you and Foster. I watched them clatter out of here. They were slavering after you like mad dogs."

"That's just the way they appeared to me too, Kate," he said, bringing the glass of beer up to his mouth. "Right now they're probably a lot madder. They're on foot—them that can walk, that is—and in a pretty dry land. They got Foster, though."

"What are you going to do?"

"How much did you tell Kilrain?"

She looked suddenly away from Longarm's eyes and plucked unhappily at the knuckles of her left hand. "Everything, Longarm. One of his men had Constancia. The girl was terrified. I was too."

"He knows what I suspect."

"Yes."

"That's all right, Kate." He reached over and placed his hand over hers. "I'm glad he knows. He'll probably figure he has to make a move against me. I've whittled down his force of imported plug-uglies some. If he comes at me, he'll make things a lot simpler."

"I'm scared, Longarm. The man has changed. He's—he's ruthless."

"He always was, Kate. Only now he's seeing what he has been building for a long, long time maybe coming apart—with me as the wrecker."

"And me too, Longarm. He knows how I helped you."

Hank entered the saloon and stood for a moment in front of the batwings. He looked unhappy. It was the first time Longarm had seen him not in a generally cheerful frame of mind. When he saw the marshal and Kate at the table, he strode over.

"Sit down, Hank."

Hank sat. He looked restlessly about him, then looked straight at Longarm, inquiringly. "You want I should stable your horse out there, the chestnut?"

"I'd appreciate that, Hank. And the one beside it."

"They're both good Jingle Bob stock."

Longarm nodded grimly. "The other one belonged to Duke Foster. He won't be needing it anymore."

"Kilrain's boys caught up with you, did they?"

Longarm glanced at Kate.

"I told Hank," Kate admitted. "I had to tell someone. I was so worried, Longarm, when those men rode out after you."

Longarm looked back at Hank. "Yeah, they caught up with me, but they'll be a long time gettin' back."

"Kate told me about Dudley McBride."

Longarm smiled. "The fake Billy the Kid."

Hank shook his head. "This here Kilrain is sure startin' to throw a wide loop."

"I guess you might say that, Hank."

Hank then looked bleakly at Longarm. "He talked Theresa into workin' for him in the Dry Gulch."

Theresa, Longarm knew, was Hank's girl, Maria's cook. "You mean she's one of Kilrain's play-pretties now?"

"That ain't what she thinks. She said Kilrain promised her all she would have to do is smile at the customers and get their drinks for them."

Kate frowned angrily. "Is that what he told her?"

Hank nodded.

"And she believed it?"

"I tried to talk her out of it. But that Kilrain sure has a way about him. Seems like he could talk a woman into just about anything."

"Ain't it the truth?" Kate said bitterly.

"I'm tired," Longarm said. "I been going ever since a very exciting picnic yesterday. And I didn't get no sleep at all last night." He smiled at Kate. "You think you could let me get some shut-eye upstairs?"

"In one of my girls' rooms?"

"It would be inconvenient, I know."

"No, it wouldn't. That girl Murales roughed up left me, ran off with a whiskey drummer. It looked like a good match, so I didn't try to stop her. You could sleep in her room."

"Fine. Now this is going to be tricky, so listen. I'm checking in at the hotel and going up to my room. I'll leave the lamp on, then sneak out the back into the alley and come here. You let me in the back way and up the rear stairs to that room. Don't tell Lazarus or any of the girls. That way I'll get some sleep, and at the same time I'll be on hand in case you have any trouble."

"Are you expecting trouble?" Kate asked unhappily.

"Hell, yes. Kilrain knows I'm back and after him, and that I sure as hell don't aim to let this here election make him the top dog in these parts. He's going to be a mite skittish until he nails me. You've been a good friend, Kate. And that means you should be careful yourself, from here on in—real careful."

Kate finished her whiskey. "I'll be careful," she said. "But I'm glad you'll be sleeping upstairs, Longarm."

Longarm got to his feet. "Just don't tell no one," he said.

Hank got up also. "I'll stable them horses, Mr. Long."

"Thanks, Hank."

"Then I think maybe I'll drift back in here."

"Who's going to look after the stable, Hank?"

"I told Maria I was quittin'. She knows why."

Longarm nodded, rested his hand lightly on Kate's shoulder, then left the table and moved out of the Lucky Lady, blinking in the bright sunlight as he walked up the street to the hotel. He was groggy. He just hoped he could make it back to the Lucky Lady without being seen. He needed sleep the way rotgut whiskey needs a chaser.

One of Kate's girls was shaking him roughly by the shoulder. He struggled out of sleep with the reluctance of a man freeing himself from a blissful embrace. He rolled over at last, his Colt in his hand, his eyes blinking up at the girl. At the sight of the gun, she ducked back, a hand over her mouth, her eyes wide with terror. It was still light. The late afternoon sun was pouring in through the one window.

"What's wrong?" he managed, aware that his mouth was sour. He needed a drink.

The girl pointed downstairs. "Kate! She send me. Say trouble!"

He swung his legs off the bed, grabbed his hat from the foot of the bed, rubbed one big hand down over his face, then holstered his gun and left the room, with the girl on his heels. He was more than halfway down the stairs when he saw two of Kilrain's hired help starting up them. When they glanced up and saw Longarm coming, they seemed startled and back swiftly down. They were still backing away in some confusion when Longarm reached the saloon floor and nodded coldly to them. Longarm saw one of them cast a swift, furious glance at the table where Kate was sitting. Kate covered her face with her hands. At once, Longarm knew what she had done—and then what she had done in an effort to erase her betrayal.

Hank was sitting by himself along the far wall. Longarm walked over to his table and sat down beside him.

"All rested up, Mr. Long?" Hank asked pleasantly. He had enjoyed that business at the foot of the stairs. He was smiling slightly.

The tall marshal smiled back at him. "I reckon we know each other well enough by now that you can call me Longarm, Billy."

Hank's expression did not change, but his eyes seemed to gleam a little brighter. "How long have you known—Longarm?"

"Since I figured out why every lawman in the southwest thinks you're a southpaw. That picture of you, the one where you're holding a rifle."

Billy chuckled. "The one with all my teeth showing."

"That's the one. Well, it was printed with the plate flipped over. Kate spotted it, saw you was wearing buttons on the wrong side of your vest."

Billy sighed. "I was wonderin' why every poster was callin' me a lefty. But I wasn't complainin' none." Billy looked shrewdly at Longarm. "You goin' to broadcast this, Longarm?"

"Right now, Billy, all I'm interested in doing is nailing this Kilrain."

One of Kate's girls, very nervous, came over to their table and asked if they wanted anything to drink. "Two beers," Billy said.

The girl nodded, snatched up the Kid's glass, and left. Two more of Kilrain's men shouldered their way into the Lucky Lady. They sauntered with exaggerated nonchalance over to the bar to join the other two.

"This place is sure gettin' crowded," Billy remarked.

"I been doing my best these past few days to shrink down this army of Kilrain's," Longarm remarked wearily, as he watched the four confused gunslicks at the bar.

"You done fine, Longarm," Billy said. "Cut Kilrain's army in half, you did. Them two that just came in must be pretty footsore right now. Just got into town sharin' a horse barely able to hobble into the livery. Them four is all Kilrain's got left."

The girl brought their beer. Longarm gave her a coin. She hurried away from the table looking as if she had just served two dead men. Longarm paid no attention to her. His eyes remained focused on the remnants of Kilrain's army. They were still at the bar, conferring nervously; something had gone wrong. Now they had to figure out what to do next. They couldn't go back to Kilrain without blood on their hands.

Longarm sipped his beer and glanced over at Kate. She had been watching him, but the moment he turned his head, she looked quickly away. When this was all over, he would have to tell her that he was not angry with her, that he had expected her to tell Kilrain where he was holing up. All he had needed was a little time for a quick nap. The hotel decoy had given him that.

Abruptly, the four gunslicks at the bar separated. They had come to a decision. Now they knew what to do. Kilrain had sent the last two in to back up the first pair of gunmen, who were supposed to have surprised Longarm asleep upstairs. Kate had ruined that plan by sending a girl up to warn Longarm, so they would just have to finish the job down here.

He finished his beer and watched the four men continue to move apart, inching their way along the bar. A quick glance at Billy showed his blue eyes dancing with barely suppressed excitement. "This ain't your fight, Billy," Longarm said, looking back at the bar.

"Them two on the right are mine," the Kid replied by way of answer.

Longarm nodded slightly. That helped some.

One of the gunmen, the one farthest to the left and the biggest brute of the four, bumped a Mexican nursing a whiskey. The Mexican had a high-peaked sombrero on and Longarm saw the wide brim turn swiftly as he looked at the fellow who had just bumped him. The Mexican said something to the gunman in Spanish.

"Speak English, you goddamn greaser!" the gunman sneered, knocking the Mexican angrily away from the bar and drawing his sixgun at the same time.

At once, another Mexican behind the gunman grabbed at him, trying to pull the gun out of his hand. This caused a second gunman, who had evidently been waiting for just such a reaction, to draw his own gun and crunch its barrel down on the second Mexican's head. As this fellow's hat went flying, there was a scream from one of Kate's girls. That seemed to do it. Instantly the men at the bar erupted in a furious free-for-all. A shot was fired. Men at the tables bolted for the doors leaving overturned chairs in their wake. Others at the bar who were closest to the door also ran from the place.

By this time, the girls were huddled around Kate's table, and out of the corner of his eye, Longarm saw Kate push the girls toward the stairway. All four of them darted around the bar and then vanished swiftly up the staircase. In a moment, Kate was alone at the table, a Mexican was lying unconscious on the floor, and three others were grappling, showing surprising tenacity, with Kilrain's four gunmen. Then a second shot exploded in the saloon and another Mexican staggered away from the melee and collapsed onto a table. The table tipped and went crashing with him to the floor.

Another shot came from the struggling group, and this time the round buried itself in the wall just behind Longarm, who left his seat and crabbed to his left, his Colt firing over the heads of those still struggling at the bar. He got off two quick shots; the rounds were high enough that nothing of value behind the bar was struck, but the quick detonations seemed to sober the Mexicans still struggling with Kilrain's men. They pulled away and, ducking low, bolted out of the saloon.

For a split-second, the two opposing forces faced each other without either side making a move. Longarm was behind an overturned table and the Kid, leaning over the table they had been sitting at, had trained his own sixgun on one of the gunmen. Kate, petrified with fear, was still sitting, defenseless, at her table. Kilrain's four men, their guns drawn, crouched with their backs to the bar. They appeared startled to see Longarm and the Kid waiting so coolly for their diversion to end. It hadn't fooled anyone, they must have realized with dismay.

The two men on the right, those closest to the door, turned and bolted from the saloon, with Billy—a wide grin on his face—racing after them. There were shots outside in the street, but Longarm paid no attention as the big fellow opposite him punched out with his Colt, thumbed back the hammer, and fired point-blank at Longarm. The act of cocking the revolver had ruined his aim, however, and the slug spent itself on the surface of the overturned table. Longarm fired once, twice, at the fellow. His first round ricocheted off the bar's solid mahogany lip and slammed up into the ceiling. A thin tracery of plaster sifted down. The second round caught the big man in the heart, punching him back against the bar. He looked startled. His eyes bugged. As he sagged drunkenly to the floor, already dead, his lone companion, with both hands steadying his aim, fired at Longarm.

Again the table, and not Longarm, caught the slug. As the marshal poked his head out, his hat went flying. Furious at what damage must have been done to it, Longarm stuck his hand out and, without aiming, firing solely by instinct, sent a round at the man. He heard the man gasp. Then came the sound of his revolver striking the brass footrail. Kate screamed, a long, high, terrified keening that raised the hair on the back of Longarm's neck. Looking out from behind the table, Longarm saw the second man—half his face gone, a gaping, streaming hole in the back of his head— staggering blindly across the saloon floor toward Kate's table. He was on his knees before he reached her, and then he was on his stomach, still crawling, incredibly, a choking, sucking sound coming from what had been his mouth. Kate, standing now, both her hands over her face, began to scream again.

In order to get up, Longarm had to duck back down

behind the table and untangle one of his legs from an overturned chair. In that instant, he heard an explosion that momentarily deafened him, cutting off Kate's scream instantly. The detonation crashed from floor to ceiling and slammed around the walls, reverberating and reechoing with awesome force. Glancing up from behind the table, Longarm had difficulty seeing clearly through the heavy curtains of smoke—and then in believing what he saw.

Lazarus, a smoking, double-barreled shotgun in his hand, was leaning out over the bar, a fixed, satisfied grin on his emaciated face, while Kate Ballard, hard against the wall behind her—her face and chest a mottled stain of ribboned flesh, shattered bone, and blood—slowly sank to the floor.

Lazarus—Kilrain's ace-in-the-hole—swung the shotgun toward Longarm. A split-second before Lazarus fired the second barrel, Longarm discarded his now-empty Colt, flung himself forward, and slammed down on the floor close in under the bar. The blast carried just over his head like a wind out of hell. Longarm grabbed the edge of the bar and vaulted up onto it, drawing his derringer from his vest pocket in the same motion. Lazarus swung the empty shotgun. Longarm ducked under its murderous arc and fired point-blank at Lazarus. The round caught the man in the right eyesocket. The bullet seemed to explode upon impact. Exiting from the rear of the man's skull, it splattered the mirror with gore and smashed into the two shelves of glasses Lazarus was always polishing, transforming them into a brilliant explosion of glittering, multi-colored shards.

As Lazarus sank down behind the bar, Longarm forced himself to turn around, still crouching on the bar, and look over at Kate. She was sprawled on the floor, close to the wall. He could not be sure, but she appeared not to be breathing. Her wounds were fearful. Longarm hoped that her death had been instantaneous. The last thing he wanted to hear at that moment was the sound of her moaning.

Billy burst into the saloon, his sixgun in his hand. "What the hell was that? The whole town heard that blast! A shotgun?"

Longarm dropped to the floor, and retrieving his Colt, slowly began to reload. "That's right, Billy. Lazarus also worked for Kilrain—and he had a shotgun."

That was when Billy saw Kate. He swore softly, bitterly. "Oh, that sonofabitch," he said. "That dirty, no-good sonofabitch."

"When Lazarus looked up from behind the bar, it looked to him as if Kate was the only one left alive. That was when he shot her, on orders from Kilrain, no doubt." Longarm finished reloading. "You all right?"

"Not a scratch. Them two grabbed a couple of horses. The last I seen, they was headin' north. And they weren't lookin' back."

Doc Cook poked his head into the saloon. Longarm glanced over at him. "Get in here, Doc. There's a woman over there hurt pretty bad. Take a look at her, will you?"

A moment later, Doc Cook got up and looked back at the two men. "She's gone. Never knew what hit her, I'd guess."

Longarm nodded, relieved, then led Billy out of the saloon. There was a crowd in the street, but the two men had no difficulty in making a path through it. As they started up the street, they saw Kilrain standing on the sidewalk in front of the Dry Gulch.

The moment Kilrain saw them, he ducked hastily back inside his saloon. Longarm looked at Billy. "I told you before, Billy, this ain't your fight."

"Hell, Longarm, I liked Kate. You know that. She was always square with me."

"All right, then. You go around back. I'll go in the front. I'll give you enough time to get to the alley."

Billy ducked quickly between the barbershop and the Dry Gulch. Longarm kept going toward the saloon, walking slowly. His Colt was in his hand, and he wished he had his rifle. There was no telling how many gunslicks Kilrain had left. But it didn't matter. There was no way Kilrain was going to miss this reckoning.

With measured stride, Longarm walked along the sidewalk, reached the batwings, and shouldered through. The moment he entered the cool, dim interior of the empty saloon, he crouched, holding his Colt out in front of him. There was a sound at the rear of the saloon, a door slammed open, and Billy was standing in the dimness, his sixgun gleaming in his hand.

"Where the hell is he?" Billy asked.

Shouts came from the street. Longarm ducked back outside. He saw townspeople in the middle of the street, pointing toward the church. Kilrain, on foot, was running across the courtyard that fronted the church. Even as he watched, Kilrain disappeared inside the building. Longarm holstered his weapon and looked at Billy.

"He must have went out a window. And now he's hoping the priest can save him. Looks like I'll have to do some more bluffing. The sonofabitch is as slippery as a greased sidewinder."

Chapter 13

"I am not armed!" Kilrain cried, flinging his hands into the air as Longarm and Billy entered the church.

Kilrain was standing with Father Chaves and Maria Antonia Lugo in front of the low railing just before the altar. Three husky Mexicans were standing beside Maria. They were a hard-bitten threesome and were dressed like working *vaqueros,* complete with embroidered jacket and pantaloons, trimmed with tinsel lace.

"Who are they?" Longarm asked Billy, indicating the Mexicans beside Maria with a nod of his head.

"The tall one is her foreman. The one behind him is the segundo."

Longarm pulled up in front of Kilrain. He had a difficult time keeping his hands at his sides. "Put your hands down, Kilrain. I can see you're not armed."

"There have been more killings, haven't there, Mr. Long?" Maria said accusingly.

"My son," said the priest, "you bring death with you, I am afraid. And now you are after this man! What has he done?"

Before Longarm could reply, an indignant Kilrain

spoke up. "I have done nothing! Absolutely nothing!" He snorted derisively. "It seems to me his problem is he doesn't like politicians. He doesn't want me to be mayor. He accuses me of bringing in those men who have been causing so much trouble. I admit, their presence in Paso Robles has been unfortunate, most unfortunate. But how am I responsible for their manners? They heard there was to be an election, with its usual attendant celebrations, and so they flocked to this hospitable little town. I had nothing to do with that!" He swung around to face Longarm. "Do you have a warrant for my arrest, Longarm? Do you have formal charges to make? What are you accusing me of, exactly? Of running for mayor?"

Longarm was impressed. Kilrain was good, very good indeed. Since, by this time, his imported gunhands were dead, buried, or fleeing the area, Kilrain no longer had their embarrassing presence to explain away to Maria, the priest, or the local Mexican population. Longarm had erased an error in judgment on Kilrain's part that might have cost him the election. And with Foster and Kate dead, there was no one left to testify to his real motives for wanting control of Paso Robles. Longarm was back to square one. Short of shooting Kilrain dead on the spot, there seemed to be no way to stop him.

Unless Longarm could lie as well as Kilrain.

"It's a long list, Kilrain," Longarm replied. "Do you want the particulars? All right, then. Conspiracy to murder, rustling, selling stolen cattle and horses, conspiracy to defraud. And there will be more, lots more, when we get down to cases before a federal judge."

Kilrain paled. "You have no proof of these insane accusations!"

"Lazarus didn't kill Kate, Kilrain," Longarm said coldly. "Oh, yes. On your orders, he tried. She's wounded, but she's going to live—and testify. And Lazarus will testify too, to keep himself from spending the rest of his life in the lockup for attempted murder. Kate knows all about your plans, Kilrain—why you need control of this town and the pass."

In a small, worried voice Maria spoke up. "Could you explain that, Mr. Long? What do you mean, control of Paso Robles and the pass?"

Longarm glanced at her. "Kilrain's been importing gangs of rustlers and seeding the hills all around here with them. He employed one gunman to impersonate Billy the Kid and lead a gang of toughs that helped to whittle down John Chisum's herds. There are other gangs as well, waiting to swoop down after his election and begin to pick on other, smaller ranchers. He's been shipping his rustled cattle through the pass and on down to El Paso. Kate gave me the name of the cattle broker who's been accepting the rustled stock. Don't you see, Maria, how control of this town and the pass would make this whole county his playground? He'd be like a pig at a trough, him and the rest of his swine."

Kilrain moistened his dry lips. Until that moment he had played a pat hand beautifully, but he appeared now to be coming apart at the seams. He looked quickly around him, at Maria, then at the priest, then back at Longarm.

"Kate's lying!" he managed. "No one would believe a woman like that!" His voice was suddenly laced with contempt. "She's a tramp! A whore! Do you know where I found her, Longarm? In the most notorious whorehouse in El Paso!"

"Charles!" Maria cried, recoiling from Kilrain in dismay. "You mean she *is* your partner? You brought her here? *That* woman?"

"Maria, you've got to understand! I—"

"I *do* understand," she replied emphatically. She

223

looked at Longarm. "Perhaps, Marshal, I owe you an apology. You seemed to have turned over a stone in my presence and uncovered something rather nasty!"

It was all over for Kilrain then. And Kilrain knew it. Longarm's bluff had worked. Kilrain backed away, his face becoming cold, almost maniacal in its mask of frustration and fury. Before Longarm could draw his own weapon, the man had reached behind him and pulled from his belt a Smith & Wesson pocket .38. Longarm cursed himself for not having frisked the man as he had offered earlier. Kilrain leveled the small but deadly weapon at Longarm and Billy.

"Both of you—unbuckle your gun belts," Kilrain ordered. "And that derringer too, Longarm." He smiled thinly. "You see, I know all about that hidden gun. Kate told me."

Longarm and Billy did as they were told. Kilrain instructed one of the *vaqueros* to dump the weapons in the sacristy, and Father Chaves was told to lock it. Then he sent the segundo after two horses, with instructions that they be saddled and provisioned for a long journey. When the segundo had left, Kilrain looked at Maria and smiled.

"Something nasty, am I? Come over here!"

She walked over to him. He reached out brutally and spun her around, thrusting the barrel of his .38 into her narrow waist. Maria winced, but did not cry out.

"I'm taking Maria with me," he told Longarm. "Desert nights can be cold, you know. But if any of you come after me—if I see riders trailing me or hear them approaching—I will kill this woman and take my chances. Stay put, let us go without harassment, and I give you my word I'll release Maria in El Paso, unharmed."

"Your *word!*" Maria spat contemptuously.

"It's all you have, my dear. It's all any of you have."

224

"You say you'll leave her in El Paso. That's not much help. That's a big city. This woman will be alone, friendless."

"I will give her enough money for a hotel room and for transportation home. That I promise."

"All right, Kilrain," said Longarm. "Your capture is not worth this woman's life. But I warn you, if anything does happen to her, I'll track you down if it takes the rest of my life."

"A fine threat, Longarm, but useless. I'd rather catch a bullet from your gun than rot in prison. I suggest you simply do as I tell you. As you say, my capture is not worth Maria's life."

The horses were soon brought by the segundo. After Kilrain had meticulously inspected the horses and the provisions, he and Maria mounted up at the rear of the church and rode off down the narrow alley, heading for the fields in back of Maria's ranch buildings. Longarm watched them go until they crossed the river and disappeared beyond the cottonwoods. Kilrain *was* heading for El Paso, then. Longarm would have to count on the arrogance of the man to do precisely that.

Billy moved up beside him. Longarm turned to look down at the Kid. "We need horses, Billy, a string of them. Fast horses, if we're going to get to that pass before they do."

Billy grinned. "Just what I was thinking. You let me pick them out. I know these horses real good."

He turned then, and spoke in fluent Spanish to Maria's foreman. The man's eyes lit as Billy told him what they wanted, and in a moment the foreman and his second in command were gone. Billy looked at Longarm. "The thing is, will he go that way?"

"And if he does, will we be able to get him without losing Maria?"

"Reckon maybe we better not try it?"

Longarm considered this for a moment before replying. Then he said emphatically, "No. I think we ought to. If we didn't try to stop him, I don't think Maria would ever forgive us. I think she wants this man nailed more than we do."

Billy smiled. "You understand, huh? She was sweet on that man. He told her a lot of fairy tales, you can bet. He was one big man with the ladies."

Yes, he was, Longarm mused grimly as he turned and moved back into the cool interior of the church. And one of those ladies was lying in a pool of her own blood in the Lucky Lady. That was sure as hell another reason for nailing Kilrain. He owed it to Kate Ballard, the unlucky lady.

Pushing their horses all the way, Longarm and Billy had gone through three mounts apiece in less than two hours of riding. The last horse in each string had just barely managed to get them to the pass; that these two horses had lasted, despite the pace at which they had been driven, was a tribute to Billy's judgment of horseflesh.

Billy was now on the other flank of the pass, out of sight, as close to the trail as he could get while still maintaining a view of the entire pass. Longarm was equally well-situated. There were only a couple of hours of daylight left, but Longarm was fairly certain that their quarry would appear well before sunset. If they didn't, that would simply be another can of worms Longarm would have to open when the time came.

There was one more problem. The range of their rifles did not give either Longarm or the Kid much of a chance of hitting Kilrain if he stayed close to the middle of the broad trail that cut through the pass. They had discussed this. All they could hope for, they finally decided, was that Kilrain would pass close enough to one of the cliffs to give Billy or Longarm a clean shot. And that would have to be it, they both agreed—one clean shot that would knock Kilrain out of his saddle, allowing Maria to spur her own mount far enough away from Kilrain to ensure her safety if Kilrain survived and was still intent on carrying out his threat to kill her.

There was only an hour of sunlight left when two dots materialized in the distance. For a while, it appeared as though the faint specks on the horizon weren't moving. Then, almost suddenly, Longarm found he could make two horses and riders. Kilrain was riding a little ahead of Maria. He was forced to stop on more than one occasion to wait for Maria's horse to catch up to his. Maria did not appear to be anxious to make the journey to El Paso with Charles Kilrain.

Longarm had already taken a three-foot strip of rawhide from one of his saddlebags. Now he tied one end to his Winchester's barrel, and the other around the stock. Next, he looped the rawhide around his upper left arm, tucked the butt into his right shoulder, then stretched the strip until it was taut. The hand holding the barrel usually weaves a bit, ruining the aim. Longarm was using the rawhide to brace his arm. The strip cut off some of his circulation, making his arm heavy and providing a solid base for the rifle.

He was lying prone on a small patch of grass. Boulders crowded him on either side, and a cliff dropped away precipitously in front, affording him a clear view of the pass. He sighted now along his barrel and caught Kilrain's chest and head in his sights. He tracked the man for a while, his fingers sweating against the wood of the stock. The sun's rays slanted, golden, across the rough ground. The rocks cast long shadows.

Abruptly, Longarm swore. Kilrain was riding just out of range, keeping his horse to the center of the trail. He was riding warily too, turning his head nervously from side to side as he scanned the distant rocky walls of the pass. The man was no fool. He knew that this passage was the most dangerous portion of his journey south to El Paso. Not until he had negotiated this neck of the bottle could he relax.

The two riders came on. Kilrain was below him now, but still out of his range—and out of Billy's as well. They kept on. Before long, they would be through the pass. Longarm swore again, louder this time. Kilrain was going to make it!

A desperate resolve seized him. With his right hand, he snatched up a rock the size of his fist and hurled it out over the cliff's edge. He heard it strike just below him, saw it bounce high, then fall again, the sound of it bounding down the steep cliffside fading rapidly.

Kilrain pulled up. The man swung his horse around and peered up at Longarm, leaning far out over his horse's neck as he did so. He could not see Longarm. It was the small avalanche of stone and gravel now sifting down to the floor of the pass that had caught his attention.

Longarm steadied his left arm, flexing it so that the rawhide strip cut deeper. He had Kilrain in his sights now. But still the man remained too far away for a clean shot. Then Kilrain turned his head swiftly. Pulling his cheek away from the stock, Longarm glanced down and saw that Maria had started to ride closer to the cliff.

"Yes, Maria!" Longarm muttered. "Yes! That's it! Keep coming! Draw the sonofabitch closer!"

Once again, Longarm found Kilrain's head and shoulders in his sights. Spurring after Maria, Kilrain grew steadily larger. Longarm waited, barely aware that he was holding his breath, that his left arm felt as solid as oak. He could see Kilrain's sandy mustache now, the lines of his face moving as he shouted after Maria. Longarm lowered the barrel carefully until the sights rested on the man's vest, and squeezed the trigger.

The crash of the shot shattered the air, snapping Longarm out of the deep well of concentration into which he had fallen. He lifted himself to see Kilrain's riderless horse pulling violently to one side, and behind it—flopping over and over on the ground—the figure of Charles Kilrain.

Longarm could not see Maria now. She was somewhere in under the cliff. Kilrain managed to pull himself to his knees—a dark stain on his shirtfront, his sixgun gleaming in the slanting rays of the sun. Longarm swiftly dropped his cheek to the stock, sighted again, and fired. Kilrain was flung backward as the slug hammered into his left shoulder.

Longarm rose to his feet then, to see more clearly. Kilrain was twisting slowly on the ground like a damaged insect. He tried to raise himself twice. Then, at last, he was still. Longarm glanced skyward. Against the red sky, three vultures, like cinders caught in an updraft out of hell, tipped and soared, then began to circle over the pass.

Chapter 14

Longarm had heard the horse ride up, and was not surprised when Maria entered the living room to tell him Billy was outside.

The Kid was waiting on the back patio. He stuck out his hand when the marshal appeared. Longarm shook Billy's hand warmly.

"Just stopped by to say goodbye, Longarm."

"I'm glad you did, Billy. I won't ask you where you're riding to. You got better sense than to tell me, anyhow."

"Guess I have, at that. I was thinkin', Longarm—now you know I'm not a southpaw, you goin' to let on about it?"

"You mean you might like it if I'd just forget you weren't a left-handed gun?"

Billy smiled. "Sure would. Never can tell. It might give me an edge someday when I really need it."

"I owe you, Billy. So why don't we just consider that our own little secret?"

Billy nodded and mounted up. "I'd sure appreciate that, Longarm." He waved goodbye, pulled his horse around, and rode off past the corrals on his way to the river—and the hills beyond.

As Longarm watched him ride off, he thought of that tall Irishman running for sheriff, Pat Garrett. Garret had impressed him, and so had the Kid. If Garrett won the election, he hoped the Kid would be able to stay out of further trouble. Longarm didn't like the thought of the two of them tangling; for one of them, it would almost certainly be fatal. As this ominous reflection occurred to him, he shivered with a sudden chill.

He shook it off, turned, and went back inside to Maria. It was siesta time, so Longarm was not surprised to find that Maria had changed into a long, dark chemise. She had combed her hair out and was relaxing on the sofa, her long legs tucked under her, a second glass of wine in her hand.

"Billy's gone?" she asked.

"He's ridden out. Heading for Texas, most likely. New Mexico is not exactly the safest place for him right now. Leastways, that's what I'll be telling Governor Wallace when I see him. I hope I'm right."

"You know, of course, why I was so anxious to protect him from you."

"He—or someone with him—killed Sheriff Brady, the murderer of your husband."

"Do you forgive me, Longarm? I was not very nice, as I remember."

"I understand loyalty, Maria." He smiled. "Of course I forgive you."

She finished her glass of wine and got up. "Then let's forget all that now, Longarm. You and Billy saw to the burial of Kate Ballard this morning, and you'll be riding out tomorrow." She smiled. "That gives me too little time to thank you for ridding me and Paso Robles of Charles Kilrain."

"You don't have to thank me," Longarm said. "And

maybe you better wait until you see how much money is left in that bank Kilrain took over."

She smiled. "It's all there, or most of it. That's all Kilrain moaned about as he rode beside me. He had not had time to loot the bank's deposits."

"I guess maybe you *should* thank me, then."

She pressed against him and kissed him warmly, the tang of the wine still on her full lips. "Stay and be our new mayor," she whispered into his ear.

He chuckled, turned, and walked with her toward the bedroom. "Hell, Maria, this town don't need a mayor. You and Chaves are all the authority Paso Robles needs. Politicians you can do without."

"Yes, perhaps, Longarm," she said, as she turned before her bed to face him, her chemise opening slightly, both arms held out toward him, "but a man like you we all need."

He didn't argue with her about that as he stepped into her arms, the lovely warmth and promise of her body driving from him completely the chill of death that had clung to him since he had first ridden into Lincoln County.

SPECIAL PREVIEW

Here are the opening scenes
from

LONGARM IN THE SAND HILLS

thirteenth in the bold
LONGARM series from Jove

Chapter 1

Longarm knew he was going to be late to the office again. It was a subject to ponder as he strode the streets of Denver in the early-morning rush. The booming town was getting famous for its traffic jams since they'd put in those new streetcar lines without bothering to widen or even pave a few downtown streets. But Longarm didn't think his boss would accept that as an excuse. There'd been a right interesting tie-up involving a brewery wagon, a coach-and-four, and a horsedrawn streetcar at the corner of Colfax and Broadway. But if he told Marshal Vail he'd stopped to assist the Denver P.D. in putting down the riot, his boss would likely want to know how come he'd been over on that side of the Federal Building when they both knew he roomed almost a mile in the other direction.

Longarm grinned wistfully under his Longhorn mustache as he thought of the redhead he'd just said goodbye to over on Colfax and Sherman. Marshal Vail was a married man, so he likely knew how a gent could lose track of the time when he was busy in bed in the morning. But the one time he'd offered that excuse, the boss had cussed him forwards and backwards, and sent home for more bad words.

That wasn't why he was late, anyway. He packed an Ingersoll watch that kept fair time, and he'd never been late getting anywhere important. It was obvious as hell what the sneaky part of his head was doing. He kept getting to work late because his job bored the shit out of him.

It wasn't the fieldwork he minded. In the six or eight years he'd been working for the Justice Department, he'd had some interesting times chasing folks. But Washington kept sending more and more fool paperwork every week, and being a peace officer these days was getting to be just another fuddy-duddy trade. You weren't allowed to just go out and pistolwhip the law into folks, these days. You had to fill out at least three fool forms every time you shot an outlaw, and Longarm's big, rawboned hands had never been designed to play a typewriter.

Longarm legged it across Welton Street in the bright morning, and caught a glimpse of himself in a plate-glass store window. It was embarrassing as hell. For the last couple of years, Justice had insisted that he report for work in a suit and tie, and he thought he looked like one of those sissy dudes from back East who likely had to sit down to pee.

He was wrong, of course. Longarm's tall, muscular frame was no more suited to the brown tweed ready-made suit he wore than his big fists were to the office typewriter. Anyone who'd ever seen a cowboy could have spotted the way he walked in his low-heeled army boots. Any cowboy would have identified the crush of his dark brown Stetson as that of a Colorado rider. Most lawmen cast at least a thoughtful look at the way the tall deputy's frock coat hung. Though Longarm wore his cross-draw rig under the coat, his double-action Colt .44 was a man-sized weapon, and the bulge it created was not easy to conceal.

Longarm found himself striding faster as he approached the side entrance of the Federal Building. He was only forty-odd minutes late, and if he kept it under an hour, Marshal Vail wouldn't bother with the paperwork it took to dock a man for being a mite tardy.

Inside the building, Longarm tried to look invisible as he strode the marble floors of the stairwells and corridors. On the top floor, he rounded a corner and almost ran over a flustered little secretary gal going somewhere with a sheaf of papers. He reached out to steady her as he smiled and said, "Sorry, ma'am, I wasn't looking where I was going. Was that your toe I just stomped?"

The girl flushed and dimpled as their eyes met, and Longarm saw that she was sort of pretty behind her glasses. She said, "I'm wearing stout shoes, praise the Lord. Aren't you Marshal Long?"

"I am Custis Long and I am only a deputy. My boss, Billy Vail, is the U.S. Marshal for this district."

"I'm Susan Honeypepper, and I work in the secretarial pool just down the corridor from you."

He said, "Well, I'm proud to meet up with you, Miss Susan, and I'd like to stay and jaw some, but I'm already late for work, so, since I can see I didn't bust your foot, I'll say adios and be on my way."

"Another time?" she suggested, looking away as she turned a deeper shade of red.

Longarm sighed to himself as he strode on. She'd been a handsome little thing, but damn it, she worked under the same roof. Since the fool government had started hiring gals, it was getting distracting as well as tedious around here. Thank God Billy Vail was an old-fashioned boss who didn't see fit to clutter up his own office with feminine help. Of course, that young fellow who was Vail's receptionist and office clerk walked sort of funny and looked like he shaved once a week, but at least he didn't give the other help a hard-on during business hours.

Longarm reached the door and grasped the handle. He tugged, then muttered, "What the hell?"

The door was locked.

For a moment Longarm thought he'd somehow made a mistake. Billy Vail had never been late to work in living memory, and even if the boss had been run over by a streetcar, the prissy clerk had the annoying habit of reporting to work five minutes early to open up.

But the gilt lettering on the door still read, UNITED STATES MARSHAL, FIRST DISTRICT COURT OF COLORADO. So Longarm tugged again, then knocked. There was no answer.

Grinning like a kid swiping apples, Longarm reached in his pants pocket for his jackknife, One of the folding blades had been filed down in a way that could have led to his arrest if he hadn't been a peace officer himself. He picked the lock and went inside.

The outer office was empty. Longarm crossed to the door leading to the inner office and picked that lock too. Then he went into Billy Vail's inner sanctum and sat down in the red morocco leather overstuffed chair by Vail's desk. As he leaned back, crossed his legs, and took out a smoke, he glanced out the window and saw the gold dome of the State House up on Capitol Hill, shining in the morning sun. He lit a sulfur match with his thumbnail, and applied it to the end of his cheroot as he swung his eyes along the oak paneling to the banjo clock across the office. Good God, it was almost nine. Where in thunder *was* everybody?

He'd smoked his cheroot a third of the way down when he heard the door behind him open. Marshal William Vail clumped in on his short, stubby legs, moved around behind the desk, and dropped a flat cardboard box on the big green blotter before he sat down and said, "Longarm, you're late."

Longarm glanced at the clock, blew a thoughtful smoke ring, and replied, "Do tell? I've been here some time, pondering the way you boys have been shirking on the taxpayer's time. I didn't know you were keeping banker's hours these days, Chief."

Vail swore under his breath and said, "Don't shit me, you tall drink of innocent water. You know damn well this office opens at eight. I've only been out of this place a few minutes. But spare me the fool excuses. As long as you've seen fit to grace us by your presence at all, I've got a field job for you. Take a look at these photographs."

As Longarm leaned forward, Vail handed him a sheaf of glossy paper prints, warning, "Careful, they're still a mite damp. I've just come from the photographer down the street. My clerk's still down there. We're putting the old glass plates on paper with that new process some jasper in New York State just developed. Ain't they pretty?" Longarm glanced down at the first photograph, grimaced, and replied, "Not hardly. I just ate breakfast."

The picture was that of a little girl about six or seven years of age. He could see she'd been dead at least a month when they'd photographed her, and it appeared that she'd died in an ugly manner.

The pathetic little cadaver still wore pigtails and a soggy-looking print dress. The flesh had fallen away from the bones of her face, and her open mouth and empty eye sockets were filled with dried mud. You couldn't tell if the child had been pretty or not, but for some reason, the perfect, pearly little teeth in the silently screaming mouth seemed more obscene than the other, more ruined parts of her.

Longarm noticed that his cheroot smoke tasted brassy as he set the first print aside and studied the photographed remains of an adult male. The second face was skeletonized and muddy, too. The skull was misshapen, as if it had been stomped flat. From somewhere in the distance, Vail was saying, "The old sepia prints don't show fine detail, and the originals on glass are untidy to keep in the files. This new black-and-white process should make it easier to keep up to date."

Longarm didn't answer. The third picture was that of a cadaver in a less advanced state of decay, and thus more horrible to look at. Vail saw that he'd come to it and said, "That one's a Dr. William York. He's one of the only ones identified for sure. His brother recognized the remains."

"His brother likely had a strong stomach. What's this all about, Billy? Have you been out to the burial grounds with your box camera? You've got almost a dozen very dead folks here. I haven't read anything in the papers about another Indian rising or a mass murder."

Vail looked pleased with himself as he said, "Sure you have. It was even in the London Times. But you've likely forgot the case. It happened six or eight years ago, about the time you started working for us."

Longarm leafed through the other photos, saw they were all just as unpleasant to look at, and said, "Six or eight years is an old case for sure. Who killed these folks and where do I fit in?"

"Nebraska. Up in the sandhill country near the South Dakota line. You know the territory?"

"Sure, it's cattle country. Mostly federally owned open range. But these folks weren't killed and buried in the sandhills, Billy. The soil clinging to their bones is clay loam."

"I admire a lawman who can read sign, even if he seldom sees fit to get to work on time. Those folks were murdered over on the Osage Trail in southeast Kansas, near a settlement called Cherryvale."

Longarm snapped his fingers and said flatly, "The Terrible Benders! I remember the case now."

"I should think you would. Every lawman in the country wasted a couple of years trying to collect that two-thousand-dollar reward. You were down near the border after those Mexican raiders at the time, but I sent you a wanted flier. Everyone from the Pinkertons to Wild Bill Hickok got one. It was a really nasty mess. That little gal was riding with her father when the Benders killed them. As far as the coroner could make out, they smashed the father's head in, but they threw the kid in on top of his corpse and buried her alive."

Longarm nodded and said, "I remember that part. I was sore enough *without* these pictures to look at! I was sort of busy with that Mexican gang, but I purely studied everybody else I met up with for a time. I disremember spotting anyone answering to the descriptions on the wanted fliers though, and to tell you the truth, the whole thing's sort of faded from my mind. You'd best fill me in some before I light out after the rascals. I've hunted a lot of owlhoots since. I've got a damn good picture in my head of Frank and Jesse James, and I reckon I'd know Mysterious Dave Mather if I met him in a dark alley. But I figured the Terrible Benders must have been caught by this time."

Vail said, "They were never caught. I'd best tell you the tale from scratch, and let you start caught up fresh. The Terrible Benders were a family of four. Nobody knows where they came from, or if Bender was their real name. They were some sort of foreigners. Some say they were German, and some allow they might have been gypsies. There was Old Man Bender; he spoke poor English and answered to the name of John. His wife was Ma Bender. She was in her fifties, and spoke even less English. They had two kids: a boy called Junior, about twenty-five, and a daughter called

Pretty Kate. She was the only one who spoke with no accent and seemed to have any brains worth mention. All four of them were big. They say the daughter was nigh six foot tall and her brother and daddy towered over her. We have a picture of Kate Bender here. The others were camera-shy."

Vail took another print from the box, and handed it across the desk. Longarm stared thoughtfully down at the picture of a surprisingly pretty brunette with big, innocent dark eyes and a slight Mona Lisa smile as Vail explained, "She gave her picture to a boyfriend—a storekeeper from Cherryvale. He was good enough to come forward with it once he learned he'd been sparking a lunatic who went in for mass murder on the nights he didn't come courting. He likely had some spooky dreams about her, for a time."

Longarm said, "She don't look like a six-foot amazon."

"Well, she was, and a head-turning handsome woman to boot. She might have been the brains of the outfit, but that ain't saying much. The Benders' neighbors hadn't suspicioned what they were up to, of course, until it was too late. But later they remembered that even Kate had seemed a mite spooky. She read tea leaves and held spirit-rapping sessions for the neighbor ladies and told more than one that she had occult powers. At the time, they thought she was funning. She didn't *look* like a real witch."

"Get to the murders. The Benders ran a boarding-house or something, didn't they?"

"No. It was a trail stop between Cherryvale and Thayer, Kansas. It was really just a one-room cabin, divided in the middle by a canvas partition. The family lived in one half of the cabin; the other half was fitted out as a dining room. Folks coming up the Osage Trail to the railroad at Cherryvale stopped there to water their mounts and rest a spell. The Benders served bad

244

coffee and awful beans at an outrageous price. So few folks stopped more than once, and business must have been slow. Lucky travelers made their way past the Bender cabin and only remembered it as a place to be avoided. Folks dropping by alone at night, when no other folks were on the trail, weren't as lucky. We know for sure that at least eleven folks who stopped for grub and water were murdered and robbed by the crazy family. There might have been more. The grand jury figured they had enough to go on after the posse dug up eleven graves in and about the cabin."

Longarm nodded and said, "I remember how they did it now. It was that canvas wall. The victim would be seated at the table with his back to the partition. While the women served him, one of the Bender men crept behind the canvas with a nine-pound sledge. The girl would suddenly shove the poor bastard backwards, chair and all, and the sledge was aimed at the bulge in the partition."

Vail nodded and said, "Yep. Later they found traces of blood and brains on the canvas. They got away with it for about a year. Then this Dr. York vanished on the trail, and his family took the time to trace his movements. York had been packing an engraved watch, and when it turned up in a Cherryvale hock shop, the dead man's brother rode out to the trail stop to ask how come Junior Bender had pawned it."

Vail shook his head in wonder as he added, "The Lord protects drunks and other fools, I reckon. The brother should have been victim number twelve. But it was broad daylight and some hands were driving a herd to the railroad as he jawed with Pretty Kate in her dooryard. She said her brother wasn't home and invited him in for some coffee."

"Jesus, he didn't go inside with her, did he?"

"Not hardly. He's still alive. He got suspicious of the wild look in the big gal's eyes and said he'd come back later. She took him by one arm and tried to lead him in, allowing they might have some fun while her kinfolks were away. He lit out like he'd just shook hands with the devil, which was pretty close to the truth, when you think about it. Kate cussed him as the passing cowhands reined in to see what all the fuss was about. But she couldn't stop the dead man's brother from riding off with them."

"Where did he go then? To the law?"

"Hell, yes. Where would *you* have gone? He tore into Cherryvale and got the sheriff. The sheriff had already heard some spooky talk about the new folks out on the trail, so he gathered a posse and rode back with the dead man's brother. He was a good lawman. When the posse arrived, there was nobody home and everything looked peaceable. But the sheriff threw well water on the dirt floor of the cabin, and as it started to dry a mite, he ordered his men to dig where the packed dirt stayed damp. They found bodies under the dining table, and more out back. Like I said, they quit when they uncovered eleven, including Dr. York."

Longarm grimaced and said, "Meanwhile, they let the whole murderous crew ride off into the purple sunset?"

"Hell, Longarm, it was open country. How far could four giants get? The sheriff sent men to cover the railroad and put the tale on the telegraph wires in every direction. He figured that building an airtight case against the Benders was more important at the time. He hauled in the gal's boyfriend, put a noose about his neck, and questioned shit out of him. The storekeeper was scared skinny and told the little we really know about the Benders. In the end they decided he was clean. He admitted screwing Kate Bender more'n the law allowed, but he had alibis for the dates the sheriff found important."

Longarm asked, "Storekeeper, huh? Wouldn't a store be a handy place to get rid of stolen goods?"

"They thought of that. He didn't have anything for sale that he couldn't account for, legal. Besides, the dead man's watch had been pawned miles away by Junior Bender. They naturally suspected the man, and kept an eye on him for a few years. But he got married after a while and moved on."

"Then nobody knows where he is today?"

"Hell, of course we do. He only moved away from the scandal, not out of the state. Every once in a while some lawman drops by to pay him a visit. They say it upsets his wife and kids. I got his name somewhere in the files if you want it."

Longarm shook his head and said, "Sounds like a waste of time, if he's stuck to the same tale all these years and he ain't in Nebraska. What makes you think the Terrible Benders are up in the sandhill country, Billy?"

Vail handed him a Western Union flimsy, saying, "This came in the other day from Deputy Harcourt. He's that kid they just sent us from back East and, as you can see, a fool."

HAVE SPOTTED SUSPECTS ANSWERING DESCRIPTION KATE AND JUNIOR BENDER WANTED FOR MURDER IN KANSAS STOP PLEASE ADVISE RE FEDERAL JURISDICTION SIGNED HARCOURT U S DEPUTY MARSHAL

Longarm frowned and asked, "That's all? He doesn't even say what township he saw them in!"

Vail sighed and said, "I know. I don't know where the department gets 'em these days. Harcourt was sent up there on another case, of course. He sent that wire from Bridgeport, on the North Platte. He was traveling on the Burlington Line, and as you see, he didn't say if he spotted the Benders aboard the train, in town as he stopped off to eat, or standing on their heads in the river."

"You wired back, of course?"

"Hell, no. I just sat here like a big-ass bird," Vail said with a wry look. "Of course I wired! I wired every lawman within a day's ride from Bridgeport while I was about it. What in hell do you reckon Harcourt meant by 'federal jurisdiction'?"

"I'll ask him when I catch up with him. Offhand, I'd say he's over-educated to be packing a badge this far west. He's new on the job and likely wondered if a federal lawman could arrest a suspect on a Kansas state warrant."

"Shit, any lawman can arrest anybody that any other lawman wants. Everybody knows that!"

"Harcourt didn't. When he spottted the Benders— if he really did—he likely got arresting powers mixed up with extradition and such. It's a natural mistake for a green hand. Where is Harcourt now?"

"I wish to hell I knew. He was supposed to pick up a government mount at Fort Robinson before riding into the sandhills. The army remount people say he never got to Fort Robinson."

Longarm whistled silently and observed, "In other words, one of our men is missing, right after reporting at least two wanted killers."

"There's no other words about it, Longarm. Nobody's seen hide nor hair of Harcourt since he got off the train in Bridgeport. Where do you aim to start looking?"

Longarm thought before he said, "Let's eat the apple a bite at a time. There's a mess of open country between Bridgeport and Fort Robinson. Can I figure the Bridgeport law has poked about some for our long-lost greenhorn?"

"Of course. If he's a day's ride from Bridgeport he's buried deep. He could be anywhere between the Platte and the sandhills, alive or otherwise. I know I've given you a hard row to hoe, old son, but it seemed like such a simple job that I never thought to send an experienced deputy."

Longarm nodded and asked, "What *did* Harcourt go up there to do, if it wasn't to look for the Terrible Benders?"

Vail said, "I sent him up near Sunbonnet, Nebraska, to evict some squatters on federal property. You know already that the sandhills are open range. Uncle Sam has put that corner of Nebraska off-limits to homesteaders. The government stands to collect more in grazing fees than it'd ever get in taxes from a blown-away farm. Bust the sod on them big rolling hills up yonder and . . ."

"I know you can't farm the sandhill country, Billy. Fill me in on these here squatters Harcourt was sent to evict."

Vail shrugged and said, "It's another one of those damn fool Utopian communities. The outfit calls itself the Church of Ancestral Wisdom. I swear, I don't know what this country is coming to. First we had the Mormons and Mennonites and such. Now we're getting even wilder folk with funny notions out here. The old-time religion has been good enough for lots of folks, but now we got Owenites and Marxists and folks who want to build octagonal houses to read Darwin instead of the Good Book. What in thunder's wrong with a square house? I've lived in 'em all my life and it's never hurt me."

"Let's stick to this Church of Ancestral Wisdom. What are they doing up in the sandhills, Billy?"

"Beats hell out of me. You sure can't grow crops there, and they ain't running cows. These jaspers picked up some fool notions from them Fox sisters back East.

They say they live by revelations from their dead ancestors."

"You mean they're part of the spiritualist movement?"

"Yep. They wear funny duds and talk to haunts. The cattlemen up there say they spook the livestock and practice free love while fencing off the only water for miles. I sent Harcourt up there with a federal judgment, ordering them to jaw with spirits and screw each other some-place else. Some of the local cattlemen have offered to evict the sect a mite more informal, but we don't want vigilantes on federal property, either."

Longarm nodded and said, "I'll keep these pictures. I'll need another copy of the eviction papers, the usual travel vouchers, and such."

"Don't you aim to look for Harcourt first?"

"Nope. Like you said, he could be most anywhere in a mess of open range. I figure the best move, right now, is for me to just take over his mission and see who tries to stop me."

Vail said, "Hell, it seems obvious enough that he stumbled over another case, got spotted by the Terrible Benders, and—"

"Back up and restudy what you're saying, Billy," Longarm cut in, going on to explain, "Harcourt's only been out here a few months. He was just a kid when the Bender case was in the papers. He might have really recognized Kate Bender. He might have made a mistake. It's sort of odd they'd be spotted so easy by a green kid when no experienced lawman has managed to catch sight of 'em for all these years."

"Ain't you forgetting something, Longarm? Kate Bender was interested in spiritualism!"

Longarm nodded and said, "I'm way ahead of you on that. Sure, a new bunch of table-rappers living out in the middle of nowhere might attrack a gal like Kate

Bender. On the other hand, Harcourt must have been thinking along the same lines. He was on the prod to look for folks who dabbled with spirits, from the time you sent him north, all hot and bothered, on his first field case."

"You mean, if folks start looking for ghosts, they're likely to see 'em? All right, let's say he just saw a big pretty lady answering to Kate Bender's description. If she and the other giant with her weren't really Benders, why is Harcourt missing?"

Longarm got to his feet, saying, "Don't know. There's nothing to tell us Harcourt was done in by the suspects he reported. I can think of a dozen reasons why a federal man could get in trouble up in that neck of the woods. The sandhills are rough country, Billy. Leaving aside owlhoots hiding out up there, the Sioux are sulking on the Pine Ridge Reservation just to the north. The price of beef is high this summer. Cow thieves get to humming around the herds out on the open range like flies, whenever the price of beef goes up."

Vail grimaced and said, "I follow your drift. It ain't like a strange lawman is a popular visitor, on the job or off."

Longarm grinned and said, "There you go. I've had folks try to gun me right here on the streets of Denver. Anybody could have had it in for Harcourt."

"Maybe, but I still cotton to the notion of Kate Bender being interested in that spiritualist bunch, Longarm."

Longarm said, "I aim to keep that in mind. But if she's joined the commune, I'll likely notice. How many six-foot beautiful women do you reckon there might be, even in a free love society?"

Longarm sat with his back to the rear bulkhead of the Burlington coach, reading the book he'd picked up at the public library before boarding the train. The book had been written a few years back by a reporter who claimed to have talked to Colonel York, the brother of the dead doctor whose murder had led the law to the Terrible Benders.

The old federal files hadn't mentioned the man as a colonel, but they hadn't said he wasn't. The colonel in the book seemed to have played a more important part in the investigation than the official report said he did, to hear *him* tell it.

In fact, the popular version was exciting as all hell, with the colonel paying visit after visit to the Bender spread and living to tell about it. He had himself playing fancy games with the whole murderous clan, even though Vail's version had them down as illiterate white trash who spoke in grunts. There was the same picture of Pretty Kate Bender, but a lot of facts failed to add up. According to the colonel, he'd not only solved the case, he'd led the posse and told them where to dig. The book was filled with gory but dubious details, such as that the one-room cabin had a deep, dark basement with blood-spattered walls. Longarm didn't think it was worth a side trip to Kansas to see if a one-room shack had been built with a full cellar by people content with interior partitions made of canvas. The sheriff's version was likely self-serving, too.

As the wheels clacked under him, he tried to picture the mysterious family. There was something wrong with every version he'd gone over. The popular version had the Benders lighting out with a herd of cattle, for God's sake. According to the sheriff, the posse had missed catching the family by minutes. The colonel had them with a two or three days' lead as he moved heaven and earth to interest the law in his missing brother. Was Kate Bender the articulate, well-dressed gal who'd advertised herself as a spiritualist and fortune teller in the

Kansas papers, or the half-wild she-brute other travelers had reported as snarling at them like an animal?

He was beginning to see why they'd never been caught. Everyone in Kansas had given a different description of the infamous family!

They could have been semi-prosperous German immigrants who kept a store and a herd of cattle; they could have been grunting savages living like gypsies in one-half of a tiny cabin reeking with blood and brains; it was hard to fathom how they could have been both.

Once the story had broken and the little town of Cherryvale was flooded by reporters from the outside world, everyone who'd ever heard of the Benders, and likely some who'd never met them, had given their own version with all the trimmings they could think of.

He saw that the writer of the book had his own theory as to why they'd never been caught. He suggested that the posse *had* caught up with them, but, enraged by the terrible crimes they'd uncovered, the possemen had killed the whole bunch, saving Kate for last and burning her as a witch while she spat defiant curses at them. Naturally, they'd then sworn to keep the deed a secret among them. It was dramatic as hell, it made good reading, but the writer had forgotten two things.

Two thousand dollars was a lot of money. Any member of the posse who had the slightest notion where the Benders could be found, dead or alive, had purely kept an expensive secret. The second thing wrong with the notion was that the posse had been *sent* to find them. They were wanted for at least eleven murders. What was to stop any lawman from killing all four of them and bragging his head off about it? If a whole posse could keep *anything* a secret, it would have been simple enough to agree that the Benders had died "resisting arrest."

So the book was just another penny-dreadful, like most of the nonsense Eastern writers made up about

253

anything west of the Hudson. Like all the men poor James Butler Hickock was said to have gunned, or like the man Billy the Kid was supposed to have killed at the age of twelve, or like a hundred other similar yarns. The reporters hadn't allowed any tedious facts to get in the way of an exciting detail or two.

He closed the book and put it in the saddlebag beside him on the plush seat. His McClellan saddle and bridle rode ahead of him in the baggage car, but he'd learned the hard way to keep his possibles and Winchester .44 in sight while traveling the rails, and, though the book was of no use to anyone, the library likely expected him to return it.

He fished out a cheroot and lit up as he gazed out the window at the passing scenery. The sunset was painting the rolling prairie orange and lavender, and they'd be getting into Bridgeport soon. He'd lay over for the night there, just in case Harcourt might have left some trace the local law had overlooked.

Up ahead of him in the car, a woman got up from her seat and made her way toward the privy at the far end. Longarm gazed admiringly at her hindquarters as she moved gracefully in time with the swaying floorboards. He knew what she looked like from the front; he'd had an eye on her since she'd boarded the train with him back in Denver. So far, she hadn't offered him any opportunity to strike up a conversation and, what the hell, he'd be getting off in a few minutes.

When the woman was almost to the narrow corridor leading to the privy and forward platform, a lean man with hunched shoulders slithered from his own seat to head the same way.

Longarm had been keeping an eye on him too. He was that chinless jasper who'd tried to start a conversation with the lady a while back and been cut off at the knees with a withering look. There was just one privy, for use by both men and women, with a door that locked from the inside. It had only one hole and Longarm couldn't see any civilized reason why a gent should be following a lady in that direction. So he sighed wearily and got to his own feet.

By the time he'd sauntered the length of the car, both of them were out of sight around the bend of the corridor opening. He kept going, and as he passed the door to the privy, he saw that it was unoccupied. The seat sat invitingly with the railroad ties whipping by under the squat-and-drop-it. He didn't have to go, so he eased on up to the platform between cars.

The gal he'd thought might need protecting stood on the platform, facing his way. She was a nicely built ash blonde, wearing a Paris hat and a floor-length linen travel-duster. She pointed the Colt Dragoon in her hand at Longarm's belt buckle and asked, "Whose side are you on, mister?"

LONGARM

Explore the exciting Old West with one of the men who made it wild!